CHRIS PEASE

Project Vanguard

For Emily x

Foreword

The journey to releasing this novel has been a rollercoaster. To put this feeling in to words is incredibly painful. As a dad, to lose a child is unthinkable and i have been lucky enough to have the most incredible support in my darkest moment. For that reason, for every book sold, a donation will be made to repay those who have supported me. And to support those who will need it after me.

Here's to the future. . . one step at a time.

Chapter 1

"Three guards ahead, two on the left wall, one on the right."

Turning his head, the soldier gestured forwards with his hand. At her commander's order, out of the shadows, a female soldier stepped forward. Walking towards the guards, she made no sound as her specialist, lightweight armour clung tightly to her body.

In the dim light, her ice-blue coloured visor shimmered, changing tints thanks to the advanced technology in use. She held a pistol equipped with a silencer as she stepped out from her cover, grabbing the first guard from behind and firing a shot from her weapon. Dropping him, she fired two more shots - the first hitting another guard in the head, the second eliminated the other before the trio had a moment to register what was happening. The soldier clicked the empty magazine from her pistol, pushing it into her belt and clicking a fresh one in its place. Holstering the weapon, she turned to face her team as they moved towards her.

Four soldiers, each wearing similar armour, moved almost invisibly in the shadows cast by the dim lighting in the corridor, their visors flickering an assortment of colours. The five were from a new generation of soldiers known as Augmented Operatives. These new super soldiers were kitted out in extremely advanced armour, the technology taken from an alien race called the Hydroxii who humankind had been fighting until recently. The war had ended with a truce. Although both races were keen to avoid conflict, both were aware the war could restart at a moment's notice. Each species believed itself to be superior to the other.

The war had given the sides unique opportunities to work together. The augments that made up the new AOs were a result of reverse engineering and splicing both technologies together as a last-ditch effort to fight back against the highly advanced and intelligent race. The operatives took on a distinctive look in the field, from their choice of visor to plating style; it was a defining point for the few who were strong enough to become a part of the augment program. This squad was, however, very special. The operatives were a major program in the Global Military Task Force, which protected Earth and its colonies from any threat. On this occasion the operatives were working with their Global Intelligence Command who were on the hunt for a major player in a home-grown, human threat to civilian lives in the galaxy. The GIC had commissioned the team to bring in rebel leader, Julian DeMarko, a French Special Forces colonel who had gone rogue and was hitting the military hard for resources to add to his own. He was able to locate humanity's most high-profile agents and soldiers in the field. This mission was the first time anyone had put a marker on him, and the intelligence service were keen to finally bring him in.

Room by room, the team cleared out the opposing force so quietly the militia barely had time to register what was happening. Julian was particularly unhappy with the recent truce between humanity and the Hydroxii. GIC had operatives placed in specific locations across not only Earth but throughout the galaxy; they had slotted in Hydroxii agents loyal to the cause.

The team pressed on as they made their way through the bunker. The team's leader, codenamed Byson, led them through the low-lit corridors. Byson was a strong command figure, a perfect operative for humanity, with his dark past and nothing to lose. He had a particular desire to bring in DeMarko after he had taken down two of his previous team during the early end of the Human-Hydroxii war, the rebels taking this as a welcome chance to strike back when the military was at its most vulnerable. His team now compromised of four AO soldiers - himself, Ice, Pyro, Trinity and Sage; the nicknames used to keep their real identities a secret from prying eyes.

The team were renowned for their ability to complete every mission, retrieve intel or shut down entire military operations. For once, they were fully prepared with lots of firepower which made them extremely dangerous. Following the operatives, as backup, was a group of marines. The two sides disliked each other, but the intelligence and military leaders picked up important information which sparked a very small alliance between the two sides.

Byson reached the end of the corridor and held up his hand in a fist. The team stopped and surveyed the room, their rifles aimed high, their bodies braced for combat. Byson lowered his rifle and placed an object against the iron door which stood in front of them. The object beeped and suddenly the audio from inside the room filled his helmet. Byson clicked the device from the door and stowed the object in his utility belt.

"Ice, Pyro, I want you two up top with the marines," Byson ordered as he leaned the rifle, checking the ammunition counter, "Trinity, Sage, you two on me, we're going in first, the others will cover us."

The two teams moved into their positions, Byson and the two operatives leaned against the concrete wall beside the large iron door.

"Okay, on three we breach and take this bastard down, agreed?"

Green acknowledgement lights blipped on Byson's heads-up display; this was followed by a small count down. He stepped forward, pulling a handful of breach charges from his belt, placing them on the corners of the iron door. Byson moved back and pushed his rifle into his shoulder, leaning away from the door. He counted in his head.

Three. . . two. . .one.

In a flash of light and blaze of white flame, the door fell abruptly. The room lit up and confused shouting could be heard from those inside. Without flinching, Bryson swung into the room firing short bursts at the militia soldiers nearest to him. The teams breached, bringing disarray to the militia soldiers, the suppressors barely heard in all the chaos. The thermal imaging built into the helmets guided the soldiers inside and to their targets.

Less than a minute later the militia soldiers and scientists were either dead, dying or had a rifle to their heads. Byson attached his rifle onto his back with a magnetic click and scoured the captured soldiers before recognising his prize, Julian DeMarko.

"Ah, there you are, you ugly bastard!"

Grabbing him by his hair, Byson lifted him upward and threw him to the middle of the large room. DeMarko grunted as he landed and slowly lifted his head. Byson unholstered his pistol and leant down to the militia commander, pistol firmly pressed against his forehead, reminding him who was in charge.

"Your reign of terror is over."

DeMarko laughed and shook his head, "You think this, this ridiculous armour makes you stronger than me? You cower behind this abomination acquired through dirty methods and you call me a monster!"

"Don't act so smug!" Byson shouted as he grabbed DeMarko's head and pushed the commander's face hard into the floor, "You will have plenty to talk about once the Intelligence command boys and girls bag your sorry arse." Byson pulled Demarko's bleeding face upward. DeMarko smiled through the blood dripping from his nose. "They're going to stick you in a black hole you won't be getting out of any time soon." Byson pushed off from the floor, shoving DeMarko's shoulders and walking towards his team.

"Nice job Byson!" Ice patted him on the back. Even as she enjoyed the brief victory, Ice sensed she was being watched.

Glancing to her right a blur moved in the shadows. Ice's visor twitched trying to give her a visual of whatever was stirring, but she shrugged it off and turned back to her team.

"Cuff this lunatic, Byson, and we'll all get out of this pit, shall we?" Ice swung a pair of handcuffs from her utility belt and held them out for Byson to take.

"With pleasure."

Taking the handcuffs from Ice he turned back and knelt down, fastening the handcuffs around the leader's wrists. He twisted the dial on them, smiling as DeMarko grunted in pain. As he pulled him up, DeMarko struggled out of Byson's grip, stepping back and brushing his face against his shoulder to wipe off the blood pooling on his face.

"I think you underestimate me," he called out, smiling wide to himself, "This pathetic attempt to silence me will not go unpunished!"

"Just shut up old man or I'm going to gag you," Byson brought out his pistol and pointed it at DeMarko, "or you and me will have some problems."

"Oh, I don't think I will be your only problem. . ."

A squad of Hydroxii paladins, adorned in very similar armour to Byson and his team, appeared as if from thin air in front of the stunned team leader. The Hydroxii soldiers were wielding standard issue plasma weapons used typically by the alien species and stood unflinching in a defensive line in front of the commander.

Byson stumbled backwards pulling out his assault rifle, pointing it from side to side. "Pyro what's your ....," Byson glanced up to the balcony where the marines and other operatives had headed but found that they too faced the same problem.

"What's going on DeMarko?"

"I'll tell you what's happening, augmented toy soldier, a new order is going to rise up and tear down the foundations of your precious Global Task Force!" DeMarko stepped confidently beside the Hydroxii soldiers and held out his hands. One broke the handcuffs with the brute force of its fist.

"We are going to do what they couldn't alone."

"Do what? Enslave an entire species?"

"No," Demarko grabbed the Hydroxii's plasma rifle and fired point blank at Byson's armour, the shielding blistered and failed as he fell backwards, "We're going to elevate ourselves above all who stand in our way, become something. . . more, starting with the cleansing of you augmented monstrosities!"

The Hydroxii units fired indiscriminately, ripping apart the marine squad. Watching, with a dark smile, DeMarko stood and relished the scene unfolding before him as his Hydroxii paladins gunned down the first of his many enemies. Finally, the time had come. He could destroy the foundations of the Global Intelligence and Military Task Force and unleash his plans to take full control of anything he saw fit to claim. The Hydroxii were hard-working, technologically powerful and extremely resentful of the current state of affairs. He could be responsible for a cataclysmic event which would set the galaxy on its head by the end of it all. It was time to do what even the Hydroxii with all their power hadn't done - end free will.

DeMarko turned to the lead paladin, who stepped forward with his arm across his chest as a sign of respect.

"DeMarko, two augments are fleeing." The paladin pointed to a large screen that hung above the room; it showed two panic-stricken operatives attempting to escape.

"Don't worry about them," he turned, handing the paladin its plasma rifle back and grabbing the giant alien's shoulders, "I have a surprise waiting for them. It's time for our shadow to rise brother."

The paladin turned and spoke in its own language, ordering its squad mates to go on the hunt. The Hydroxii paladins crossed their arms and each camouflaged themselves as they turned to leave. The lead paladin stared at the monitor. Revenge would be sweet for Nag-Adeer, Supreme Commander of the Hydroxii.

Ice grabbed Pyro and pulled him behind a crate as a swath of plasma flew towards them, scarring the concrete walls as it sparked on contact. Looking down at her rifle's ammo counter, the reading of '0' gave her a disappointed, sad feeling. Ice turned to her squad mate and leaned in.

"Pyro, I'm all out," she pulled her pistol from her belt and twisted it in her hands as the digital readout counted the bullets leftover in the magazine, "down to maybe one clip of pistol rounds."

Pyro twisted on the spot as plasma continued to beat the area around them, the shouts of the Hydroxii closing in made it awkward and uneasy.

"I'm down to my fist. . . so I can see we have a problem." Pyro threw his empty rifle across the room in disappointment and tapped on the data pad strapped to his arm. Tapping on his digital screen, every button command brought up a red error marking, "No way to communicate with our exit either, damn it!" Pyro slammed the data pad against the crate. Ice peeked around it only to spot a large squad of Hydroxii soldiers holed up by the exit.

"Jesus. . . I count at least fifteen paladins, all special forces spec, armed with a mix of weapons." Ice pulled her head back to avoid the incoming barrage of plasma and sighed, "Any ideas on an exit strategy?" She leaned her helmet against the crate, which shook from the impact of the plasma hitting it, and turned to a disheartened Pyro who was slumped against the wall. "Merrick please?" she twisted and knelt in front of him, his visor glinting a mix of red and orange as they heard the sound of the plasma barrage ahead of them.

Pyro lifted his head, the fact she used his real name made him realise how scared she really was. Pyro shook his head, reaching at the join between his helmet and body armour. He lifted and removed the helmet, throwing it aside.

"Listen Jane," he grabbed her hand and smiled, "we're not going to make it, you realise that don't you?"

Jane turned away unable to meet Merrick's eyes. Placing her depleted rifle by her side she tried desperately to plan her way out but came up short as the plasma fire drowned out her thoughts. The incoming Hydroxii moved ever closer to their position. Jane swiveled on her feet and pulled Merrick to his feet.

"Then let's go down fighting," she smiled as she took her pistol and placed it into Merrick's hands, "Fighting the good fight!"

Merrick smiled and placed his hand on to Jane's shoulder, "Let's do this."

Jane sprinted across the dimly lit concrete corridor and pushed her back against a crate. She turned and unloaded the pistol, counting exactly how many bullets she had left. Jane pulled her arm back and breathed out. She unclipped the magazine from her pistol and read her on-screen display. Four. Four bullets against fifteen heavily equipped Hydroxii special forces soldiers. Easy. She pushed the clip back in and looked over her shoulder ready for Merrick's signal.

Merrick rushed up from his cover, pulling on his red and orange engraved helmet and walking up to the Hydroxii. They raised their plasma rifles, aiming squarely at the incoming human. Merrick held his hands high, his helmet now in his hands and shouted loudly, "Okay, okay! I surrender!" He stepped towards them.

Despite the fifteen strong squad, the augmented soldier continued moving his way towards them unphased by the overwhelming force, smiling as he did so. The Hydroxii, confused by the ignorance being displayed by the human, were becoming edgy, their fingers twitching on the triggers of their weapons. A Hydroxii soldier, donned in a commander's helmet, scarred across its left eye, raised his hand for his unit to hold its fire and stepped forward himself. Merrick continued toward them.

"Human, do you finally accept your fate?"

Merrick made no effort to slow down, "Oh no., I'm here to even the odds!" Like something seen in a western movie, Merrick flicked his pistol from its holster and emptied the clip into the commander's chest causing him to fall backwards. The Hydroxii raised their rifles but were caught out by the incoming fire from across the room. The Hydroxii commander shook his head and stared in confusion as the human jumped at him with his fist clenched. The Hydroxii commander scrambled for its plasma blade but found the human had already reached him and begun to flail punches at him.

Jane twisted from the crate and ran as fast as she could towards her teammate. Pulling herself over the railing, she landed, throwing her empty pistol at the closest Hydroxii soldier, landing a punch on its head as she side-stepped the huge alien. Jane grabbed the nearest Hydroxii and threw it to the floor, ripping the plasma rifle from its grip and firing into the tightly packed alien squad. Throwing the rifle at the closest Hydroxii paladin, she reached out and grabbed one of the plasma grenades clipped to its belt and pressed it against the chest of another of the paladins who was trying to flank her. Sparking a light blue, the Hydroxii pulled frantically as it tried to yank the grenade away from its armour, but the plasma had fused to it already. Jane kicked the paladin into a wooden crate in time for it to detonate, splintered wood spraying all around inside the confined room, knocking the feuding races to the ground.

Desperately trying to find her balance, Jane pushed hard on the ground. To her surprise somebody was helping her to her feet. It was Merrick. After all those heroics he had somehow survived.

"Merrick, move!" Jane pulled the combat knife from Merrick's chest holster and pushed him aside, stabbing it into the throat of the Hydroxii commander and dropping its plasma blade to the ground, sparking along the floor. Merrick clapped as he laid on the floor and Jane arrogantly put her thumbs up before turning and planting her fist firmly into the closing paladin's helmet, relieving it of its rifle.

"Jesus, now that was ice cold stuff Jane. Not even a flinch!" Their celebrations were cut short by the firing of a plasma cannon as the Hydroxii brought in reinforcements.

"Okay Ice, one last run, okay?" Merrick called as he took the rifle from Jane, "You're going to get back to Earth and warn them." Before Jane could refuse Merrick was already running at the Hydroxii soldiers, plasma rifles flashing across their path. Jane made a break for it and didn't look back, side stepping and rolling between their ranks she pushed on hard.

Dragging herself through the doorway, Jane moved closer towards the exit, wondering just what was going on here? How did a militia commander manage a union between the Hydroxii who could hardly stomach working alongside the humans in the current truce state? It was going to be quite the de-brief.

She reached the hatch they had entered through and ran into the door, knocking it open. To her delight, she was greeted by a team of augments. However her delight was quickly replaced by shock and bewilderment - what the hell was really going on here?

Jane fell, stumbling as the blast from a large shotgun hit her chest, the armour doing as much as it could to help her survive. A human figure blocked out the daytime sun and stared at her as she lay on her back, breathless. Before she could muster a word, another soldier stepped up to her, unholstered its pistol and fired.

Chapter 2

The room was beginning to heat up. It felt like someone was holding a magnifying glass up to the sun, amplifying its intensity. Despite the heat she continued to pour the hot coffee into the mug, not the corporate mug everyone else had, this one was special. Well, kind of special. Grabbing the mug, she set off down the corridor ready for the early morning rush of police officers as they made their way to their desks. Kayleigh Crawford had been on the Atlanta State police department for eight years now, having been promoted to Sergeant for exemplary actions during the Human-Hydroxii War. Kayleigh had bravely taken on a Hydroxii soldier in order to rescue a family from a crashed car. After doing so she received a commendation and, with it, a promotion. She pulled the chair back and sat at her desk and sighed. Paperwork mounted relentlessly in her in-tray. Kayleigh tapped her fingers along the desk, putting the cup to her mouth and taking a long drink.

"Time to get to work."

Slowly she leaned across the desk and began to pull the files one by one, flicking through the non-essentials and quick reading the notes written by various officers. But something was distracting her, gnawing away in the back of her head. It had been distracting her for over a year now. Swiveling on her chair she leaned against the back rest, turning to a long digital screen and tapping a few times until she found what she was looking for.

Kayleigh had an eye for the strange and often tricky cases, but this one in particular was really worrying her, it was more than a mystery waiting to be solved. Over the past year seven bodies had turned up with unexplained injuries. The thing they all had in common was the dark purple bruises, but the truly strange part was the fact every one of the victims was full of an unknown toxin. And it wasn't just a minor detail, it was circulating around the bodies. Since victim number one, the 'symptoms' had been more and more severe, to the point where the state disease control team had declared an emergency. Was it a new drug? Or something far worse.

What troubled her further was the fact that the Global Intelligence Command were always on the scene, taking over using their powerful authority. She never received any answers and as more bodies turned up in the city, they simply vanished and the case was closed. As easy as that. She hoped nobody was aware she was trying to get to the truth. They would only tell her to stop.

Swiping the data across the screen from side to the side, she was so absorbed in her own thoughts she barely noticed her partner, Greg, sneak up behind her.

"So Kay, what ya working on?" Greg side stepped another officer, nodding as they muttered under their breath.

"Nothing," she replied almost falling off her chair, "Just old cases. And stuff. Things."

Greg shook his head and smiled. The kind of smile that somebody gives when they know you're not doing what you're supposed to be doing.

"Sure, anyway, we need you at the scene of a body dump."

"Another one of those. . .?" she asked, raising an eyebrow.

Greg nodded and waved his hand, gesturing her to follow him. Moving off her chair she swiped the case files across the screen and picked up her coffee. Downing it in just a few big gulps, she half-heartedly pushed her up-to-date case files together in a neat mess and pulled her police jacket from the back of her chair, heading to the lift.

As Kayleigh stepped into the lift, there was an awkward silence before Greg finally turned to face her.

"Kay, please tell me the truth." His comedic demeanor had changed, and she suddenly felt uneasy.

"Okay, about what?" she asked knowing full well what he was alluding to.

"You know exactly what, those zombie looking guys we've been picking up all year! Tell me you're not investigating, please!"

She turned her head glancing to the button panel, toying with the idea of pushing the emergency stop to avoid the glare he was giving her. She clenched her fists and turned suddenly, "And so what if I am? What's it got to do with you?"

Greg kicked the elevator door, "Dammit it, Kay. I knew you were stubborn but, Jesus Christ, what if those idiots at GIC find out?"

"But what if there's something going on Greg?" she snapped back, "What if this is some Hydroxii conspiracy?"

"This has nothing to do with the Hydroxii, I'm sure we would know by now if it was. They're not the kind of species to lightly poke the bear," he put his hands on her shoulders and closed his eyes, "Seriously. Please stop looking into this, okay? We turn up, we do our jobs, we go home, that's it alright?"

She turned away but knew he wouldn't stop pestering her if she didn't agree and nodded, "Fine fine...," she replied, feeling like a child getting a telling off.

"Great, now I can keep my job and not end up in a black hole," Greg called as he exited the elevator and headed towards their patrol car. Kayleigh pulled the door open and climbed in. She was a little caught out by Greg's reaction to her looking into the victims but, as her partner, he had a right to criticise but not to know the full extent. That's how partnerships work.

Arriving on the scene, the distinct flash of red and blue emergency services' lights was almost distracting in the shade before the busy highway tunnel. Greg came to a steady stop and the pair unbelted, climbing out to assess the crime scene. It had been sealed off and preserved perfectly - police barriers up, officers holding back and dealing with the press, blockades up to avoid a media snap of the crime and the unusual daytime heat to add to it all.

Stepping around the blockade and through the holographic police barrier, Kayleigh entered into the crime scene 'zone'. A large tent and been placed over the area to keep anyone who shouldn't be there from handling evidence and to stop any drones getting a peak of the crime scene.

Pulling back the old school tarpaulin, she lifted the material, holding it out for so that Greg could step in. In front of her laid the good old yellow numbers indicating each piece of evidence that had been documented so far. Before her feet lay a thin streak of blue liquid which led to the body of the victim - a common drag scenario to hide the body. The assailant was obviously caught by surprise and had had to abandon the body.

Kayleigh pulled her notebook from her breast pocket and began to scrawl. She twisted around and found the beginning of the drag mark. There was an abrupt line, probably where the boot of whatever vehicle had brought the victim here had been. What was strange, however, was the way in which the body had been dumped without much attention. Simply discarded and propped up in a back alley on a busy road. The rush hour traffic not too keen on being held for 'another one'.

The people of Atlanta had been through a lot over the past few years. When the Hydroxii finally mustered the strength to attack Earth, its major cities were the main targets during their High Command's crusade to wipe out humanity. Hydroxii capital ships had hovered over the city and released a swarm of fighters and drop ships; in seconds the beautiful city was a burning fireball. Kayleigh was on patrol that day and could remember how the entire city had paused in disbelief as the Hydroxii glided into orbit. Eventually, their disbelief had changed to shock and fear, panic reigning supreme.

Sidestepping around the first indicator, Kayleigh turned to her left and stared down the road at the queue of cars, a similar view to that of the day she almost lost it all. She recalled how a Paladin drop pod smashed down into the ground, tarmac and concrete splintering around it. Out came the nightmares the military had warned the world about. Quickly dismissing her painful memory, she stepped up to the officer guarding the body, looking kind of lost.

"Hey, its Danny, right?" she asked with a smile.

Turning in shock, the rookie jumped a little and patted himself down, "Yes Ma'am, Danny Mayland."

"You new here?"

"Ye-yeah, yeah just got in actually."

"Alright, well first things first, talk me through the scene."

The recruit stood for a second staring at Kayleigh wide eyed like an animal caught in the headlights.

Danny cleared his throat and held out his hand, "Ermm yeah so. . . ," he stepped aside and pointed towards the tent entrance, "Well the victim was dumped over there dragg-"

"Yes, I get that but I'm looking for something else," Kayleigh tapped her pen against the notepad and indicated for the recruit to continue.

"Something else?" he stuttered, a little taken by her questioning,

"You're giving me the obvious, what I've seen as I walked onto the scene, give me something I don't already know."

"Okay, well I-I-I ermm figured the tyre treads leaving the scene have to be from a GM-31."

"A GM-31? Like a marine class?" she asked puzzled as she wrote quickly.

"No Ma'am, civilian class."

"And you know this how?"

"Tyre sizes Ma'am, marine GM's have wider tyres than civilian ones."

"There we are," she patted the rookie's shoulder, "Easy hmm?"

The rookie nodded, gave an awkward smiled and almost jogged away from her to avoid further embarrassment.

Kayleigh knelt beside the body currently covered by a sheet and pulled it back. This was another of her 'mystery cases' and one she had just been told to avoid. The typical blue veins were far more apparent this time around. The victim's blood had almost become the very liquid oozing from the body.

"So Greg, what am I to do and say about this then?"

"Well," he replied stepping forward, "I say chemical re-action to something, the swollen eyes suggest a reaction, so purely accidental."

Kayleigh looked at Greg and shook her head. Bullshit, she thought to herself, "Bravo Greggo, excellent detective skills used there."

Greg shrugged and walked away to talk to Danny who glanced awkwardly to and from Greg back to Kayleigh. Kayleigh turned her back and examined what she could of the body. Despite its dramatic look, it resembled a lot of the previous victims - blue bruises, blue veins, but something else stood out this time. The victim had extreme muscle mass on the left side of its body. The muscles had physically torn the body leaving rips in the upper arm where cloudy blue matter had seeped out but not from the fatal wound. This was something she had not seen with the previous victims; new, more severe symptoms were showing up and yet nobody would give her an explanation without slapping a huge 'classified' stamp across every single word, even the date for crying out loud.

As she couldn't trust anybody to hand over any or all the information, she had decided to document the scenes herself before the intelligence division pulled a fast one and threat-ened them with the 'black hole' punishment. They had a habit of making people or things disappear, whether good or bad, yet this time these infected bodies were appearing in broad daylight, media documented and almost common knowledge. More were showing up and with increasingly distressing signs of physical damage. Was it a side effect of some kind of test? Maybe the GIC were using test subjects? Perhaps a new method to create the augmented soldiers?

She shook off the questions before the idea, and the smell, made her sick. Stepping back out of the tent, she took in the scene from a distance. Kayleigh walked back to the patrol car and clicked the button on the boot, revealing the inside of the car. Rooting inside she pulled out her data pad from her backpack and began taking pictures of the notes she had written at the scene. She would make sure that there was a log on their records back at the station, one way or another.

As she began uploading her data, the ominous sound of a tyre squeal reached her ears. Black tape was coming – the GIC.

"Shit!" Pushing the data pad back into the car, Kayleigh jogged back to the tent. As she fell through the tarpaulin door, she came face to face with GIC agents and armed military police. And so, the black tape began. Kayleigh stepped towards the GIC agents but was stopped by a pair of military policemen.

"Do you want to call off your mob please?" she growled, her arms outstretched. She was itching for a fight.

The GIC agent talking to Greg turned and waved his left hand down - the stand down gesture. Kayleigh muttered an expletive under her breathe and barged past the guards. Grabbing the lead agent by his shoulder she spun him around.

"Why are you interfering with police matters again?"

"Actually Officer Crawford. . .," the agent grunted as he turned and patted Kayleigh's hand away, "you should know by now the way this works"

"Oh, I do, but I don't like it." Kayleigh folded her arms and eyed the agent, he was always the one to shoot her down.

"You don't have to like it. You have to deal with it."

"Not without authorisation," she smiled smugly knowing that the agent had intended to force his authority on the police rather than do things by the book.

"Listen Crawford, you are great at your job, and I'm glad you were promoted for your heroic acts," the agent grabbed her shoulder and squeezed tightly, "but that shiny commendation won't save you from a dishonourable discharge."

Kayleigh lowered her head and sighed, she knew she could only do so much but things were beginning to get out of hand, she had to fight her cause.

"You still need a warrant of some kind or blank paper at minimum."

Greg let out a small laugh only to be met with a fierce scowl from the GIC agent who waved his unit out to the delight of Kayleigh and her police force.

Greg applauded lightly, "That was impressive."

"Aww thanks Greg, don't use up all your compliments in one go, will you?"

"Oh, I won't but I think that a world class trip to the jobs fair might be coming." Greg patted her shoulder and made a slow walk to the exit.

"I'm just trying to do my job," she replied putting her hands in the air.

"Yeah? Well try keeping your job too."

Greg walked out of the tent and left Kayleigh standing with the rest of her squad giving her mixed reactions. She shrugged it off and walked back to her patrol car. She pulled her data pad from the boot once again and began working away, keeping her mind on the job. Carefully she began documenting all the information, swiping pictures and notes across to the relevant folders, connecting her data pad back to her desk at the station. She pulled up a new folder, this new body would be the eighth victim on the streets. Eight too many.

Swiping the files she had just written on the new victim,

the similarities between each of the cases was obvious. At the start of the year, the first victim was recognisable to the public and to Kayleigh; sadly it was close to home and the victim was her friend Tyler Poulson. He had gone missing two weeks previously; he'd been discovered in mysterious circumstances. He had no enemies, kept himself to himself and worked hard to give himself a chance in life. No one could really give her an explanation as to what was going on or what had happened to him, just the fact it wasn't an accident. When the second body turned up, things started to get more secretive. The second body was that of a shop worker, another strange disappearance, this time just one week before being found. The body more grotesque this time - an eerie pale grey colour, where the neck had some kind of strange intestinal rope around it.

This is when the GIC started to take over and push their noses in, taking the cases from them. Months went by before the next victim turned up; the Atlanta Police Force were almost breathing easy until one of their own disappeared. A city-wide manhunt ensued in an attempt to stop them from becoming another statistic, but they were too late. The officer's body turned up in the car park in a busy shopping district in the patrol car he had used before his disappearance. Again a week covering the time scale. From then on Kayleigh had made it personal and intended to close the case herself, however, she was constantly overshadowed by the black tape of the GIC and the inability to get any backup to hunt for who was responsible. Everyone was too scared to push the GIC into assisting them. Now six more bodies in two months had shown up all over the city. Since then the military and intelligence divisions had conducted raids, publicly announcing their intentions and reports or part of them, to show the city they had been doing something. Nothing ever came up in their investigations worth mentioning, or so they said.

Kayleigh pushed the data pad into her backpack and turned to find Danny walking towards her.

"Be careful Ma'am, those intelligence guys don't seem too happy."

"That's because we're doing our jobs properly," she smiled and closed the boot of the car. Across the road she saw Greg talking to someone on his radio. Glancing across he pocketed the radio and jogged back to their patrol car.

"Are we going now or are we going to be causing more trouble?"

"That depends if you have finished being a wimp," she scowled and folded her arms.

"Come on Kay you know I can't hassle those guys."

"You can and you know it. It's wrong and we need to be seen as trying to uphold the law, or some of it."

"This is not our war," Greg started up the car and accelerated away, "This is between the GIC and the militia."

"The Militia?" she turned with a puzzled look.

Greg paused with his eyes wide, shaking his head as he tightened his grip on the steering wheel, "You didn't hear that from me."

"So it's the militia then? Interesting, I didn't even put a thought in for those guys, I thought they were disbanded to some degree."

"Well it could be, I don't know exactly," he fumbled around with the dial of the car radio and turned it up louder. Her cue to shut up.

The journey back to the station was long and awkward, neither of the two officers spoke after that, not even to shout at the bad drivers attempting manoeuvres in the city.

Arriving back at the station Kayleigh was the first out of the car. She opened the boot to pull the backpack from it and stormed off to the elevator they had used before attending the scene. Greg locked up and pulled out his data pad. Heading to the lift he expected her to hold it, instead she pressed for the fourth floor and left giving him a cold stare.

"Dammit it!" he muttered to himself as he held tightly onto his data pad. He needed to be careful with what he said but it would become difficult to keep certain information from her. He pushed on the button to call the elevator back, the light flashing for just a second before going off. Angrily, he pressed it several times before resorting to a quick punch and a step back; this partnership was about to take a turn for the worse. He turned to the door next to the elevator to make the long walk up the stairs to the fourth floor and her glares.

Back at her desk, Kayleigh slammed down the backpack, causing her colleagues to give her awkward glances which she returned with another of her glares. She pulled out her data pad and placed it down on her desk, pushing her bag carelessly onto the floor. She began looking into her past cases and sorting files out, creating a new folder where she intended to map out the timeline from victim one to the latest eighth victim. As she began to work, she was unaware of the sudden change of mood in the station and the uncharacteristic silence which was setting in.

Stepping through the door leading from the stairs came a disgruntled Greg, he came to a sudden stop. Out of the elevator stepped out the GIC agent who had had the standoff on the scene with Kayleigh. Alongside him were two soldiers in military police blue armour. They didn't glance at any of the officers in the station as they followed the agent through. Kayleigh looked up from her screen, noticing the GIC personnel, and slowly got to her feet. Greg walked up behind her and pulled her back as she tried to step forward. Kayleigh quickly glanced at Greg who shook his head. Ignoring him, she pulled her arm free and walked behind them. The GIC agent walked into the police force Captain's office and closed the door behind him. As Kayleigh tried to walk in the soldiers pushed her back.

"This is official GIC business Ma'am," the soldier informed her calmly.

"I don't care, this is my station," she grunted trying to force herself through.

"Ma'am," the soldiers pushed her back, "I won't warn you again, step back." This time he raised his weapon a little as a warning. Looking down she saw the rifle wasn't on safety. She stepped back and raised her hands as the door opened and the Captain stood, with a stern look on his face, glaring at her. With the wave of a finger she knew that she was in trouble. Shoving her way past the soldiers, she stepped into the office, grudgingly standing alongside the GIC agent in charge.

"Kayleigh, I presume you have met Agent Falaney?" the Captain asked indicating the agent who turned and smiled at her.

"I believe she has."

"I have had the displeasure of meeting this man, yes," she replied not making eye contact with the agent.

"You know who he works for then?"

"Yes I do sir but-"

"But nothing Kayleigh! The Global Intelligence Command

have jurisdiction over everything!" the Captain shouted as he interrupted her, "We uphold the law in this city for the people in it, they uphold the law that we can't."

"Sir, with all due respect, we have no idea who is behind these killings, so how can they claim jurisdiction over them?"

"Actually we do. We believe it is the Hydroxii."

"Bullshit!" she snapped, "If it was the Hydroxii there would be more than one body by now, there would be hundreds, and they would remind us of who did it. This isn't them."

"I would tell you how we know but you're not on the same page."

Kayleigh turned to the Captain, "Sir, please, I have a link established between the victims and have an idea of where to look."

The Captain shook his head, "No, I'm handing all the data we have on this to the GIC and they're taking complete control of the investigation." He pointed out to the office where GIC personnel were setting up desks for themselves, "We are giving them control of the station so they're first on scene, we just uphold the peace."

Kayleigh turned and stormed out of the office almost knocking over the soldiers on guard duty.

The two high ranking officers stood next to each other.

"As mentioned, my team and myself will accommodate you." The Captain offered his hand.

"Appreciated Captain, but I don't think some of your company feel the same," the Agent replied as he watched the Kayleigh storm past her partner and out of the building. They may need to do something about persuading her to toe the line.

Chapter 3

Jack fidgeted, the painfully solid plastic chair making the wait all the more agonising. He watched on as dozens of men and women, everyone from scientists to marines, were all hard at work, not giving him a passing glance or even a nod of acknowledgement. Jack put his head in his hands and sighed. How long did it take to start a meeting?

He was ready to give up when the door to the office finally swung open and a pretty faced secretary stepped out and smiled, "General Kato will see you now." She stood aside and gestured to the doorway. Jack stood, smoothed down his trousers and made his way through. As he approached, a team of four augmented operatives walked down the corridor, the lead soldier glancing towards him as they passed.

Shrugging it off he entered the room, smelling the distinct aroma of cigar smoke. Trying not to cough, Jack stepped up to the desk and offered his hand to the General. Dressed in a bulky black suit, Kato looked up and leaned to the side, nodding to the secretary to close the door. Jack awkwardly retracted his hand and stood to attention.

"So marine, you have quite the record," Kato spoke to the data pad in front of him, making no eye contact as he flicked through the marine's military record, "Some might call it exemplary."

"Thank you, Sir," Jack held his head high, keeping an eye on the General's unmoving facial features.

"You proved to the military task force that you are a leader, strong in combat, smart on the field, but here at the GIC, we require more. Much more."

"Sir," Jack replied tilting his head a little as he tried to catch the man's attention.

"Here we do what the military boys and girls can't. We kick the bad guys when they dare to do us harm. Not just on their knees," he stood up from his chair and walked to Jack turning him around and pointing out of the window, "but on their arse. You see those AO soldiers out there?"

Jack nodded.

"They are some of the meanest bastards we have. They do what needs to be done. No questions, just actions."

"I have already gone above and beyond fighting the Hydroxii several times," Jack replied, a bite in his voice.

"Yes marine, I read your exemplary combat record, but I need somebody who can lead those men and women and do what needs to be done, no matter the cost." Kato turned and sat on the end of his desk, folding his arms as he took stock of the soldier who stood before him, his suit tight to his body and his composure unmoving despite the General's questions. "There's no hesitation here. We do the job whatever the outcome. We always complete the mission."

Jack turned back to the General, "Sir, what do you need?"

"I need a new team leader, Jack," Kato picked up a paper dossier from the top of the desk and handed it to him. Jack noticed it felt extremely light. Opening it up Jack looked up at the General, then back at the paper.

"Sir, it's all blacked out," Jack forced the dossier back into the General's hand, "Is this some kind of joke?"

"No not at all. That is the world you're walking into – a black hole where nobody knows who you are, in fact nobody cares. You will disappear into a new war." The General stood up and pointed to the augmented operatives that passed Jack while he waited outside. They were talking and laughing amongst themselves. "You're going to lead them." Jack turned and checked out the four soldiers. Each operative had their own unique armour preference. They stood out from other operatives he had seen. It wasn't just their armour, or their colour choices, it was their attitude - without even speaking their demeanor spoke for them - their confidence, their power; he wasn't surprised they were chosen to become an augmented operative.

"Sir, who am I replacing?" Jack asked without turning,

"Who says you're replacing anybody marine?"

"They look pretty solid to me. A good team. Most squads are made up of five. There's four."

Kato smiled and placed his hand back on to the dossier he had just passed to Jack, "The man who's file I gave you."

"It was all blacked out. How am I to know who he was, how he led? I get the need for secrecy, but what was he, a ghost?" Jack asked calmly,

Kato handed him the file again and pointed to the top. Hidden within all the blacked-out text and pictures there were just two words: *Codename: Byson*

"You're his ghost,"

The General moved to the office door and ushered Jack out. Stepping out, Kato nodded at Jack to follow. The pair headed out of the office to go to meet the augmented team that Jack would be given leadership of. Jack, however, was a little uneasy. Despite over thirty-five operations during the war, over hundreds of fights against an alien race hell bent on putting the human race into extinction, the task of leading this particular unit was quite a daunting task in comparison.

As the pair approached the operative squad, their jovial attitudes soon become dull glares as they eyed up the 'new kid' who was walking towards them. Jack fidgeted a little to try and put his mind at ease. It wasn't working.

"AOs, I want you to meet your new squad leader, Major Jack Halliday," the General sidestepped to allow the team to give the new guy an even more disapproving look.

"It's a pleasure," Jack casually held his hand out to offer a handshake. The lead soldier looked down at his hand and back at the Major.

"There are no pleasantries here, Major," the soldier turned back and sat down on the crate behind him. Jack tried hard not to cringe at how awkward this meeting was becoming. Without him noticing, one of the other soldiers had stepped up behind him.

"Don't worry about him," the female's voice calm and sarcastic, "He's always grumpy. So you're here to lead us, hmm?" She placed her hands on her hips, "I think you need to show us what you can do before we accept you." The General gave her a scowl. "Although we will anyway. We don't have a choice.".

Together the two remaining soldiers of the team stood with their arms folded. The pair stood side by side with Jack and gave him an up and down glance.

"Well, he is certainly ugly."

"I agree, this is perfect."

"Really? I can't be led by an ugly man. Byson was ugly enough."

The joking soldiers both got a dig from the female soldier. "Have some respect you idiots he's MIA."

"Sorry ma'am," the two soldiers replied in a quiet tone as they stepped back awkwardly.

"Sorry about that. Those jokers haven't got much respect," the female soldier called out.

"That's okay. Can I ask what happened to your squad leader, Byson?" Jack quizzed as he took a shot at talking to the team while they dropped their guard.

"No one knows," she leant forward and whispered, "He went out with a team on a special op and never came back."

"But I thought you said he was MIA, surely that means he could be out there?"

"We're always marked as missing in action," she glanced down, her emotion showing a little as she moved about the room, clearly unsettled, "He was a good man, I hope you're better. And ready."

The four soldiers stepped out of the corridor and began wandering away. The soldier who had been sitting on the crate rose from his spot and faced Jack.

"If you're really keen to get to know us. . ." he pulled his rifle from his back and threw it towards Jack, "Show us what you've got."

Jack grabbed the rifle and twisted it in his hands before he nodded to accept the challenge.

The General patted him on the back, "Well you made an impression, not bad."

"What did he mean by showing them what I've got? Are we

being deployed already?"

"We have a combat arena here in the base. These guys train against each other. The best, training with the best. The only way to be the best is to beat the best. And that's what your job is. To be the best!"

The General walked away, leaving Jack standing in the corridor; he heard the quiet murmurings of the scientists and marines wandering by as he weighed up the situation. He was about to enter the hidden world of the intelligence division. Here you go in and often enough never come back, and no one knows you were even alive. A new kind of warfare was about to begin.

Jack swung open the door to the armoury open and stepped inside. The room was filled with all kinds of weapons, armour and technology from standard equipment to infiltration gear. Any normal soldier would have thought they had entered a research facility. The weaponry on display was impressive and deadly. Walking through the armoury, he was met, almost nose to nose, by one of the soldiers who had challenged him earlier.

"Alright Halliday, it's time to show us what you've got." He reached into one of the ammunition lockers and tossed a box of training rounds at him, "We, your wonderful team, want to see you at work."

Jack turned back to the wall lined with assault rifles and pulled one from the weapon rack, pushing one of the magazines into it then pulling back the loading pin. The ammo counter, on the weapon's digital display, adjusted as it counted the magazines capacity.

"You can call me Spider by the way," the soldier called out as he selected an unusually shaped rifle of his own from the adjacent wall.

Jack stepped slowly to the side, the rifle firmly in his arms as he watched the soldier adjust the weapon in his hands. In his hands was a light grey rifle, its barrel a cold blue colour. The weapon's gunsight was moulded to the weapon and, as Jack continued to slowly step across the room, he noticed one distinct feature which stopped him in his tracks. The weapon was a Hydroxii plasma rifle, adjusted for human use and modified with pieces of human technology. This was slightly unfair Jack thought to himself.

"So why do they call you Spider?" he asked casually.

"You're about to find out aren't you!" the soldier replied pushing a glowing blue cartridge into the plasma rifle.

"This is slightly unfair, isn't it?"

"We augments live for an unfair fight, Jack, you should know that."

Jack followed Spider out of the room. He found himself inside another vast space, this time it was filled with body armour stands and various base staff who were running diagnostics across many of the consoles in the room. Littered around were five large machines connected to several uniquely designed helmets. The helmets were unusual, and Jack couldn't put his finger on their design. They weren't standard marine helmets or even Air Force. As he pondered their origin, Jack stood trying not to show his surprise as he watched the operative, Spider, pull the helmet from the stand and put it over his head. Pushing a button on the back the man was almost consumed from his head to his hands and then covering his entire body. Once the armour had finished covering Spider, he gave Jack a thumbs up and entered into the next room. This wasn't the marine core anymore.

From behind him, the three soldiers making up the rest of the team stepped up to the other armour stands and pulled over their own helmets, again each one different to the others. Subtle colours painted their armour giving them their own unique style. Finishing the armour wrap process, the soldiers selected their own plasma rifles from the weapon rack and exited the room.

Jack stepped towards one of the armour stands and peered from left to right. Nobody made a move to help him and so he decided the last helmet must have been assigned to him. The helmet was without colour. He imagined the colours all had different meanings within the team. Jack pulled the helmet free and examined it briefly, rolling it from side to side to get a feel of its weight. It was incredibly light to hold, and, with a quick breath, Jack pulled it over his head, standing in surprise as the inner visor blinked and revealed an array of information and data. He stumbled and dropped his rifle as the armour suddenly engulfed him. Within seconds it was wrapped tightly around his body, but he barely even noticed it. It was like a second skin. It was close-fitting but not connected; it was an unusual sensation.

Turning around slowly in bewilderment, Jack started as one of the scientists stood in front of him with the rifle in his hands.

"I take it the armour fits then?"

Jack nodded.

"Excellent. The armour is Hydroxii by origin, but we managed to pry it from one of the fallen Paladins and well. . . with the spoils of war, we reverse engineered a set and made new armour. Now be careful, this is extremely expensive and valuable. I will bill you for damages."

"Wait, is this not mine?" Jack asked, his voice altered

slightly with the helmet's in-built mouthpiece.

"We shall see Major. In you go!"

The scientist indicated that Jack should turn around. Jack jumped slightly as the scientist pushed the rifle against the backplate of his armour, its magnetic lock clicking quietly over the sound of the helmet, providing endless amounts of data onto his heads-up display. Turning back to face the scientist, Jack felt a pistol pushed into his hands. The scientist patted his side and Jack placed the pistol against his leg, it was instantly magnetised to his armour. Lastly, the scientist attached a small data pad to Jack's leg. Once satisfied, he pointed to the exit door and gave Jack the thumbs up.

"Good luck Major, you're going to need it."

Jack pushed through the door and found himself in an extremely large room. Shaped like an arena, the room was filled with tall rectangular pillars covered in unusual markings. Before he could fully take in his new surroundings, flashes of electric blue plasma splattered the pillars besides him, lighting up his armour and room like a torch. Jack pressed himself backwards against the nearest pillar, bracing his body as the plasma fire cracked the stone around him.

Jack was briefly stunned as he considered the exercise he had just stepped into. He wasn't even thirty seconds on the squad and was already involved in a live fire exercise, and it was a no holds barred match.

Jack grabbed the rifle from his back and pulled the loading pin, arming the weapon in his hands. Flicking his body around, he took aim, firing short bursts in the direction of the incoming plasma flares, hoping to give himself an opportunity to move. Jack paused as his visor briefly marked the hits on his display, quickly realising this wasn't designed to be fair. The training rounds were not normal training rounds. They were just paintballs.

General Kato walked into the room and the nearby scientists stood to attention. He gestured for them to get back to their work and walked up to a team who were studying the various screens displaying a barrage of information, from heads up display visor feeds to heart rate monitors.

"So. . . how's he doing?"

The lead scientist turned to face the General before laughing a little as he glanced back to the screen, "He is not happy, talk about into the hornets' nest."

Kato watched the camera feed as Jack braced behind cover, "Let's see if he's as good as he says he is."

Kicking the pillar with the heel of his armoured suit in annoyance, Jack spun round, this time aiming down the sight firing shots at the higher vantage point. The small paintballs covered the area in a multitude of colours giving him a chance to sidestep to a different pillar. As he prepared to fire more shots, the panel below him slid away forcing him to move out into open space, taking a shot to the chest which knocked him down. On his back, Jack jolted forward as he attempted to find his feet in the unusual armour. His frustration turned to panic as the panel revealed a large mechanical turret. Jack rolled to avoid the weapon's large rolling barrel as it ripped up the panels where he had just been laid, the high calibre bullets ripping them apart with extreme force.

Attempting to get his breath amidst the dirt and concrete flickering around his head, a pinging sound filled his helmet. On his leg, a data pad flashed the name 'Hunter' repeatedly.

Lifting it, he pressed frantically on the screen trying to figure out what it did, praying it wasn't a decoy as the firing was beginning to switch sides and angles. They were on the move and had the homefield advantage.

On the screen a large button appeared with the words 'Push me!' written across it. Pressing the data pad, his right leg flashed a light purple, and the heads up display inside of his helmet flickered and was replaced by a purple outline. Jack's visor flickered briefly to a dark purple and inside his helmet the unusually cheerful voice of a female echoed in his head.

"Hello Hunter, my name is AI54-3C or Harley if you prefer, I will be- "

The AI was cut short by plasma shots skimming Jack's helmet and he bit back in anger, "Seriously I do not need an automated- "

"I AM NOT AUTOMATED!" his HUD shuddered as the AI shouted into his earpiece, "I didn't choose to be your AI. . . this was Kato's ridiculous idea to help you and if you don't want to embarrass yourself you will listen to me NOW." The AI brought up a radar on his visor display and four dots pinged back in red, "There – your targets."

"I gathered that – but I'm a little pinned, if you haven't noticed, and very overpowered," he snapped.

"Push on the panel above you, it'll switch the battlefield around."

Jack looked up and slammed his palm against the pillar, his handprint remained on it as the arena shook.

"Now. . . run!" Harley shouted as the arena's large pillars began to lower and adjust in size and positioning.

"I thought you were helping me!"

"Just run and keep your head down!"

Jack darted across the lowering pillars and stumbled as new formations rose up to give him the cover he needed as he slid behind one. He pushed the assault rifle over the top of the covering formation and fired short bursts into the now exposed soldiers who found themselves without any cover, the paintballs splashing across their armour. One soldier threw down his plasma rifle in disgust as he staggered out of the arena.

"One down, three to go," Harley called, marking out one of the four crosses on Jack's heads up display.

His delight was quickly drowned out by the blast from a pulse grenade, its shockwave knocking down a nearby pillar and almost crushing him. Peering over the crumbled pillar, Jack came face to face with one of the soldiers who was raising his rifle ready to shoot. As he lay there, the damaged pillar began to crumble and tip to its right. Grabbing his rifle, Jack jumped to his feet and charged at the enemy, who for a moment, lowered his sight in surprise.

Jack flipped his rifle around and smashed the butt into the corner side which brought the pillar down in front of the dueling soldiers. Seizing the advantage, he threw his rifle to the ground and grabbed his pistol firing the entire magazine, lighting up the body armour in a rainbow of colours. The soldier threw his rifle to the ground and put his hands on his hips as he wandered out of the arena. Another one off the field.

"Nice job Hunter," Harley called encouragingly, dropping another cross off the board. The celebrations, however, were cut short by the thud of boots hitting the floor as a barrage of fire sparked across Jack's armour. As he stood there taking the hit, he found himself mesmerised by the shimmering shield wrapped around his Hydroxii armour.

Firing blindly, he stepped from his cover only to come face to face with another of his combatants. The enemy soldier punched the pistol from Jack's hands and planted a fist into his helmet, his shield shimmered from the force. The punches kept on coming and soon Jack found himself unarmed and in a predicament. The soldier's relentless punches kept him pinned to the floor. Jack flailed around and landed a punch in the soldier's chest sending him stumbling back, but not fazed by the attack.

Lunging forward, Jack swung his fist entirely missing his enemy who, with incredible strength, flicked him onto his back, leaving him winded. Another punch landed on his helmet. This 'training' exercise was starting to seem brutal and personal. Placing his arms across his helmet, Jack blocked the punches as best he could. As the soldier let up for a moment, Jack knocked him back with an uppercut. Jack grabbed for his pistol, ripping it from his utility belt, and fired repeatedly till his shields fell and he was forced backwards. With the final rounds, Jack emptied the magazine before grabbing the paintball-filled pistol from the ground, firing it with a smile on his face. The soldier slammed his fist into the ground. Jack reloaded as he awaited the final encounter.

"Well, that was interesting, nice grab!" Harley called in excitement.

"I'm no stranger to bad odds, Harley." He propped himself against a pillar and leaned out.

Jack spun around as he spotted his last target and fired his remaining shots. The target was a hologram and the shot passed right through it. He threw the pistol to the ground and reached for his assault rifle as his last target fired a barrage of blue plasma at him, his shield failing immediately.

"Jack, careful that's just knocked your shield off entirely."

"Thanks for the obvious," Jack snapped back as he took a punch to the helmet before another barrage of plasma fire lit up his armour. He turned on his heel and kicked the pistol at the soldier's helmet.

"Oh and you're all out!" Harley shouted.

"I noticed!" His sarcasm was cut short as he was thrown against the nearest pillar after taking another punch. Giving a quick jab in return, Jack pushed the soldier back. Whilst he had the chance, he launched himself up and on top of the pillar, out of reach. Staring at the soldier, he couldn't tell who it was and wouldn't find out as they slammed the pillar nearest to them shaking the room once more. This time it revealed a large array of sentry guns sitting high across the back of the arena.

"RUN!"

"On it!" Jack jumped to his feet, leaping from pillar to pillar as they were torn apart by the heavy rounds fired by the sentries' large barrels. As he ran, the soldier giving chase fired a shot unbalancing Jack dropping him back into the maze once more.

"Harley, please, I need some help!" Jack groaned as he lay on his back.

"I'm out of options. I've been locked out!"

"Great!" Jack pushed himself against a nearby pillar and tried to come up with a plan on his own.

"Jack, I have an idea, just hold out for me!"

"Wait, won't you then be in the system?"

"Yeah, but we want to win, don't we?" Harley laughed as Jack pulled the data chip buried in the data pad. With the chip in hand, Jack pushed it into the pillar which lit up with a purple light.

"Don't mess up now!" she called as she disappeared into the system.

Jack's heads up display stuttered as it changed back to its standard blue. It was now missing a few key features. He leaned away from the pillar to get an eye on his target but was met with a sharp jolt of plasma. Knocked back, Jack side stepped back into the maze in an attempt to guess his target's next move, but the shots seemed to come from all directions making it an almost impossible fight.

Trying to plan his next move, his thoughts were once again cut short by a crack of light, this time followed by a fist pushing Jack into a pillar where he was subjected to more hand-to-hand combat. Unable to get a hit in, Jack raised his arms in self-defence and attempted to hold his own. The soldier throwing the punches was all too aware that he was in control and Jack found himself being thrown across the arena to another pillar. In agony, he lifted his head to see the soldier, plasma rifle in hand, wandering towards him. Placing the rifle over his head, Jack's eyes were wide.

"Oi!" a voice boomed across the arena. The soldier holding the rifle looked around trying to figure out what was going on.

"Hunter, now! Hit the pillar!"

Accepting Harley's order, Jack slammed his palm against the pillar. Stunned the soldier spun around coming face to face with a turret. The turret opened fire and knocked the soldier onto his back. He lay there winded, coughing heavily.

Jack got to his feet and wandered towards the turret; a hologram of a female was projected from it. The artificial intelligence was a light purple, her clothing strangely that of a punk rocker from days gone by, her hair a wild mess of dark purple standing out from her light purple scalp.

"You miss me?" she joked flicking the hair to one side, her hands on her hips.

"That was impressive."

"Get me out in the real field and see what we can do."

"Deal." Jack pulled the AI chip from the turret and wandered back into the armoury where he was greeted with applause and cheering. During the fight, a fairly large crowd had been watching and Jack found himself the hero of the hour. The female soldier was the first to congratulate him.

"Not bad for a cheat," she laughed as she patted his shoulder, "The name's Venom by the way, no personal names here." She walked back into the crowd and two more soldiers stepped forward.

"Well, I'll let you off, using her like that," the first said as he put his arm around his comrade.

"Yeah, I guess I can be happy you're my man in charge," the second said bringing Jack round to join the huddle.

"We come as one."

"A duo or a duet depending on the weapon of choice."

"But you can call me Dragon."

"And me Draco, see you on the firing line!"

The pair walked off and Jack smiled to himself. A quick shove followed as he was pressed up against the computer panel. It was Spider.

"Don't get smug now, this is a battle not for the faint-hearted." Spider let go of him and stepped back, "You're going to need a strong head or you're going to be dead and useless to me." He stepped up to Jack, almost in his face, "And I will be the one popping you." He walked off and threw the plasma rifle across the room.

Jack brushed off his armour and shook his head. Harley appeared on the console in the middle of the room, one hand on her hip.

"I wouldn't worry about that guy, he's all bark and no bite. He's just pissed he didn't get the squad leader role." She watched as Spider kicked the door open and walked away. She turned back to Jack, "But you're way more suited for that job."

"Thanks and cheers for the assistance." Jack put his thumbs up seeing as he couldn't shake her hand.

"My pleasure, honestly that was fun. I've not been in a combat scenario before. It's nice to see someone without trust issues here."

Jack watched as Spider talked to the team, the team he would be leading into an unknown war, one he was extremely unprepared for.

Chapter 4

Jack hovered impatiently over the table. The heat from the Valkyrie dropship's engines, though they were cooling, still warmed the space around him. The dropship was thin, like an arrowhead, its cargo bay doors etched into the rear. Jack had spent a number of encounters stumbling out, rifle first, into enough firefights to recall every inch of this particular dropship's firefight history. On the other side of the table a tall, well-built, young engineer hauled out crates of all shapes and sizes. Jack peered around looking for a particular crate in. The pilot hopped over the crate half laid across the Valkyrie's ramp and headed over to Jack.

"So you're the new kid, eh?"

"I am, yes," Jack replied bluntly as he tried to look over the pilot who was now standing in the way.

"The name's Grant, Sir," the pilot smiled as he held his hand out, "I hear you gave your own team an ass whooping!"

"Yeah, but it wasn't that special."

"Wasn't that special?" the pilot squeaked with excitement, "Man you just gave those stubborn arse augments an ass whooping. . . single handedly!"

Jack let a small smile slip across his face, the story of his initiation wouldn't sit well with Spider, but he didn't mind, maybe it might ground the stubbornness from him. Besides, the pilot didn't need to know the real story.

"Anyway, it was pretty awesome."

The pilot finally carried out the crate Jack was waiting for and placed it in front of him. Jack finally shook the pilot's hand. The pilot saluted and turned back toward the Valkyrie to continue.

"I think you might have made a name for yourself, Jack," Harley chuckled into the intercom covering his ear.

"There you go sir," the engineer finally relinquished the dropship of the one bit of cargo that Jack wanted, placing it into his hands.

"Excellent, thanks Private!" Jack lowered it to the ground and began to disconnect the latches. Carefully lifting the lid, he began to rummage through the crate. Checking the contents over briefly, he smiled to himself as he closed the lid once more. He proceeded to lift it up and headed out of the loading bay.

"Come on, Jack. So what did we just stand around waiting for?" Harley buzzed in his ear

"Just some personal stuff from my old base, Harley."

"No one owns ANY personal stuff that they get that excited about, so spill your human emotions please."

"You know, for an AI, you are more like a nosey child than a complicated line of code."

"Hey, I'm a few million lines of code actually and I'm incredibly intelligent, best in class if you must insult me."

"I don't understand though, for an AI you're pretty mobile. Don't you have to be plugged in or something?"

"I'm more than just an AI, I'm unique. Only one of my kind to reach a level where I can move this freely."

"So how come I've never heard of AI out in the field? Are you Hydroxii?"

"No, I'm not. I'm a breakthrough in artificial intelligence Jack, not a technological mess like those suits you insist on wearing, for which, by the way. you're welcome."

Jack continued down the corridor and continued to haul his crate gleefully, the contents jingling along as he carried it through the base. Since arriving he had not been the most welcome human being, but the arrival of personal items should have a hand in altering his feelings about being on the base. Without him noticing, Venom had snuck out from one of the corridors and had started following him. She stalked him as he wandered throughout the base without a care, speaking to Harley through his intercom. Nearly the entire base was on comms or a communication device, but Jack stood out like a sore thumb. His mood was different to that of everyone else on the base, probably because they hadn't broken him in yet.

"Jack you must really enjoy drawing attention to yourself or something," Venom called from behind him.

Jack turned, narrowly avoiding a scientist walking idly by, "Ermm, no. Why?"

"Oh nothing, just you're talking to yourself and causing rumours about us already," she stepped in front of him and spun round to hold the door open, "I think you enjoyed that fight, didn't you?"

"A little, but those rumours haven't come from me," Jack replied calmly trying to stay on her good side.

"Relax kid, I'm joking.".

Jack finally reached the locker room and pushed his way inside.

It was like stepping into a black abyss. The lack of colour and row after row of grey lockers made it difficult to even tell the walls from the lockers. Jack stumbled up to his locker number and pulled it open. Putting down the crate, he began placing the items inside, taking care not to damage them.

"You know, for a young guy, you are very odd," Venom laughed as she watched him attend to his locker, "How did a guy with a life, end up in the dark and dangerous world of intelligence and espionage?"

"A step up," Jack replied, barely turning his head.

Venom laughed again and shook her head, "Well, I'll give you that. . . it's certainly a step up."

She sat down on the bench behind Jack and peered around him as he picked up a picture.

"Family?" she asked politely.

"A team become your family, don't they?" he replied smiling, "This was my old team back on Base Gorda."

"They look quite the bunch."

Jack slotted the picture into the slit of the locker door's lining and closed it up, "They were a great team, sadly-."

As Venom was about to pursue the answer further, the light in the room turned red and the ominous sound of sirens wailed through the base.

"All combat personnel to combat ready positions, this is a Code Alpha Six. I repeat all combat ready personnel to combat positions, we have a Code Alpha Six."

Jack looked around and tapped his intercom, "Harley what's going on?"

"I don't know but Kato wants to see Viper One in the briefing room," she replied with a sudden seriousness.

Jack jogged out of the room and headed down the corridor

to the briefing room. Venom sat for a second and breathed slowly. Reaching down to her utility belt, she double-checked her equipment and eventually got up to join him.

Entering the briefing room, the blazing sirens were toned down, the flashing red lights not so blinding as he met up with the rest of his squad. General Kato stood, with his arms folded, staring at the large screen, data moving across it revealing streams of information, small video screens pinned to the right-hand side. Just behind Kato were Spider, Dragon and Draco who huddled in front of the large screen. Spider turned as the door opened, the sirens blaring through as Jack stepped in; there was no emotion on his face as he turned back to the screen. Jack stepped towards his team and placed himself next to Draco, who gave him an acknowledging nod.

"Nice of you to join us, Hunter."

"Sir?" Jack stood with a puzzled look on his face as he was addressed by an unfamiliar name.

"That's your new operational name, Hunter. Consider it an official housewarming gift. Anyway, back to the task at hand." Kato's expression barely changed as he turned back to the screen, "For those of us joining us late, Camp Kyreel is currently under attack by militia forces." Kato flicked across the screen with his hand, "These are not standard militia, they're heavily armed and have plenty of armour on site already."

"Sir, where did they get all that firepower from?" Spider asked raising his hand to the monitor, "Last dealings with them were hardly this much fun."

"I'd like to know that myself. We know they have been putting a lot of effort in lately to gather a force, but this is not what we were expecting." Kato folded his arms in a disapproving stance, "Anyway enough questions. Harley. . ." He turned to the pedestal on his right and Harley appeared, her appearance slightly different from the last time she was in person.

"Thanks, General. The militia are using their tanks as mortars to bombard the facility to cover their troops on the ground," she turned on the pedestal, twisting her hand and bringing up a new screen of information, "Hunter will bring you in along the eastern side, here you will neutralise the tanks and proceed to assist anyone left alive on the inside."

"Couldn't we use a team of Valkyrie dropships and assault jets to do that? Seems a big ask of five augments to be the only ground operation." Spider asked puzzled.

"The Valkyries will provide air support only once the asset is retrieved. We need you on the ground. The base is home to the command node for a new orbital defence cannon." Harley turned and flicked her wrist, revealing new images and layout plans of a giant space cannon, "If the militia get hold of this, then we are in trouble. Your job is to stop them from accessing this at all costs. Besides air support can't retrieve this on their own."

She gave Spider a smug smile and turned to Jack, "You will lead the squad in and out, no backup."

"No backup?"

"Not on this occasion."

Jack stared at her.

"Don't worry, it shouldn't come to that."

Venom darted into the room, "Sorry sir!" she called as she sidled in alongside Jack.

"Hunter, will fill you in. Suit up Vipers," Kato turned and

passed the soldiers, nudging Venom as she stood a little out of place.

"Nice of you to join us. . . oh wait," Spider joked as he pushed past her with force. Venom flicked her head to say something but thought better of it.

"You alright?" Jack asked as he held the door for the rest of his squad.

"I'm fine," Venom barged past and headed to the armoury with the rest of the team.

Jack turned back and walked to the pedestal Harley was displayed on, "Oh well, this should be fun, moody teammates and tanks! Perfect!"

She put her hands to her face and shook her head, "Yeah whatever, come on."

Jack headed out the door as Harley's digital image faded away and she spoke into the earpiece, "You'll be glad to know I've chosen you a new set of boots."

Jack walked into the armoury, the team had already donned their armour, their equipment human this time. Stepping up to the helmet, Jack pulled it from its stand and twisted it in his hands before pushing it over his head. As it engaged around his body, he still couldn't grasp what the armour was or how it exactly worked.

"The armour is a mix of Hydroxii and nanite technology, lots of science. . . Oh and you have purple gloves." Jack laid his hands out and sighed. "Hey don't sigh!"

The team gathered at the lockers and chose their weaponry. Spider grabbed an assault rifle and clicked it to his back plate before adding two pistols to his utility belt. Dragon and Draco weren't joking when they'd said they were as one as they both took Battle Rifles from their holders. These rifles were specially designed and featured a red and orange dragon design on their sides, the red laser sight replaced with a black infrared scope. Venom hovered slightly over the locker, not exactly choosing weapons but thinking. Jack pulled out an assault rifle, angling it low to switch the rifle to single shot mode and opted to add a small sub machine gun which clung to his thigh.

The Valkyrie lurched from side to side as it ploughed through the low-lying clouds which were providing cover for them on route. The team sat not uttering a word as they prepared for battle, only the sound of the pilot's out of tune humming was heard through the aircraft.

Jack stood, reaching for the handrail above him, and stepped awkwardly to the cockpit's door, "ETA?" he shouted through his intercom.

"Two minutes Sir, breaking cloud cover in ten seconds. Should give you a visual in just a moment," the pilot tapped his comms off and began to make adjustments on the dropship's dashboard.

"Okay Viper One, I know there's a bit of frustration with me being team leader, but we have a mission to complete. Let's leave the banter at home."

Apart from Spider, who continued to adjust his rifle, the rest of the team gave a unanimous nod. Jack shook his head and shrugged off his teammate's reaction, "The armour on the field is modified Wolf class standard battle armour. With quick turret rotations speeds, we want to be under their noses fast." Jack walked through to the back of the Valkyrie and grabbed the panel perched on the rear of the dropship to hold himself steady. "Once dealt with, we will move on the base and neutralise any targets on the way to the node. With the cannon on offer, we need to hit them fast and cover it till we can call in support." The team nodded silently in response and rose to their feet.

"Viper One, this is Echo Five. Five, you are clear to. . .jump." The pilot clicked off the comms and the rear panel lit up green, the Valkyrie's rear hatch lowered steadily as a blast of air filled the now open rear space. As it lowered completely, the dropship landed briefly above the ground, the grass tearing up underneath the roar of the engines.

Jack pulled his rifle from his back and stepped off the ramp, the steady sound of armoured footsteps that followed meant they were boots down and the mission was a go.

"Hunter, I'll be on point for as long as I can from a distance. Clear those mortars and I'll do what I can from there," Echo Five called out over the intercom as the dropship's hatch closed and it lifted swiftly into the cloud cover.

"Copy that. Hunter out." Jack aimed high and stepped quickly toward their objective, the team following in unison as he jogged over the hill accompanied by the sound of tank shells. With the evening light covering their backs, they might enjoy a small element of surprise, but they needed to get in fast or they would need searchlights and flares to call up support. Jack knelt down and poked his head over the hill. In a line, the five Wolf class tanks shook the ground around them like an earthquake as they fired almost in unison. Observing the area, the team followed suit and were quickly alongside him.

"Alright Jack, plan?" Spider asked awaiting orders.

Jack continued to eye up his enemy and his options, "We take them out one at a time, move fast on each target, use their own tanks as cover."

"Let's hope they don't mind shooting at each other," Spider laughed sarcastically.

"It's alright, you're on." Jack turned and Spider could sense a smirk despite his visor completely covering his face.

Spider moved across the hill into a position where he could get the jump on the armour from behind, allowing the rest of the team to move in and distract them.

Reaching his position, he had one last glance over the area before placing the rifle onto his back plate. He sat for a moment, trying to count the time between the shots. Over and over, he counted until he was happy that he could time it just perfectly, he could jump over the hill, board the armour and do some damage without being knocked back by a round. The target fired its shot. In the time between the firing mechanism slamming the shell into the cannon and out, Spider was already flinging himself over and down the hill, eyes firmly on its rear plate. Pushing off from the soft grass Spider lunged at the Wolf tank, holding firmly to a metal arm sticking out from the back of its large turret. The impact from the soldier's armour alerted the tank crew who spun the turret around allowing easy access to the entry hatch. Jamming his hand under the sealed latch, Spider dug in and began to pull till the lock clicked and was flung open. Swinging into action, he jumped almost cleanly across the tank's wheel arch. Landing and finding his balance, he looked up and saw the militia driver armed with a pistol aiming straight at him. Ducking, Spider lost his grip on the tank and rolled away. A short sharp burst of rifle fire splintered across the tank and eventually landed on the armour, the driver slumping back inside and reversing across the field towards him. In desperation Spider rolled across, narrowly missing the armour's larger, modified wheel treads as it crashed hard into the next Wolf tank in line. In the confusion, the tank crew had fired a shell landing directly underneath the opposing tank. The armoured pair both lit up in a ball of orange and yellow fire, destroying them both in the process.

Spider jumped to his feet and punched a fist in the air, "Look at that, two in one!" he gloated.

"Alright Spider, enough, next target we're on route," Jack replied calmly as he waved his team onwards pushing a fresh magazine into the rifle. Making their way to their next targets, the four squad members took cover behind the burning tanks, their armour shining in an amber glow.

"Spider, those remaining Wolves kn-," Jack tucked in as shells pummeled the ground around them as the remaining armoured unit switched targets.

"I hear you and I'm on it!" Spider replied confidently.

"Echo Five, you here still?" Jack shouted into his comms piece over the armours' shelling,

"Yeah, I'm here, two minutes till I'm zeroed in though," the pilot crackled in reply.

"We need you to give us some support for as long as you can, three Wolves East of our position."

"Copy that, on it."

"Okay, once Echo brings the fire we move, clear?" The team nodded and waited for the guns to pass over.

The three Wolf tanks rotated their caterpillar treads and began heading straight for them. The ground began to shudder as the large treads tore up the grass beneath them. Jack impatiently checked over his shoulder as he awaited the Valkyrie's arrival, the wait seeming like an eternity with the inbound armour threat.

"Echo, we need you now!"

"Almost there, Sir," the pilot spoke trying to reassure the Major.

"Not good enough. Team on me, we're moving on three."

"Jack there are three heavily modified mortar tanks closing in on us, you intend to hit them without launchers?" Draco questioned.

"Improvise."

"Jesus Christ!" Draco shook his head and gripped his rifle tighter in his armour.

Jack peeked over one more time and held out his hand, three fingers acting as their countdown. As the team twitched and readied themselves, Jack slowly withdrew his fingers and gripped his rifle tighter. With the clench of his fist, the squad moved over the burning tanks and ran at the remaining armour. As they made it past the burning wreckage, the objective seemed a tough ask as the clearing opened and there was no cover in sight. In a blast of warm air, Echo swung the Valkyrie over the hill, the jet thrusters pummeling the ground as it flared up above the wreckage. The dropship dipped its wings at an angle, halting in midair as it positioned itself over the squad to provide cover fire. For a moment, its heavy machine guns lit up beyond its reach and tore into the nearby armour.

"Nice timing, Echo," Dragon called out with a chuckle in his voice as he sprinted across the field, "In fact I think we should rename this moment-"

"Not now, Dragon. Echo, suppress those tanks, were moving on them," Hunter butted in, swaying his finger in front of his teammate, who shrugged in response.

Venom swung herself around the wreckage and brought her assault rifle forward. She aimed low as she fired shots at the armour's barely noticeable window hatch. The tank swung its turret around but stopped midway as the shots ricochet off the armour plating. Continuing its swing, the armour brought its turret to a halt and fired its large machine gun at the incoming soldier, the ground popping beneath her.

Sliding to the floor, Venom slithered up to the tank. Swinging an arm up onto its wheel arch, she hauled herself up. Hunter watched as Venom elegantly climbed the tank, nothing but pure finesse as she negotiated the large iron body work.

"Venom in position," she called as she planted her fist into the hatch of the Wolf tank's driver's seat.

"Dragon, Draco, jump on that last bit of armour. Echo let's finish up here."

"Loud and clear, Major." Echo tapped away on his dash as the large cannons tore into the final tank, its explosion not fazing the team as they poised to eliminate the remaining tank operators.

Spider, who had already boarded, had begun dismantling the Wolf tank and had released the hatch to reveal a very stunned driver. Dragging him out by the scruff of his neck, Spider launched him up and out before turning to come face to face with the co-driver, who had climbed free of his machine-gun post. Aiming down the rifle's sight, Spider fired. The militia co-driver pushed the rifle to the side before pushing him back. Off balance, the soldier reached for his pistol and aimed. Jumping, Spider landed on his back, the militia soldier followed but he was struck down by a short rifle shot. Spider turned to his left to find Jack running to his aid.

"I owe you nothing, Jack," Spider grunted as he was helped to his feet.

"Seriously, I thought you guys didn't use names?"

"Rookie problems, my bad."

Jack shook his head and led the team to the next Wolf tank. Climbing the tank, Jack unclipped and dropped a grenade into the pilot hatch and disabled it for good., the team rushing past to take on their last target. Venom fired her rifle, hitting the Scorpion's militia driver, calmly dropping a grenade into the cockpit of the tank. She stepped down as the explosion closed the cockpit off for good.

"Talk about drama bomb," Draco held out his fist.

Venom blanked her teammate and headed toward Jack, "Clear Major," she said triumphantly, "Next-" Venom was cut short as a rocket ploughed into the hull of the Valkyrie, the blast knocking the Viper team off balance slightly. Before the squad had time to scramble, the dropship landed on top of them. Hitting the ground, the fuel ignited into a large orange fireball, the blast whipping across the field outwards before retreating and leaving the downed Valkyrie clear for the squad to see just as it landed on top of them.

Chapter 5

Jack rolled over coughing, the armour pushing out the smoke from his helmet. He pushed himself forward and checked the situation and the squad's position. Stepping back into the fight, the team dragged and pulled their way back to their feet and soon found themselves together again.

"Everyone alright?" Jack asked as he tried to make his assessment.

"I've been in worse," Venom replied as she pushed away a large piece of debris.

"Well I've scratched my nice new helmet," Dragon said sarcastically, "Apart from that I'm peachy."

Draco jumped and picked up his rifle, wiping away the large amount of grass which had become embedded in it. As he cleaned it up, he glanced around and surveyed the area. The militia forces were now well inside the base, the local forces were probably also struggling somewhere inside.

"Jack, we need to go now. The guys inside will be struggling now despite the loss of the enemy artillery."

"Agreed. Spider you still out there?" Jack called out as he turned back.

"Still here Jack, seems to me you needed some help."

"Hilarious, now meet us at the bottom of this field, we will meet up on the south side."

"On it."

Jack turned and waved the squad, minus Spider, over the brow of the hill towards the now almost unrecognisable, base wall. The team hurried across the open field to avoid being seen, although the in-house fighting seemed to be keeping both sides extremely busy. As they reached the wall Spider met them at the entrance.

"They all seem to be fighting inside, no guards so we should easily get in without being noticed."

"Excellent. We'll head in as a squad and rush as many as we can, cause a little chaos," Jack turned to face the squad who nodded in agreement. "Alright, on me," Jack raised his rifle high and took the first step inside passing through the ruins of an old doorway, the team following suit.

"Jack watch yourself; they have the entire base to themselves. I can't get a read on the severity of the situation," Harley cautioned.

"We have no other choice, we're the only chance they have of surviving this."

The team entered the base with their rifles held high, as they stepped down the battered and bullet-ridden corridor the losses from the fighting were clear, both sides taking heavy losses. Spider leant down and pressed two fingers to the neck of a barely moving soldier. The faint pulse he felt at first was soon gone and the soldier slumped down releasing the grip on his pistol. Dragon turned away. Whilst they were distracted, a team of militia soldiers had covered off the front and back of their current position and was laying fire to the squad. With the flick of their wrists, the AO's had their rifles aimed and fired before they were even straightened, returning shots as they destroyed their attackers in mere seconds, their firepower much greater and far more accurate. As soon as one group was put down it was quickly replaced; appearing from the side door leading to the old cafeteria, another group of militia took charge. Dragon twisted round and rammed the butt of his rifle into the nearest soldier's face, breaking his nose instantly. The soldier alongside received Dragon's now free hand to the face as he knocked back the two attackers. Switching to his pistol and firing four times at the two soldiers on the rear guard, the magazine was now empty.

"Dragon, heads up!" Draco called out as two more militia fell through the door. Dragon sidestepped and pulled the pistol from his teammate's holster, firing two headshots before holstering it again.

"Wow," Draco applauded, "Hands of god, hey?"

"God's got nothing on these beasts," Dragon joked as he high-fived his teammate.

"We've got to keep moving, we're sitting ducks in these tight corridors," Jack called out.

"Oh come on, Jack, you were a little impressed, weren't you?"

Jack stared at the pair, turned back around, and waved them forward.

"Well, you can't please everyone!"

"I was fairly impressed," Harley called out, "for an AI."

The squad continued through the base, taking out any militia forces on their route, not stopping as they began to push the enemy back. As the enemy were busy hitting the stunned local soldiers, the Viper team were hitting them from behind just as hard and without any remorse, a bit of counter offensive.

Taking out some militia stragglers, the team came to yet another crossroads.

"Jack, the door to the left, get in there and link me up to the system," Harley requested in a rushed tone.

Jack kicked in the door and scanned the area for enemies, his assault rifle acting as his eyes; the team following him in and doing the same.

"Clear."

"Okay, link me up in the mainframe in that data port," Harley illuminated a particular computer in the room with a purple outline on Jack's HUD.

Pulling the AI chip from his data pad, he pushed it into the console, her purple silhouette graced the screen.

"Ah nice to be out, right the mission..."

"Excuse me?" Spider asked puzzled as he stepped up to Jack, "I thought our mission was to insert ourselves into the base, eliminate the militia scumbags and go home."

"Not quite. . ."

"Not quite?" Jack stepped up to the console and lowered his rifle, "Care to elaborate, Harley?"

"This isn't a normal military facility. It's a. . . ermm. . ." Harley stuttered, "black site."

"Oh fantastic," Spider replied with more sarcasm.

"What's so important, or bad, about this particular black site?"

"It's home to some particularly potent Hydroxii tech, particularly the weaponised kind."

Jack turned away from the console and peered towards the open doorway, "Regardless of what this place is, we have a mission. Harley what are we doing here?"

"The facility is housing an artifact and we need to extract it before they do," Harley threw out a hologram of a container. The container had Navy Intelligence over it, the silver edging slightly visible in its darkened position.

"What is it exactly?" Draco asked.

"Classified, now stop asking questions, you are all wasting time, the artefact is -" Harley became distorted as an explosion rattled the entire building, the walls of the room becoming ever more fragile and the roof somehow not caving in.

"What was that?" Jack asked.

"The inner wall has been breached; they have the artefact!"

Jack pushed the rifle into his shoulder and prepared to move, "Where are they Harley?"

"Bottom floor, two corridors to your left, I'll mark it on your HUDS."

Jack pulled the data chip from the access port and pushed it back into the slot in his data pad and ushered his team outwards in pursuit of the militia. As they reached the entrance way, the blast had lodged the doors firmly apart for easy access. Edging nearer, a barrage of plasma fire flickered out of the darkness of the corridor and scarred the concrete walls with a light blue burn. It reflected all the colours of their armour as they were pushed back against the walls.

"What the hell are the Hydroxii doing here?" shouted Spider as he swung his rifle over the wall and returned fire.

"It's not the Hydroxii Spider, look!" Harley buzzed in the team's radio.

Spider dropped his rifle a little as he knelt down behind a partially melted wall to take in the situation. Through the chaos of the bullets and plasma, a squad of armoured militia soldiers stepped out, Hydroxii plasma rifles at the ready.

"Where'd they get those from?"

"Over the course of the war we've kept a stash of them for research."

"Wonderful" Spider propped himself back up and returned fire. As the militia stepped out of the darkness provided by the underground entrance, the team stood and prepared to push forward. The lead soldiers fired up energy shields which acted like a medieval knight's shield, their assault rifles poking out from the well-placed indentation in them, providing them with perfect cover.

Jack twisted back to the wall and turned to his squad, "This is getting out of hand." He pulled the empty magazine out and replaced it with a fresh one, "Draco, Dragon, move up, we need to push them back in-"

"Jack get back!" Venom pulled Jack back as a shell detonated along the roof of the corridor, spraying green plasma lightly across the squad.

"Let's try that again. You two on me, were moving up!" Jack swung round and stepped confidently toward the enemy, firing wildly into the approaching unit, the bullets flickering off their energy shields. Draco pulled a stun grenade from his belt and slammed it into the wall, the flash lighting up the room, the squad's vision, however, unchanged thanks to the active visors in their armour. Distracted, the augmented soldiers pounced on the militia lead soldiers. Jack grappled the front soldier, managing to slip off the energy shield from his wrist, before firing a short burst to stop them.

"Jack behind you!" Draco called out as he glanced across to a militia soldier running at him.

Jack slipped the shield onto his arm and fired it up, swinging round to use it as a riot shield, pushing the soldier back. Dragon fired a number of shots, downing the soldier before he could react. Caught off guard, the militia soldiers stepped back, blindly firing at the incoming threat who were now using their tactic against them. With a few short bursts they eliminated the militia and regrouped.

"Harley, where's the artefact?" Jack asked bluntly.

"It's on the move, they were a distraction."

"Where is it?"

"It's right next to us," Harley spoke in a low tone, confused as she figured out where their target was. "But how were. . ."

As Harley tried to pinpoint the location of the artefact, Draco was knocked to the ground and hit hard by a plasma weapon. The squad reacted and turned to their attacker, only to come face to face with nothing but a blur. Rifles aimed high, the squad scanned the area but came up short. As if out of thin air, bolts of plasma tagged the team, causing them to stagger and stand apart. Spider aimed down the sight and flashed the thermal imaging up on his visor, seeing a black, cold silhouette. Firing, Spider made the most of his position but found himself knocked back, more plasma bolts tagging his armour. Stepping back, he quickly found himself frozen on the spot, his chest and upper leg armour had locked from the plasma bolts. Unable to retaliate, the blur knocked hard into Spider, and he found himself laid flat on the floor with limited movement.

"What's happening? Harley, give me something!" Jack ordered as the target continued its attack.

"I can't find it, it's like a blur! No heat signature at all!"

"Then make this thing stand out!" As Jacks frustration continued to grow, he too found himself pushed onto his back, although he managed to roll aside to avoid the plasma bolts. Looking up, the blur was barely noticeable, yet the faint trickle of light movement made it stand out enough for him to figure out the target was on the move.

"Jack, whatever it is, it has the artefact. Move!" Harley shouted as Jack jumped back to his feet and began to make chase.

As he ran down the corridor, the walls of fallen concrete and broken containers littered the area and made the chase far more difficult. As Jack got closer, the blur turned back and fired more shots, hitting him in the chest, locking his armour down completely.

"What is that, seriously?" he called out.

"Some kind of EMP energy at a guess–"

"Just fix this!"

"Hold on, I need to unlock the system. . . and done. Go!"

Jack pushed off the wall he had come to and darted round the corner. As he made his way to the exit the blur slowed and stopped. A Valkyrie dropship swooped down to pick the target up. Attempting to fire, Jack stepped forward and pulled the trigger, but no bullets came out. Frustrated, Jack watched on as the blur became a more distinguishable form. Although its true identity was still unclear, the armour was extremely distinct. The figure turned its head back to give a passing glance to Jack who had boldly given chase. What shocked him most was the enemy's armour. The soldier wore similar armour to the Viper One squad. Jack froze and lowered his rifle as he watched, wondering how the militia had got their hands on a set of armour they were all adorned with. Had they stolen it, or did they have their own? The soldier stepped onto the dropship and stared at Jack as it took off and left the battle area. Behind Jack the rest of his squad caught up and stepped out of the building, firing at the escaping dropship but leaving no mark on its armoured hull.

"Damn it, what just happened!" Spider shouted as he threw his rifle to the ground, "Since when did the militia get so damned good?"

"That wasn't a normal militia soldier, Spider," Jack replied.

"Oh I get that, Jack, I would never have thought that that was normal."

"No, I meant whoever just kicked our arse was wearing our hybrid Hydroxii armour."

The squad paused to take in what Jack had just told them.

"So we have someone who thinks their incredible?" Venom asked.

"Strangely, it was modified, but not like your current spec," Harley replied.

"First generation maybe?"

"But why?"

"There is something going on here. The militia have just punched us right where it hurts and shown just what they have up their sleeve," Draco pointed out to the mess inside of the base.

"I agree, but they are terrorists, they terrorise. This was a coordinated attack," Dragon replied.

The squad were interrupted by the firing of another Valkyrie dropship as it entered their air space. From the North side of the base the dropship was rising and was heading into the atmosphere.

"Guys, they have the orbital key. . ." Harley mumbled.

"This is Viper One calling home, we need a ride to the station now!" Jack tapped on his helmet and paced as he tried to take in the situation. An enemy Operative with Hydroxii style weaponry and armour technology was going to prove difficult to take down and would become a difficult enemy in the field.

"Viper One, this is home. Valkyrie on route loaded with EVA boosters," the crackling voice of home base was faint but just intelligible enough to be understood.

Jack had never fought in space before. This was sure to be an experience.

Chapter 6

The squad huddled in the bay of the dropship and adjusted their weapons. Jack turned to face them once more.

"Right, they may have a hybrid suit, like we do, but we can't let them take the Orbital cannon too," he ordered as he leant down to pick up Spider's rifle, scuffed from his tantrum, "We will deal with that later, okay?" Spider grabbed the rifle and gave an uneasy nod, stepping back to the squad.

"Jack the militia will need to enter the key manually. It's an unmanned station, no inner structure," Harley buzzed in.

"So, we're going to be in the open?"

"Yeah, but we just need to deactivate the two overrides, it'll keep the station intact but inoperable." Harley played a short video across his HUD to prepare him for his task.

"Great, Viper One form up, we're heading out!"

The Valkyrie ride out to the station was thankfully short for the squad, their setback back at the base being rubbed in by the loss of the artefact and the Orbital Defence Cannon key. The squad pulled on their EVA thruster packs to prepare themselves for any space combat which might ensue. Along with the team was ODC command operator, Dr Tyson, who looked like a bulky marshmallow man in his standard space suit.

"Two minutes out Vipers, ready up," the pilot called from the cockpit.

"You heard the man, suit up and load up, we have business to attend to." Jack stood and looked over to the operator who was becoming increasingly anxious. "Don't worry, doctor, there isn't a lot to be concerned about," Jack reassured him, "Just don't miss the jump." The doctor slowly looked up with wide eyes, Jack smiled in return and patted him on the back. "Thirty seconds! Good luck!"

The squad stood and the dropship fell silent as the pilot locked himself inside of the cabin and the Valkyrie decompressed to become better suited for space travel. The red light above the ramp changed to green and the dropship's ramp lowered revealing the bright sunshine, the moon just out of their initial view. As the Valkyrie levelled itself out, the first console in question came into view.

"Okay, we'll split up. I'll take Dr Tyson and Venom, the rest of you stay here and head to console two," Jack ordered, the squad members nodded in acknowledgement.

"Good, let's move." Jack stepped to the edge of the ramp and fired the EVA thruster pack once to give himself an initial boost over. The gap was huge in real terms, but the effects of space made it extremely easy to move with such long strides. Jack glanced beneath him; the sheer size of the station was clear as his sight was covered by its huge hull. No wiring or electronics were visible, the engineers who built the station made sure everything was hidden out of sight to hide its true power. This made Viper Ones mission harder given that the terminals to access the cannon were behind large metal doors on its outer hull. Jack lightly swung himself to the left as he approached the terminal's hatch. In the corner of his eye, he glimpsed Dr Tyson, in a full astronaut suit, just behind him carrying a briefcase full of equipment.

"How long is this going to take, Doc?" Jack asked.

"A couple of minutes, maybe longer."

"Don't be too long, I expect the militia to be lurking and this isn't the place for a firefight." Jack glanced over his shoulder away from the doctor and fired the thruster, balancing his weight and coming to a steady stop on the landing's edge.

"I'm just estimating Major, the systems we use are–"

"Complicated. That's fine, just keep your head down," Venom butted in as she boosted to the landing just behind Jack.

Doctor Tyson brought himself to the landing and shuffled his way across the ledge, the sun lighting up his darkened visor. Jack pressed himself against the hull of the station and glanced across its vastness and the space it was in. As he backtracked, he noticed Venom glancing from side to side in a nervous fashion.

"How you holding up, Venom?" Jack leaned over and bumped her shoulder. Venom jolted a little, as much as the effects of space allowed.

"Jesus, Jack. Do you mind?" she snapped at him, just resisting the urge to lift her rifle to his helmet.

"Wow, nice and relaxed, I like it," Jack replied sarcastically as he leaned away. As he continued to survey the area, a flash of light popped up from the opposite of the station, turning into a sniper bullet as it sparked across Jack's visor.

"Sniper, move!" Jack ordered as he pushed the doctor out of harm's way into a metal column.

"Major, we need to do this now, we can't afford to lose time here!" Tyson fidgeted, "If we can at least prolong its use–"

"Copy that. Venom cover me. I'll boost out to the upper pillars and hold them off."

Venom nodded and pushed the doctor across in a hurry. Tyson stopped himself from walking any further and clicked his visor up, revealing a clear visor in its place, as he began keying in the code to access the command node. He seen very little combat man in his time so the sparks of light from Venoms rifle, despite them being quiet, bugged him.

"Could you fire a little further away please?"

"Doc, shut it and do your job. I'm saving your arse."

"Excuse me for not being a combat engineer!" Tyson continued to key in the numbers as he hurried the process as best he could, his fingers not so nimble under combat stress. Stream after stream of data rolled across the screen, most of it unreadable to normal people, but every letter made sense to Tyson as he pushed on the console to select the relevant options and keys to get in. The console hissed as the final keys were inputted with the screen lifting out and up to reveal the command node.

"Okay Major, node open, activating lockdo-" Tyson stopped as his body become cold, his eyes wide. A bullet sparked and slowly flicked across his visor. In panic, he tried to keep himself straight, the sound of thrusters hissing in his ears, leaving him feeling safer. As he found himself being rotated around, he came face to face with Venom. Attempting to mutter, he opened his mouth only to be stopped by three more bullets that had been fired. He froze completely and stared into her visor; her emotionless state showed all the intent. She threw the pistol aside grabbing hold of the doctor and twisted him away, pushing him out into space.

"Sorry Doc, nothing personal." She watched as his body

floated off, the blood trail following.

Jack boosted over the column and back into view. "Where's Tyson?" he shouted, scrambling for a hold on the station, "What happened?"

"Militia snuck up on us, Tyson's down," Venom's tone was low as she tried to sound remorseful.

"Damn it!" Jack fired up the EVA thrusters and grabbed onto the console, "How far did he get with this?"

"I think he just needed to input something to lock the node down."

"Fantastic, Spider we have a problem!" The disappointment was clear in his voice.

"Besides the odd militia nut job and space rock it's peachy, what's up?" Spider joked.

"Tyson's KIA. How do we lock the node down?"

"You need to put the station key into the node housing and turn it, simple as that."

"Copy, on it" Jack boosted around, placing the rifle on his back, and grabbing the briefcase Tyson had previously had hold of which hovered steadily beside them. Jack pushed the briefcase against the hull and clicked it open. Inside a long, thin blue key was housed inside. Jack carelessly pulled off the security cover and threw the case aside, letting it float freely into space. Venom glanced back to see a couple of militia soldiers closing in, she raised her hand in a hold signal and the pair nodded. Venom leant forwards, reaching for Jacks pistol. Pulling the pistol from its holster she pushed back.

"Jack behind you!" Spider shouted over the radio. Venom looked up to see the rest of the team above the station preparing to fire. She turned and fired two shots at the helmets of the militia soldiers killing them instantly. Jack pushed the key into the node and turned it, the entire station began to glow a calm blue as it began to power up and then down again, the light more of a recognition of the key.

The team turned around as their Valkyrie dropship came back into view, arriving to pick them up.

"Nice job, Jack," Harley called as she stood using the on-board holographic projector, "I knew you could just about do it without my guidance."

"It was almost easy," Jack turned and pointed to Tyson's body, "Damn, poor guy. Someone should get him."

"On it," Spider called as he boosted towards the scientist, grabbing his body, and spinning round to return to the Valkyrie. The team boosted in and took their places. As Jack stepped in their position was quickly shadowed by a much larger ship. Looking up, Jack took in the view of the Global Military Task Force carrier that was now stationed over them.

"Thanks for the save, Viper One, but I think we have some fixing to do," the ship's captain's voice called in from the radio.

"It's all yours sir," Harley called as she flickered away from the projector, "We're heading home."

Jack pulled himself in and punched the door controls, the ramp lifting up and the decompression commencing.

"I'll need that back," Jack pointed to the pistol Venom had taken.

"Oh yeah, sorry." She handed it over and looked away to Tyson's body. She stamped her foot and put her head back against the headrest, things were becoming tricky and the whole situation was about to become far more dangerous.

Chapter 7

Kayleigh threw the pen on the desk and sighed heavily, there was so much paperwork that it was hard to tell where the desk started and the paper ended. She glared at the screen on the desk as yet another message was received and was added to the ever-growing list of cases to complete. Since being pushed aside by the agents who had taken up residence in the station, the workload seemed a lot higher than usual. The cases were large and tedious, the evidence was non-existent and the chances of putting anyone away was either too low or too much hassle for a lowly police officer. She glanced up as her partner Greg wandered over, hopefully to offer her something more exciting to do.

"Greg please, for the love of god, tell me you have something for me to do."

Greg eyed up the paperwork on her desk and laughed, "I don't think the amount of work is the problem, is it?"

She turned to the pile of paper and tilted her head, "It really is the problem."

"Well, I have a lead on a drugs case, bit of a home visit, if you fancy seeing the outside world?"

"I was hoping for more excitement, but alright then."

Kayleigh stood and pushed the chair back. She grabbed her ACPD jacket and swung it over her shoulder. Kayleigh ran her hand along the holster, satisfied she was armed, and headed for the door. The pair entered the lift and descended down to the police parking garage.

"So, the case, what is it exactly?" Kayleigh asked curiously.

"Last week we got intel on a dealer on the east side causing some problems." Greg handed Kayleigh a file. The pile was light, not much paper attached to it. As she opened the file, she scanned the information and spotted a photo.

"That guy, Hernandez, is young and wanting to make a name for himself," Greg tapped his finger on the picture and pushed the button marked 'Garage'.

"So what's with the personal visit and interest?" Kay asked as she flicked through the file.

Greg smiled as he found a particular document and placed it on top, "Well, it turns out he's been seen stocking weapons for known militia contacts. . . and has a tendency to kidnap people for ransom."

Kay shot a look at Greg who smiled back, "Thought that might perk your interest."

"But I thought you were against rubbing shoulders with the intelligence guys?" she responded handing the file back.

"We need to keep the peace and besides, you're right, this will only get worse."

The lift reached the parking garage and the pair stepped out, heading for an unmarked car.

"Problem is getting to Hernandez. He's difficult, the guy's buried deep in loyal soldiers so we're going after one of his lower ranked men called Ryan Traviss."

"Well, let's do some real police work then," Kay smiled as

she opened the car door and stepped inside. Greg started it up and headed out into the bustling streets of downtown Atlanta.

An hour later and the pair had reached their destination, the rugged streets on east side. This side was particularly notorious for its drugs problems, unemployment and weapons trafficking. It was a black hole for corruption. Kayleigh looked around as they drove slowly through the desolate streets. The litter that blew carelessly in the wind unable to hide the shack-like buildings people had to call 'home'. As they turned a corner Kayleigh found herself looking into the eyes of those she knew all too well. They were Hydroxii eyes.

"Apparently, some of the Hydroxii Knights were left to fend for themselves, they found a place here amongst the chaos of the war," Greg spoke, not taking his eyes off the road as he tried not to make eye contact, "A lot of alien gear comes in and out of here, but we're not here for that. Don't make eye contact."

Kayleigh followed the stare of the Knight, its dark red armour glimmering in the murky light as it stood up from its resting spot. The armour was damaged; blade marks scratched into the alien's chest, probably wounds from a fight during the war. Despite the war being pronounced over both sides were reluctant to hold a truce, after all millions of deaths on both sides could not be forgotten and cast aside. As Greg accelerated down the lane, Kayleigh couldn't help but feel nervous with the Hydroxii for company. She cast her mind back to the day she had rescued the family from the Hydroxii Paladin during the siege of Earth. She had never told anyone that before the famed kill, she had been on her back about to accept the fate of the moment. Weird how stories about heroic acts got twisted. Caught by surprise, the car came to abrupt stop. Greg looked very anxious.

"Alright Kay, first things first," Greg stuck the magnum into his holster, "Keep your eyes peeled, anything is off and you tell me, okay?"

Kayleigh sat staring forward, "Okay."

"Then let's go."

The pair stepped out of the car and made their way towards the apartment block ahead of them. The blocks were falling apart, huge chunks of concrete missing from their huge, towering walls allowing a clear sight inside like a mousehole. As they approached the doorway Kayleigh slowly unclipped her magnum.

"Kay, it might be best not to wave it around just yet," Greg stated, pushing Kayleigh's hands back down to her side. Grudgingly she placed the pistol back into its holster and wandered in. Inside the building was in a lot worse condition than it was on the outside. The beams holding the upper level in place were cut, rotten and, most likely, blasted from plasma fire judging by the scorch marks blazed across them, a sure sign of a battle and why this part of the city was left on its own. As they cautiously stepped through the main entrance, eyes from all over appeared to follow their movements as they made their way. Greg pushed open the stairway door and hurried Kayleigh through.

"Okay, all awkwardness aside, we need to head for the fifth floor," Greg pulled out the notebook from his back pocket and scanned the notes he had written, "Keep your head down."

Kayleigh nodded and followed Greg. Climbing the stairs, the distinct smell of urine, potentially from both species, and other powerful odours filled the air making it almost impossible to breathe without gagging. Kayleigh tried to hurry Greg along, eager to escape the disgusting stench. As they ascended, all kinds of colours filled the gaps in the stairs. Red being the most distinct.

Reaching the fifth floor Greg slowly pushed open the door and glanced from side to side. The apartment blocks were incredibly eerie; sometimes shouting was heard from someone passing by and then, in an instant, it was replaced with silence again. As they crept out into the hallway, doors quietly closed besides them, providing an uneasy and very unwelcoming atmosphere. Greg stopped, putting his hand in the air, he drew Kayleigh to a halt too. Pulling out the notebook once again, he took one last glance before stuffing it into his back pocket.

"Alright, this is it, Ryan's known address," Greg stepped aside to allow Kayleigh to stand beside him, her hand on her magnum as a precaution.

"Ryan Traviss, ACPD. Open up!" Greg beat on the door. No response.

"Ryan Traviss, this is the ACPD open up or we're coming in!" This time Greg beat harder on the door. As Greg concentrated on his task, Kayleigh heard the creek of another door as it was propped open. Turning her head slowly, she looked around to check her surroundings. Opposite the suspect's address a door was being opened a little, not by a dangerous adult, but by a curious child. Kayleigh turned to face the child who pushed the door closed a little to hide their face. Kayleigh placed her finger on her lips and pointed back to the child. The child slowly stepped back into the darkness as loud footsteps were drowned out by the slamming of a door. Kayleigh turned back to face Greg.

"No one home?"

"Doesn't look like it."

"I'm going to kick it in." Greg readied himself. Suddenly the sound of footsteps filled the silence.

"Wait, please don't kick my door in!" a voice shouted from behind the door, "Please, just hold on!"

Greg sighed as he released the door frame and pushed back from it. "Was it something I said?" he muttered as the clicking of locks filled the hallway with noise.

Suddenly the door swung open and a small, rugged man staggered into sight.

"Please guys, I have nothing on me, I'm clean, you don't need to look in I'm-"

"Shut up, were coming in," Greg pushed past the small man and stepped inside.

"Oh come on, this isn't fair. Get a warrant or whatever, come back later please!"

"You sound like you have something to hide, Ryan?" Kayleigh stepped over the mess at the front door as she stepped inside, inspecting the apartment.

"No, it's just I haven't tidied up and you know."

"We're not your parents, Ryan, we're police officers, we have questions," Greg flicked around and poked his notebook into Ryan's chest, "And if you don't talk. . . well."

"Come on man, what do you want?"

"Hernandez," Greg stood with a blank expression on his face as he watched Ryan squirm on hearing the name.

"No way man, he'll kill me!" Ryan shouted as he tried to back out of the room, only to bump into Kayleigh who was standing firmly at the door.

"No one here is listening, so what's the prob-" As Kayleigh tried to reason with him, her hair stood on end as a Hydroxii

Paladin stepped out of the kitchen, a plasma rifle in its hand, aimed directly at Greg. Kayleigh grabbed her pistol from its holster and pointed it. Greg made a move for his pistol as the Paladin fired a blast of blue plasma, grazing his arm.

"That is the only warning you get human," the Paladin stated from beneath its helmet. Its eyes flicked towards Ryan, "And I should kill you where you stand," it growled. The Hydroxii's armour glinted slightly in the poor lighting, its previous battle scars making Traviss fearful.

"No, please, I haven't said nothin', honest!"

"I don't believe that." The Paladin fired the plasma rifle once more, this time scorching Ryan and sending him into the wall. Greg dived out of the way and unholstered his magnum as he took cover behind a table. Kayleigh left the room and pushed herself against the wall as the plasma barrage followed her out. She leaned her pistol around the doorframe and fired into the room, towards the last location of the alien.

"Greg, you there?" she called out in a panic, "Come on, don't slack on me now."

"I'm here," Greg shouted from the room, plasma interrupting the conversation, "Get out and get up to the roof!"

"I'm not leaving you; you're not being a hero." As she popped the empty magazine from the weapon, more plasma fire sprayed down the corridor skimming her arm and forcing her to drop her magnum. Kayleigh glanced into the room as two more Paladins entered. "Jesus Christ Greg, there's more!" She dropped quickly to the ground, fumbling for her weapon as she rolled and took cover behind a dresser, which was conveniently placed to cover her as she reloaded. Pushing a new clip into the weapon, Kayleigh fired back, hitting an old fire extinguisher which threw up a ball of white foam and fog to cover her exit. Pushing off the ground, she leant against the nearest door and kicked it with her back foot, falling backwards into some small feet. Kicking the door closed she rolled over onto her stomach and looked up to see the same small eyes she had seen earlier. "Hey you!" Kayleigh spoke trying not to sound scared, "Where are your parents?"

The child, showing little emotion, pointed to the opposite room but made no effort to go in. Kayleigh gulped, expecting the worst. The sound of shots magnum, followed by the scream of plasma fire, drowned out the squeaking floorboards as she stepped into the room. Kayleigh paused as she entered; she stared at the human pair who were slumped against the fridge, hand in hand. Cautiously, she wandered in, trying to make sense of the situation for the child's sake Running her hand across the kitchen countertop, its cold surface felt like a knife edge. Kayleigh froze as she took in the sight. Two vials, more than three quarters empty, sat at the end of the countertop, they had clearly contained the liquid substance drooled onto the surface. Kayleigh picked up one of the vials and shook it; its colour was a light blue, the liquid seemed to move on its own. She knew this was what had caused the victims' deaths, and the bodies' features backed that up. As she stared at the vial, parts of the mixture seemed to be moving . Kayleigh felt her grip disappear as she thought about where this drug was from. Was it the same drug found in the victims that were being littered across the city, or was that a coincidence? The vial slipped out of her hand and smashed onto the floor. Returning to reality, she turned to find the child almost in tears and the growls of Hydroxii Paladins ever closer. Kayleigh quickly grabbed the second vial, wrapping kitchen roll around the needle end so as not to not lose any of the mixture and to prevent injecting herself. She stuffed it into her armoured vest and turned back to the distressed child.

"Let's get out of here, shall we?"

The child nodded slowly and held out its hand to her. Taking it, she moved them into the living room and scanned it for a way out. At the back of the room an air vent, just big enough for a small adult, was bolted to the wall and would be an easy route out, so long as it didn't lead to anywhere worse. Deciding it couldn't possibly get any worse, Kayleigh grabbed the vent's cover and began to pry it off, it squeaked as she did so. The Paladins nearby used their plasma rifles to blast down the door as Kayleigh fell back with the vent cover firmly in her hands. As they rushed in, Kayleigh hurried the little child into the vent and fired her magnum at the approaching pair. The Paladins took cover at the doorway as Kayleigh entered the vent. Inside, the sounds were amplified, the barrage of plasma fire which scattered the wall partially slamming in the vents, lighting them up in a blue glow. After several minutes of crawling through the tight space, they reached the end. Kayleigh stuck her hand past the child and held the cover open slightly so they could both climb out. Her relief quickly turned to disbelief as the chasing Paladins stepped out of the room, their plasma rifles aimed directly at them. Kayleigh wanted to shoot back at them but didn't want to risk the safety of the child. One of the Hydroxii, dressed in battered white armour, stepped forward and waved its plasma rifle downward, indicating to her to lower her weapon.

"Lower your weapon human," the Paladin growled beneath its helmet.

"Alright. . . alright," she slowly laid the magnum on the ground and put her hands in the air.

"Now hand over the child and the vial and maybe we will not kill you."

"Not a chance. Whatever you're planning I won't let it happen!"

"You can't possibly understand what is going to happen."

"What exactly are you planning? The war is over, we have no fight with you," Kayleigh lowered her hands a little as she tried to reassure the child who was starting to panic.

"The war didn't end for all of us, human. The fight has moved underground as you humans tell me."

The Paladin nodded at its teammate to move forward. Kayleigh primed herself to grab her magnum and leaned down a little. As she readied herself, the four of them were caught out as the door crashed open causing the red-armoured Hydroxii Paladin to fall out onto its teammates; Greg spilled out with it. In the chaos, Kayleigh pushed the child aside and grabbed her magnum, firing the entire clip into the closest unsuspecting, blue-armoured Paladin. As the blue Paladin fell, the Paladin in white turned and tried to fire its plasma rifle only to have it blasted out of its hands by Greg who had managed to roll away. As she tried to reload her magnum, the Paladin she had just confronted charged and tackled her to the ground, knocking the pistol out of her hands. Kayleigh attempted to crawl to her firearm, only to be pulled back and thrown across the hallway by the large Hydroxii Paladin towering over her. Attempting to get to her feet, she found herself being lifted by her throat, the Paladin's hands like a vice as it picked her up. Plasma rifle in hand, the Hydroxii laughed, relishing the moment as it prepared to fire. Kayleigh closed her eyes expecting the worst. The blast of a shotgun filled her ears; she fell back with the dead Paladin landing on top of her. Kayleigh shuddered as she forced off the bleeding alien corpse and came face to face with the barrel of a shotgun.

"Get up!"

Kayleigh slowly lifted her head to see who had rescued her. The man lifted the shotgun upward, hurrying her along.

"Okay, I'm up, I'm up," Kayleigh mumbled as she got to her feet, "Thanks for that."

"Shut up and get out."

"Let me just-" she turned to see how Greg was doing and was relieved to see the other Paladin unconscious and in restraints.

"Fine, we're done here."

Kayleigh moved over to Greg. Pushing her shoulders under the Paladin's arms, she helped him haul the asset off the floor.

"Well, that was exciting detective work," she joked, grunting under the weight of the alien she was dragging towards the lift.

"Just a bit, but this could be important if we take this giant in and that vial in your pocket. . ."

"We need to get something out of this thing before those idiots get in on it," Kayleigh could feel herself tighten up with rage just mentioning them, "You think this Paladin is Hernandez?"

"I don't know," Greg adjusted the alien's weight across his shoulder, " I was expecting another human but this complicates things because this is no drug op, it could well be chemical warfare."

Kayleigh sighed and looked over her shoulder, the child she had saved was being tended to by the man who had saved them. The child turned and gave a smile and a thumbs up as the pair left the hallway and hauled the Paladin into the lift. Pressing the ground floor button, Greg grunted and released his grip from the alien, allowing it to slide to the floor.

"Nice job back there."

"I think I owe you after those dramatics."

"Yeah, you can buy me something afterwards," Greg laughed as he checked the restraints on the Paladin.

"So what do you think this big guy knows?" Kayleigh asked peering around the Hydroxii's large body.

"Something, I presume. There is no way, these Paladins are here without some kind of agenda."

"And there I was hoping the war was over."

"Once we get this guy back, I'm betting you we will get five minutes max alone with him." Greg got to his feet as the lift stopped and its doors opened, "So get as much out of him as possible, anything at all that could be useful."

Kayleigh jumped to her feet, grabbing the Paladin and putting its arm over her shoulder, carrying it to the exit.

"You know, we are going to end up in so much trouble for this."

"Yeah, but I think deep down he wants us to keep digging." Greg pushed the entrance doors open and sidestepped the Hydroxii out of the building, "There's something off with the guy but I think we can get something out of him eventually, he can't keep us out of this forever."

Kayleigh nodded and opened the door of the patrol car under the watchful eyes of the districts' citizens. Something was going on and the quicker they got out, the better. Stepping into the car, the weather had become clearer, the run-down area was a complete. She wanted to avoid any confrontation with the locals and hurried Greg into the car; they needed to get back to the station and interrogate the Hydroxii before they lost any valuable intel.

As they stepped out of the elevator the entire place came to a standstill. Absolutely nobody moved as they hauled a living, breathing, Hydroxii Paladin right into their station. Kayleigh surveyed everyone in the large office space, nobody spoke, either they were too afraid or too amazed. Greg was rushing ahead now, the unwanted attention not what he enjoyed, making Kayleigh nearly lose grip of the huge Paladin they had to carry around.

"Get him in here. Leyton open the box now," Greg ordered as he walked by an officer who wasn't really sure how to react.

"Leyton, if you don't open this door, I'm going to beat it down using your head. Now do it!"

This time Leyton moved quickly, awkwardly scanning his ID badge against the panel. The door opened and eyes were wide as the pair hauled the large alien onto the small iron chair. Greg stepped back and pulled out some restraints from the side of the room, tying the Paladin's leg to the chair.

"Leyton, your cuffs," Greg asked with his hand out. Leyton obliged, this time without hesitation, and threw his handcuffs inside.

"Cheers man," Greg thanked him as he restrained the Paladin's other leg.

"Now Kay, you have shot. Do not mess this up."

Kayleigh nodded and pulled up a chair directly opposite the Paladin. "Wakey, wakey!" Kayleigh shouted as she stamped the heel of her boot into the foot of the unconscious Paladin's armour. The Hydroxii jumped, nearly taking the metal chair with it as it awoke from its unconscious state. Kayleigh winced as the remembered just how tough their armour was, "Time to talk."

The Paladin steadily looked around the room, taking in its

new surroundings. Calmly, the Hydroxii soldier leaned back in its chair, the metal creaking from its weight, "Human, you cannot command me," the Paladin growled as it lowered its head to assess the situation further.

"I think I can do what I like, now answer my questions first time of asking," Kayleigh laid back in her chair as she tried not to let her fear direct her actions, "What were you doing in a run-down district with lowly human drug dealers like Traviss?"

"You know what makes your species weak, human?"

"I asked you a question, now answer it."

"You show fear in your actions even as you try to portray yourself as the bigger character here," the Paladin ground its jaws together as it tried not to laugh.

"I'll ask you again, what were you doing with the likes of Ryan Traviss?"

"Waiting."

"For what exactly? A ride home?"

"A meal," the Paladin leaned its head back and chuckled.

Kayleigh glanced over her shoulder, three taps on the window meant that she should hurry up.

"Alright, enough," Kayleigh brought her combat knife from her vest and slammed it on the table, "Answer the question."

The Paladin slowly pulled its head forward and breathed heavily into its helmet before placing its tethered hands onto the table.

"You do not scare me, human. You believe the war to be over, to be won, but it is not."

"I don't believe you're here on winning terms."

The Paladin brought down its fist like an iron hammer, growling beneath its battle worn armour, "Watch your tongue!"

Kayleigh shuffled nervously in her chair before composing herself for another round, "Come on, you can't just sit there and give me nothing. You Hydroxii are so proud, does it mean dishonour to be captured by your enemy?"

"The war is over, human. Besides, I am not here to suffer by your hands. I am here for something else," the Paladin's eyes fell on the syringe in her vest pocket, "To monitor that."

"So you created this? You killed those civilians!" Kayleigh leaned forward and pulled the knife from the table. She pointed it towards the Paladin as she pushed herself from her chair, the knife inching closer to its arms.

"Not the Hydroxii, no, we simply inherited the mixture," the Paladin backed away a little as it tried to play, this time to its advantage.

Kayleigh poised to ask another question just as the doors burst open and three heavily armed military police officers charged into the room, rifles aimed at them both.

"What is this?" Kayleigh shouted as she threw the knife to the tabletop and stood up, "This is an interrogation, you idiots!"

"Not anymore, Kayleigh," Greg stepped in and pushed her back a little, "Our friends are here."

"What happened to stalling them? I was about to charge him with espionage."

Kayleigh looked over Greg's shoulder to see Agent Falaney at the door.

"I really don't think you could put an espionage claim on a Hydroxii Paladin who openly defected and hid from his own kind during the battle over Atlanta. Besides, all Hydroxii interaction is our business." He waved his hand forward and the officers closest holstered their rifles and uncuffed the burly Paladin, replacing its handcuffs with far more sophisticated energy restraints.

"Be seeing you," Falaney pushed his way back through the door with the three officers in tow as they pushed the Paladin out with them.

"Oh, and Officer Crow," Falaney turned and held out his hand, "the mixture."

"What mixture?" Kayleigh tried to conceal the syringe but a military police officer took it from her grasp.

"That mixture," the agent smiled and continued on his way out.

Kayleigh angrily slammed the desk with a fist and closed her eyes; every time they had some evidence, Falaney was already there, on the case, and would step in to take the glory. She knew something was definitely going on and it smelt a lot like a Hydroxii insurrection. Kayleigh thought about all the blood that had been spilt during the years the two species fought over territory, all the sacrifices both sides made to end it all, undone by some shadowy figure in the background. But why? Deep in thought, Kayleigh barely took notice of Greg staring at her as she tried to not release any more of her pent-up anger.

"Come on Kay, it wasn't a complete disaster," he spoke trying to reassure her.

"Are you kidding me? We just took on some rather tough Hydroxii Paladins, for what? A stuck-up snob to take the glory!"

"Not quite so," Greg grabbed her shoulders and smiled, "Follow me."

Greg pulled Kayleigh to the interrogation room and pointed to her vest, "Paper towels don't stop leaks."

She looked down to her vest pocket and pulled out a paper towel she had used to try to contain the mixture from the syringe. It was wet, the mixture still visible.

"It wasn't all in vain, we have something."

"Get this to the techs now, I want it deconstructed ASAP."

"On it, Kay!" Greg gave a huge grin before grimacing at the paper towel, "I'll wash my hands though after this."

Kayleigh laughed and watched as Greg hurried through the station to the tech lab. It was the first real lead which might link the deaths to anything. Finally they were starting to play catch up with the shadowy intelligence division - and without bending all the rules to get there, almost. As she began to relax and try to piece everything together, the door to the Captain's office swung open.

"Kayleigh, Crow, my office now!"

No sooner had the call gone out than the door had been slammed shut. Everyone in the station turned and gave Kayleigh the look nobody wanted. Kayleigh breathed in deeply and began to stride over to the Captain's office. With one final deep breath inhaled, she opened the door and readied herself for the insubordinate accusations, but it would all be worth it once she proved her case.

Chapter 8

Jack stared at the monitor in front of him, taking in all the details. Blueprints and pictures of the attacked Kyreel base and the space cannon filled the screen, directional arrows drawn crudely across them to indicate the sight of attacking points of both the enemy and friendlies.

"Major, are you listening?"

"One hundred percent."

"No you're not, be honest!" Draco called from behind him.

"Enough, I think the point of this has passed," Kato sighed and put the data pad onto the desk in front of him, "And I require you to go back. We need something bringing back that the militia, thankfully, didn't find."

"I thought just the cannon was of importance?" Jack asked pointing to the monitor.

"You haven't spent enough time with us to understand that we don't just have one secret to hide."

"So what is it we're looking for?"

"A datalogger," Kato flicked a new display on screen to show what looked like a black box used in aircraft, "It houses sensitive data on key Navy Intelligence personnel and where they are stationed, so I don't need to explain the importance of that."

"How did they not find it if it's on site?" Spider stood and held his hands out, "They seemed to know about the cannon node, how did they miss that?"

"Clearly they only wanted the cannon, or simply didn't know about it. Either way we need it returning to us before they decide to come back for another round."

Jack stood and grabbed his helmet from the nearby table, "It's hardly worth sending your best down to retrieve it, Sir."

Kato shook his head in response.

"Sorry Sir, I'm just being honest here. If they were still on site, I would agree but it's a safe zone now, surely a team of techs could retrieve it?"

"No, I want it in your hands and no one else's. Understood?"

"Yes Sir."

"Okay. . when you find it, we can let our good friends know that they are free to roam their base again."

Jack turned to his team, "Alright Viper One, let's move out."

The rest of the team stood, picking up their helmets as they left. They had been in de-brief for hours as they assessed every option and problem the militia had picked up on. The fact that they had such a heavy force in action on Earth was the most concerning issue they faced. The big question and talking point was how they had transported so many heavy weapon vehicles into attack such a high value target. Most of the discussion was about concerns of an internal issue, a rogue agent or someone selling secrets. Plans were to be put in place to discover the source. Lots of questions raised, hardly any satisfactory answers, but that wasn't Jack's or Viper One's problem.

As the team stepped out of the briefing room, Jack grabbed

Venoms arm, "You alright?"

Venom gave Jack a hard stare and batted his arm away, "I'm fine."

"Clearly not. Am I missing something?"

"We have a mission to complete Jack." Venom stormed off down the hallway pulling on her helmet, allowing the unique armour to cover her body as she prepared for the mission. Jack shook his head and stepped into the armoury.

"Wow, what's her problem?" Harley buzzed over the radio as Jack shook his head.

"No idea but something's going on."

"You can tell all that from an emotional response? Emotions are cruel things."

"No, it's the way she acted after the mission, she also had my sidearm."

"And that's an issue how?" Harley's tone changed trying to make sense the situation.

"She had her own belted to her, she didn't need mine." Jack pulled on his helmet, the armour skin covering his body, and began to follow the team as they geared up for the upcoming mission.

The armoury was busy as the base personnel equipped the team in fresh gear and equipment for their next mission. Jack had been team leader for only a few hours and was already feeling the pressure of what was to come, not knowing what was unfolding in the shadows around them.

This time there wasn't much need for specific ordnance or heavy weapons, although the uncertainty of whether the militia had only taken the command node was on everyone's mind, small arms were all that were deemed required. Picking up the assault rifle, Jack selected a fresh magazine and pushed it in, pulling the slot to lock it before placing it onto his back plate. He stepped back grabbing the pistol as he walked over to the hangar door to board the Valkyrie dropship.

As he approached the dropship, Spider pulled Jack aside, "Something's not right here."

"What isn't?"

"The whole thing. Even I don't think were being told the whole story here. There's no way the militia just jumped down our throats without someone on the inside. Now we are conveniently sent back in."

Jack stood and thought about it, trying not to put the blame on anyone, but he had his suspicions, "Between you and me, keep your head down and don't say anything. Just pay attention."

Spider let go of Jack's shoulder, turning to board the dropship. Jack slowly stepped up to the Valkyrie, now concentrating on the fact that Spider was confirming his own suspicions. He didn't realise what Venom had really done. Putting that thought aside, he stepped into the Valkyrie and pushed the door control, bringing the ramp up behind him, sealing the team inside. The dropship rocked as the pilot fired the thrusters and brought it up and out of the facility, moving quickly on route to their next mission, back at Kyreel.

The journey to Kyreel was slow, Spider spent it head down not saying anything, Venom too was unsure of what to do. However, the duo of Draco and Dragon had plenty to discuss as Jack had discovered. The pair were like inseparable brothers who had so much in common it was hard to tell them apart at times. Their almost matching armour colours were giving Jack a hard time.

"ETA one minute," the pilot radioed in.

"Thank the digital gods, I can't handle those guys anymore. Do they ever stop?" Harley spoke sarcastically.

"I didn't realise AI got agitated?"

"We do, I hate modern science."

Jack stood, balancing himself as the dropship arced and finally landed. Moving over to the door controls once more, Jack pushed the release and watched as the door hissed and opened. Stepping down from the dropship, Jack met the steely gazes of a squad of marines and their officer.

"Welcome back, Sir," the middle marine saluted as Jack stepped off the ramp.

"Not sure I expected to be back. Kind of left this place in a worse state for you," Jack replied.

"Carnage is the word to describe this."

Jack slowly turned to the marine who had spoken. He was standing, clearly unintimidated by Jack's appearance, "Alright, don't push it. Are you in charge?" he asked as politely as he could.

"No Sir, that would be Captain Young," the marine turned, pointing to a man dressed in standard issue marine armour. The man was the spitting image of a campaign poster, leaving Jack to wonder if he had been given the promotion for being the embodiment of the marines.

Jack nodded and headed towards the Captain, behind him his squad followed.

"Well look what the cat dragged in," the Captain threw a cigar to the floor just missing one of his Corporal's boots. "If it isn't Viper, let's blow everything up, One,'" he stepped up to the team leader and attempted to make himself look bigger, "Or do you prefer-"

"Enough Captain, whatever your problem with me and my

team is, I suggest you act a little more professionally at least."

"Oh well, I'm sorry!" the Captain stepped back and made a bowing gesture, "Wasn't aware the King was in town."

"What's your problem marine?" Spider stepped out from behind Jack and stood as close to the Captain as possible, "Is it a case of who's tougher?" Spider grabbed the Captain and propped him up, "Because we can have that conversation."

"Well Hybrid, because of your stupid research project I lost a ton of good men."

"Listen Captain, I get it, you don't like us," Jack stepped in between the feuding soldiers as they slowly stepped back from one another, "Where is the vault?"

The Captain brushed himself off, laughing as he spun round to walk away, "Inside, first door to your left."

Jack shook his head and headed for the base. As they walked through the crumbling walls of the base, Jack thought back to the Hybrid comment that the marine had used when addressing Spider. Was it the armour he was referring to or something else? Jack's armour wasn't any different to the rest of his team's, but something about that comment irritated to him. Bullets were littered all over the floor, every footstep causing a bullet casing to skitter across the floor. Scorch marks flickered up and along the corner revealing the scars from the plasma weapons, that had been stolen and used against them earlier. As they stepped into the corridor Jack couldn't help but notice two medics carefully placing a dead marine onto a stretcher. They both leaned down, the lead medic catching Jack's stare. Jack nodded at the medic who nodded in return.

As they headed towards the vault, the corridor became more of a maze. Mechanics, rescue workers and builders attempted to keep the place structurally sound. Reaching the vault entrance a scientist hurried to them, his clipboard flailing alongside.

"And who are you?"

"My name is Major Halliday; we've been sent by Navy Intelligence. This is Viper One." Jack answered, gesturing towards his team.

"And that means what to me?" the scientist folded his arms.

Jack tried hard not to sign loudly, "Kato sent us to retrieve something from the vault."

"Oh. . . then you're here for the key?"

"The key?" Jack asked puzzled, "No we're here for the data-"

The scientist flailed his arms as his calm demeanour crumbled like the walls around him, "I know, I know just. . . I'm no good with this naval stuff, I'm always doing something wrong to you guys."

"Listen, we just want the 'key' and we're out of here, Venom here will go with you to pick it up, right?"

The scientist looked across at Venom's scarred armour and gulped, "If you insist Major." He turned and hurried towards the vault. Venom slowly stepped up and sighing as she followed the scientist into the vault.

Stepping inside, Venom flicked on her helmet's flashlight and scanned the area slowly. The vault was much wider than she had anticipated, the entrance looked tough with its giant steel bar locks and high security blast door, meaning to get in with such ease had to have relied on breaking into the facility's firewall. Stepping off the final step, she scanned the vault door to find blast marks from the inside panel, the main locks completely destroyed by some sort of plastic explosive.

"So, you're Venom, huh?" the scientist asked nervously.

"Yeah, that's me."

"Why the nickname? Surely you have a real name?"

"I do but Navy Intel don't let you be a somebody," she turned to face the scientist, "Easier to forget you when you've become expendable."

"Oh. I guess you guys don't socialise much?" the scientist laughed, "I just thought it was some weird codename like the pilots use."

"Nope. Just a randomly assigned tag."

Venom continued to wander around the room, spying all of the unique assets held in the vault, all the tech captured from the Hydroxii-Human war - experimental pieces, including the prototype armour they were currently using. Venom stopped and placed her hand on the cracked helmet and closed her eyes, recalling the intricate surgery she and the team had endured in order to become one with the suit. There were many painful memories linked to it, but without those early days and that agony, the war may never have concluded in the way it did. The scientist tapped on the damaged inner door and urged Venom to carry on. Following the scientist inside, she crawled through the door panel and stood inside a box room.

"Welcome to the inner sanctum!" the scientist called with excitement in his voice.

"It's a bit basic."

"This is the real hardcore stuff. Only those with certain clear-ance are allowed in here unless you have a large incendiary bomb, but enough of that. This is what you Navy guys want," he dropped to one knee and began tapping away on a pedestal which stood in the middle of the room.

"Is this where you kept the command node for the orbital cannon?"

"No, that was on another side of the facility where you were having your own firefight. This is like a war vault."

Venom continued to wander around the room before stumbling slightly as she reached a large object. She activated a number of visors to determine if it was what she was looking for.

"Ah, so you found it?"

"What is this?"

"Well, we're not sure really. It's not Hydroxii and certainly not human. It was uncovered off world somewhere, I forget the details, but this was the only surviving one. Incredible, isn't it?"

Venom stared at the sarcophagus, "Maybe." The markings on the front of it resembled something obviously inhuman. The shape of it was unlike anything she had seen before. Tucked behind the left-hand side stood at vial of dark, blue liquid. Venom leaned in and steadily removed it from its holder. As she carefully rotated it in her hand, the heavy clang of a panel dropping brought her attention back to the job at hand.

"And that Venom, is your datalo-" the scientist stopped suddenly as he struggled to breathe. Raising his arms slowly, he could feel that the needle that had gone straight into his neck.

"Thanks, but I really have to stop you there." Venom pulled out the needle that was attached to the vial and placed it into a concealed ammo pouch, stepping back from the struggling scientist. Screaming in pain, he began to roll around as he tried to control himself, but the substance was already coursing through his bloodstream and within seconds was changing him.

The scientist screamed as his body tensed, his veins wriggling inside his body as the blue liquid began to take effect. Venom stood motionless, watching him wither on the floor. After a moment, the scientist gasped as his body began to vapourise. The sarcophagus lit up behind him and cracked as his energy began to flow into it. The sarcophagus momentarily become black before the front of the panel fell with a metallic clatter and the being inside slumped out. The machine was humanoid, like an exoskeleton. The machine's body twisted and locked into place. Venom ran her hand along her hip and held her pistol firmly by her side. The being screamed and fired a blast of energy, knocking Venom to the floor as the pulse shattered the room around them. On her back, she brought the pistol forward and fired multiple shots, bouncing off the being's armour. Caught out, it frantically moved out of the inner sanctum and into the base.

Venom changed her communications link in her helmet and holstered her weapon, "Test complete. Successful transference."

Chapter 9

Jack picked up a plasma rifle and weighed it up in his hands. It was fairly heavy but weighted evenly so would prove effective in battle. In all his years of combat he had never held the Hydroxii's tech before, it was a little strange. The weapon was covered in measurement tools used by the facility's engineers. Wanting to avoid any confrontation, Jack placed the rifle back down and wandered to the door. He paused as a rush of scientists began streaming past.

"What's going on?" Harley buzzed in Jack's ear as the base lit up in a blaze of concrete dust and an ear-splitting roar, "You guys don't keep animals here, do you?"

Jack popped his head out of the room and grabbed his rifle, more scientists were running down the corridor. Jack stepped out of the room and pinned one of the scientists.

"What's everyone running from?"

"Something came out of the vault, it's attacking everyone it sees!" he stuttered, "Your hybrid is still in there!"

Jack let go of the terrified scientist and stepped back into the room.

"Alright you three, on me. We're going in after her."

The team nodded and grabbed their own rifles, following

Jack down the hallway past the barrage of fearful scientists. Pushing themselves through, the Marine Captain greeted them.

"Are you messing with my base a second time, Major?"

"This is no time for jo-" as the two men stood, the ground beneath them shook like an earthquake. Further screaming echoed down the halls adding to the chaos.

"Where do you want us?" Young smiled and leaned his rifle to his side.

"Cover the side exits and stick some marines on the vault entrance. We'll go inside and extract our operative and anyone else trapped inside."

"Copy that. Move out marines, you heard the man!" Young swung his rifle over his head and Jack watched as the marines moved to cover their respective positions.

Venom jumped to her feet and brushed dust from the earthquake from her armour. She paused for a moment as she recalled the force of energy that seemed to emanate from the suit that the scientist had been transferred in to. What a weapon on the field that would be, given a chance to control its raw power. Venom stepped up to the vault door and paused.

"This is ARC Three Two. Requesting confirmation of test."

"Confirmed test. Is the key active?" the muffled and distorted voice responded.

She pushed off from the door frame and stepped back inside, slamming her fist on the pedestal, and swinging the wall panel once again to reveal the datalogger. Pulling it from the mount, she slotted it into the pedestal, the data stream on top glowing green as the data was downloaded into it.

"Key is active."

"Mission directive?"

"Destroy test."

Switching to her Navy radio signal she winced as she was hit with a barrage of incoming radio chatter.

"Venom, do you read me?"

Venom forced herself to cough as she responded to Jack's call, "-in there, over!"

"Repeat Venom."

"There was something in the inner vault, some kind of weaponised armour."

"Jesus. . . Are you okay?"

Venom paused before responding, "I'm fine, but this thing isn't like anything I've ever seen."

"Copy that, on route to you now."

Venom swung her rifle from her back and loaded a magazine. Suddenly she realised her mission was going to become quite tricky. Destroying the evidence was going to be tougher than anticipated with her squad on route, and she had lost sight of the asset. She stepped back and immediately fell out of the vault. In a flash, the suit of armour had returned and was shimmering in the dark. Venom fired at it as it lunged with incredible speed, pushing her against the wall and finally across the room onto the floor.

Dragging herself to her feet, she darted out of the room and slammed the panel on the entrance wall, watching as the vault closed. With the vault door closed, the steel locks clicked into place and the monster slammed on the door. Lifting her head, she watched as Jack and the team came to join her.

"Is it in there?"

"Yeah, and I got the datalogger but. . . something happened."

"What do you mean, something happened?"

"The scientist. . . he just vapourised in front of me."

Jack lowered his rifle, "He did what?"

"I know it's strange, but there's this suit, the scientist was showing off this pre-war find and it was like he was transferred into it."

"How did something transfer matter into a robot suit?" Harley asked puzzled, "That's a physical impossibility."

"I don't know, okay, it just did!"

"Either way we have to stop it, we need that data logger," Jack butted in, "Open it up, we have to stop this thing before it moves on."

Jack raised his rifle and nodded to Venom who pushed the door panel, retracting the steel locks. She stepped back in line with her squad who had spread out ready to fire. As the vault slowly clunked open, the suit dived at the open door and was met with a burst of assault rifle fire, knocking it on its back. The suit of armour shuddered on the ground, leaking blue liquid from its protruding veins. Clicking empty, the team reloaded in unison and took aim again as they stepped up to the armour. It stopped struggling and relaxed. The team carefully moved in, their rifles aimed firmly at the armour.

"Is it dead or as dead as armour gets?" Harley asked.

"Only one way to find out," Dragon pulled a grenade from his belt and held it up, "This should solve the problem."

"Good plan. Venom grab that datalogger."

Venom re-entered the vault and stepped over the armour to seize the datalogger from the pedestal. As she grasped it, the armour shone, a bright blue liquid around its body. Grabbing Venom by the leg, it launched her across the vault. Flying across the room, the datalogger fell out of her hand and bounced across the floor towards a stunned Viper One as they watched the armour re-activate before them.

"What is this thing made of?" Harley called over the radio.

"Your guess is as good as mine, Harley, but I'm not asking any more questions. Take it down!" Jack raised his rifle again and emptied the clip into the creature, the rest of the team joining in. As the bullets hit the target, the armour didn't seem phased at all and was solely set on attacking Venom. The armour rattled as it took more hits from the assault rifles, its sturdy alloy barely registering a scratch from the squad's combined firepower. The squad moved in unison as the armour lunged, swiping its fists towards them. As they reloaded their weapons, the armour shuddered, releasing an ear-splitting noise, causing the squad to drop to the floor before a powerful shockwave pushed them hard into the wall of the vault.

"This thing just isn't going down!" Dragon shouted over the squad's radio.

"I'm glad somebody's paying attention," Harley joked, "Jack, the armour seems more intent on going after Venom. If she gets out of the vault, we can get it out in the open and get more firepower on it."

"Good plan," Jack grabbed the grenade Dragon was going to throw, "Venom get down!"

Unpinning the grenade, Jack launched it into the path of the armour as it darted for Venom once again. Venom dodged of the armour's path and dragged herself across the room, frantically trying to escape as it continued its pursuit.

"Do it Jack!" she braced for the explosion as Jack threw the grenade. The grenade's explosion rocked the vault as the team were knocked back by the force.

"Is it disabled?" Harley asked only to have the question

answered by a loud, high-pitched scream as it levitated off the ground, the blue liquid flowing through it, rushing around the armour, "Or not!"

"Venom get outside, now!" Jack called out, as he stepped aside to allow her to sprint past. The armour tracked her movement, sprinting out of the vault as it followed her.

"Captain Young, get your marines outside now, an unidentified combatant is heading outside in pursuit of one of my team and she needs backup."

"What do you mean' unidentified'?" Young shouted into the radio.

"Something from the vault is the threat, potential robot malfunction, I don't know but this thing is strong."

"Copy. Heading outside now. Get your squadmate to the courtyard, we can meet up there," Young replied as the radio static interrupted the remainder of the message.

"Captain? Damn it."

Jack stood and lowered his head; something was off about the situation. Why did the armour seem so intent on Venom? The team had no ties to the facility or the military base housed within. The armour attacking them was powerful, but not Hydroxii or human by design. What had they uncovered and what had they unleashed?

"Squad move out, Venom is going to need all the support she can get," Jack waved his team on ahead. Stepping forward, something caught on the ground, glistening in the darkness. Turning slightly, Jack spotted a large cylindrical object on the ground. Kneeling, Jack picked it up and rotated it, "Harley, any idea what this is?"

"Not a clue Jack, nothing like anything I've ever seen. Nothing in the database either. Certainly not Hydroxii."

"What's the liquid? It seemed to be flowing inside the armour."

"Again, nothing I know of. The liquid is foreign to me. My concern is the armour, does it not seem sentient to you?"

Jack rose and surveyed the vault one last time, "It did. Didn't seem to be defending itself tactically, but in a frenzy. Maybe we can get it back home and figure it out."

"Do you think the scientist activated it somehow? Was it dormant and suddenly active? Is this a key? So many questions!"

"Jack something is really wrong here," Harley appeared in front of him via the pedestal in the centre of the room. She held her hair to one side and thought, "Do you think we have a mole?"

"Too many questions to answer right now. We need to regroup and take the armour down." Jack stepped up to Harley who turned to face him, "Harley, we keep this between us two, no talking to anyone else about our suspicions." Jack pushed the object into his belt and pulled his assault rifle from his back, "Right now we deal with this situation."

"Okay. But I'm doing some digging when we get home," Harley sighed and dematerialised from the pedestal, her voice echoing in his intercom again.

Jack exited the vault and headed to the surface once again.

At the top Spider peered over his shoulder and rocked his head a little, "Jeez Jack, talk about dawdling."

"Sorry, Harley wanted to do a quick scan," Jack replied trying to cover his tracks.

"Hey-"

"Whatever. Anyway Venom's gone AWOL and that armour has somehow gone into hiding."

"Where's Young and the marines?"

"Outside, the exits are covered. We're waiting on you."

"Right, Dragon and Draco, you cover the west side and push out onto the courtyard. Me and Spider will cover what's left of the east wing," Jack glanced at his team who nodded in approval, "If you see the target, we need to get it outside into the courtyard. We need to take this thing down before it gets anymore out of control."

"And it seems particularly pissed," Spider added jokingly.

"Alright, move out," Jack tapped Spider's shoulder, who stood and followed the Major into the remnants of the east wing.

Dragon leaned up against the broken doorframe and waited for his teammate who quickly joined him. Draco nodded and the pair stepped through with their rifles raised.

"Clear!" Draco announced as he lowered his rifle slightly, "Joe, can you please tell me how a suit of armour just suddenly springs to life?"

Dragon turned and shrugged, "How the hell should I know?"

"I don't know, I just find it hard to accept that a suit of armour can just run around smashing the place up."

"Sorry Ben, I'm not paid enough to think this hard."

"You get paid?"

Joe shrugged, "I'm not as expendable as you, obviously."

"True, but there was that one time-"

"Anyway, shouldn't we be concentrating on this rogue armour hunt?"

"Okay-" Ben was cut short as the roof came crashing down, covering the soldiers in dust and debris. Knocked off guard, their confusion quickly turned to panic as they jumped up from the floor, fumbling with their rifles, trying to find the cause of the cave in. As Joe turned to scour the room, he came face to face with the armour they were hunting. Before he could fire, he was knocked back by its powerful arm and sent flying across the room.

"Joe!" Ben flicked back across and side-stepped through the dust; the visor unable to help make out the armour. Firing, the air spluttered and metallic sparks flickered ahead of him, successful hit markers. With a wild scream, the armour stumbled back giving Ben time to jolt forward and cover his teammate.

"Joe, you alright?"

"Yeah, yeah, fine. Just get me up."

Ben pulled Joe from the rubble, he nodded in thanks, "Plan?"

"Get it outside-" As Joe spoke, he turned away to scan the area and came face to face with their attacker. Lifting his rifle he tried to fire, the armour grabbed the weapon; using its enhanced strength, it kept the rifle pointed away from itself as Joe fired. The armour roared and grabbed him by the throat. He held his hands up to the armour's one lone hand which was clasped firmly in place. Choking, he tried desperately to release himself from its grasp. The armour stepped forward and held him against the wall. Dropping the rifle, Joe slowly opened his eyes and stared frantically at the armour's helmet. It had the resemblance of a human and moved like one. Leaning forward, it moved as close as possible to his helmet and screamed silently.

Joe lowered his hand from his throat and held the pistol on his belt. Desperately trying to understand what was happening.

The armour growled, as if it was clearing its throat, and

leaned closer. This time the audio came through his helmet. This time Joe was taken back slightly.

"Traitor!" the armour released the soldier and dropped him. It stepped back and swiveled on its feet slamming into the wall, crashing through in a mess of concrete and dust just as it had done when it arrived.

Ben stepped up to his teammate, his confused look was not hidden well even behind the helmet, "Did that thing just talk?"

"Yeah, and it said traitor."

Jack climbed onto the table, scouring the room for clues.

"How the hell did everybody lose track of this thing? It's a seven, maybe eight, foot suit of armour!"

Jack held his hands out as a shockwave rocked the room, the rest of the team glancing round trying to figure out what just happened.

"I think we're in the wrong part of the building, Jack," Spider peered out of the room trying to get an idea of where the shockwave came from. Jack hopped off the table and tucked the assault rifle into his shoulder.

"Dragon, Draco, status?" Jack glanced across the room and shook his head just hearing static.

"Comms are dead."

"Let's go then, I'm not missing them getting their arses kicked," Spider laughed and Jack followed him as he moved away. As the pair reached the end of the corridor a shadowy figure jumped from the doorway behind them and slammed Jack to the ground, who found himself staring down the barrel of a pistol.

"Venom!" Jack shouted, puzzled as he squirmed on the floor in frustration, "What the hell are you doing?"

Venom stepped towards Jack, holding out her hand to pulled Jack up.

"Sorry Jack I-" she glanced down at his hand and slowly looked up, "You alright?"

Jack clenched his fist and pushed himself off the floor, pulling his rifle towards himself as he rose from the floor, "I'm fine. Where's the armour?"

"I don't know. It was on my tail for a while, I think I lost it in the end. What exactly is it?"

"No idea, some sort of sentient suit of armour. Could be anything. All I know is we need to stop it before it gets out of hand."

Venom propped herself against the wall and peered around the corner. She pulled her pistol from its holster and watched the ammunition counter tallying up her remaining count.

"Jack, I'm running low here, I'm going to be no good."

"Alright. Venom, Spider-" As Jack turned to issue an order, the adjacent wall crumbled as a blast of blue energy and blistering heat obliterated the area around them. The team grunted as they rallied themselves back into action. Jack rolled over, his heads-up display scanning furiously within the dust and debris to give him a visual. When the display finally focused, he watched as the armour picked up Venom's limp body and rotated its hand preparing another energy blast. Jack scrambled across the floor and grabbed his pistol, aiming and firing at the armour. The bullets ricocheted off it; it was seemingly impenetrable.

The armour turned and screamed as Jack fired the remainder of his magazine at the armour. Caught off guard, it dropped Venom who slunk to the ground and pressed her body against the wall, attempting to stand. The armour screamed as it placed a well-timed punch into Jack's stomach, launching him across the room. Spider stepped out of the chaos and fired his entire assault rifle magazine into the armour, stepping as close as possible to it. The armour rotated and slung its arm at Spider knocking him back. Accepting the enemy soldier was down, the armour searched the room for its prey and lit up more brightly as it's hand rotated a light blue energy ball.

Venom panted as she stumbled to her feet, raising her hand, the heads-up display noted her empty magazine and she sighed. Staring at the armour, Venom braced herself for the blast and crossed her arms over her shoulders. As the armour fired its energy weapon, the room lit up for a moment and Venom closed her eyes.

Chapter 10

Venom wheezed as her heads-up display desperately scanned the area but finally gave in; the visor colour fizzled out and she groaned as she attempted to move. Pushing herself off the ground, she held out her hands in front of her and was surprised to find very little damage, just a huge amount of dirt. She pushed herself further and wiped the grime from her visor, finding Jack in front of her rising to his feet.

"Jack?"

"You okay?" he asked, his armour shimmering purple before dissipating around his body.

"Yeah."

"Good. Now let's finish this, okay? Get behind me."

Venom scrabbled to her feet as Jack stood with his assault rifle raised aiming into the building the blast had just pushed them from.

"How. . . what happened?"

"Something new!" Harley buzzed excitedly over the radio.

"Harley can create shields, new thing apparently."

Venom adjusted her footing and put her hand on Jack's shoulder, "Thank you."

"You're welcome."

As Jack pushed the rifle into his shoulder, the armour strode through the almost nonexistent wall, shuddering as it stepped towards them. Glancing to each side, Venom spotted a number of marines step up to form a line in front of it. As the armour let out a scream Jack fired on it and the marines followed suit. The bullets sparked, lighting up the armour in a barrage of yellow and blue before all of their rifles clicked empty and the soldiers slowly lowered them.

In dismay, the armour shuddered and let out another scream.

"Jesus, this thing just won't die," Spider exchanged glances with Jack before turning back to the armour.

"We need a bigger gun," Venom grunted.

Jack moved steadily back and the remaining force followed his rhythm, "Valykrie-55, this is Viper One, come in. We need rocket support now, are you in the vicinity?"

"55 copies, two minutes. Out Sir."

"Copy. Danger close."

"Copy, Viper One, on route."

Jack turned and waved at the marines to move, "Alright everyone, get back, air support on route. Move!"

Jack ushered the crowd of marines on and hurried them back behind the cover of the various vehicles they had used to arrive on site. Venom followed before dropping to the floor in pain, grasping desperately at the ground beneath her.

"Valkyrie-55, one minute out."

Spider stopped and took stock of the situation before glancing back to Venom who was sprawled out on the ground, the armour slowly stepping towards her, "Venom's still in the mix."

Jack spun round and glanced at both the armour and Venom,

"Damn it!" Pushing Spider aside, Jack sprinted back into the battlefield. As he ran Jack glanced up and spotted the Valkyrie in the sky.

"Are you stupid? Don't be a hero!" Spider shouted but could only watch as Jack sprinted out to their vulnerable teammate.

"Harley, think you can do that again both for two?" Jack asked as he adjusted his sprint path.

"Ergh, I really don't know, it was a momentary thought," Harley stuttered.

"30 seconds," the pilot called.

"Can you do it again?"

"I don't – Yes!" Harley shouted.

"Good enough!" Jack slid on one knee as he reached Venom and grabbed her tightly. The Valkyrie steered into view, its thrusters whipping up the air around them and, without hesitation, released its missile barrage at the armour just inches away from the pair. Venom flicked her head up and stared at Jack as he put his arms around her.

The Valkyrie levelled off and the silos opened up releasing a salvo of missiles from the dropship. The missiles launched forward and rocketed towards the pair. As the armour turned to face its new adversary, the rockets smashed into it and exploded across the battlefield releasing a fireball of hot flame and burnt dirt, the marines tucking in behind their cover to avoid the shockwave.

As the blast fizzled out, the dust hung tensely in the air as everybody shuffled on the spot. The marines wiped their visors and, aiming their rifles, glanced at each other as the dust began to settle and clear. Spider edged slowly away from his cover; his rifle covered in dirt.

"Jack," he coughed as the helmet's air filters desperately

attempted to filter out the dirt, "Venom you there?"

Spider stepped into the dust, raising an arm to block out the incredible bright light emanating from the blast zone. As the dust settled, the light dimmed and he dropped his arm, amazed at what he was seeing. In the clearing within the dust, an outline with a bright purple glow flickered gently. As it weakened, two figures appeared underneath it and Jack finally lowered his rifle.

"Jesus Christ, Jack, do you have a death wish?"

Jack slowly released his squad mate, stumbling painful onto his back as the energy dissipated from around them. Venom untensed her body and rose painfully to her feet, holding her arm out to Jack once again.

"Nice trick."

"Don't mention it," Jack grunted as he allowed Venom to pull him back to his feet.

"You alright?"

"Oh–He's–F–" Harley stuttered over the radio.

"I think so," Jack laughed patting the dirt from his armour, "Nice job, Harley."

"You–A–Id–" Harley stammered again in response.

"You okay, Harley?"

"No you idiot, Im–hav–a meltdown, god I–"

"Thanks Harley," Venom coughed again and patted Jack's shoulder, "I appreciate the save."

"No problem," Jack responded in unison with the AI.

Turning to the gathering crowd Jack stumbled back as Spider grabbed him and shook his hand, "Not a bad effort that," the pair stepped back and nodded, "Not often I say that either."

The trio turned to the sound of applause as Dragon and Draco stepped up joined by Young who had his hands on his hip.

"You're a mad one, Viper One," he turned to the ruins of the base, "I hope you have what you came back for, Major?"

Jack pulled the datalogger from his belt and shook it gently before putting it back.

"Excellent, now kindly get off my base," Young turned back and waved the marines to the armour that had not been damaged in the blast.

"55, I believe you now owe me a ride?" Jack joked as he turned to the open doors of the dropship which was stabilising behind them.

"The pleasure is all mine."

"Good, now keep her steady. . . because I fully intend to nap after this one."

As the team trudged back onto the dropship, Jack stopped before boarding and stared at the armour which lay scattered across the battlefield, "Harley I want a team to pick up the pieces and bring them back to base."

"Copy that."

"We're missing something and I want to know what," Jack boarded the Valkyrie and walked past his team to give orders to the pilots. In the back, Spider gave Venom a long hard stare, his helmet tilted though she wouldn't know it; he knew something was up, he just couldn't think what. They had all been a part of the Viper One unit for years, but recently, there was something out of place. For a well-trained unit, they weren't acting or even reacting as expected.

The Valkyrie rocked as it levelled off and prepared to land as it hit the landing strip. Jack walked up to the rear door and waited as the ramp descended giving access to the base once more. The rookie who had helped Jack pick up some personal items greeted him as he disembarked.

"Welcome back, Sir. Eventful mission, I assume?"

"You could say that."

Jack continued past the rookie pilot who looked lost at the simple response and lack of interaction. The rest of the team followed his lead as they headed for another debrief. The soldiers exited the hangar through the armoury and were greeted by a small group of eager scientists. This time, Jack was in no mood to stop and disarm, instead he barged past and kept on walking. The team quickly passed on their weapons and jogged on after their disgruntled squad leader who had just barged into the debriefing room.

"Kato, when I signed up I expected some level of co-operation, not a game of hide and seek."

"Okay, Jack, calm down and-"

Jack threw down his assault rifle in anger, "No! We've just had two very different outcomes here on the same piece of land. How little intel do you intend to keep giving us, you're so-called elite squad?"

Kato stood and took it all without flinching, "Major, I understand your frustration but you have to understand-"

"Understand what exactly? First you have us on a defence op to maintain control of a high value asset then you have us go back for a simple retrieve mission. Only, what was hiding in your R and D lab nearly killed us all! What exactly was that place anyway?"

"Let me show you," Kato held out his hand, "The key?"

Jack pulled the datalogger from his belt and placed it into the General's hands, watching as he pushed it into the pedestal, revealing a layout of the base they had just returned from.

"The facility you just visited is indeed a research and development facility. Their operation is predominantly to test weapons, it's where those suits came from, especially your mark two version, Jack."

Jack glanced to his teammates and their armour trying to ascertain the differences.

"The operation to protect the base was solely that. We were as surprised as you the militia even knew of the facility. After you ran off, the main force eventually recovered the firing key. We knew they had realised it was a major asset for them. Your mission to remove the key was valuable in itself."

Kato moved his hand over the map revealing an array of small red lights, "These blips are intelligence agents, everyone from operational agents to deep cover spies, all over Earth and beyond in the new colonies. This logger holds some of the most important data in the humanities information war. This would give the militia, or the Hydroxii, enough ammunition to take out and end all ties and operations we have on the go and well. . . war would be inevitable."

Jack stood upright and stared at the screen, not sure whether to continue to be angry or accept that he had stepped into some extremely big boots.

"Major, I know this way of working must be difficult for you but working under these 'need to know conditions' is likely to keep everyone safe. You've reported an enemy combatant in armour only your team wear and have taken out a potentially dangerous suit of armour from origins unknown."

"I just want more information, Sir. I don't like being left in the dark. How can I lead my team into the void?" Jack gripped the rifle and tilted his head, "If I know of something's importance I can co-ordinate more effectively, that armour was almost indestructible."

"But it wasn't and we now know what its strength is. You led your team well, protecting them where necessary, that's all I want and need. We will look over the data and evaluate the situation."

Dragon stepped forward and stood by the Major, "Sir, I agree with Jack here. Something was off in there. We can't honestly admit we missed all of these major talking points and that nobody was aware of an overpowered mech?"

"Perhaps you're all right, but right now we don't know and the techs will overlook the data and the armour. Let's keep moving forward," Kato pushed open the door and waved a hand, "Jack, Spider, you two with me I have a mission for you." The pair followed the General out and left the rest of the team standing around.

Dragon unhinged his helmet, pausing briefly as the armour retracted from his body. He breathed a sigh of relief, "Well I'm not envious of those two, right now I need a nap."

"I need a damn shower after that excitement!" Draco called as he hurried out the door with Dragon following slowly behind.

Venom stood on her own and watched the data on the screen intently, wincing as the bruising from her fight began to come out. She stepped slowly from behind the desk and swiped steadily at the data on each screen before landing on a particular one.

Chapter 11

Kayleigh stared blankly out of the window, avoiding the Captain's angry stare, words pouring out of his mouth.

The captain stopped and waved for her attention, "Jesus Crow, are you even listening?"

"Yes, you we're reminding me how much of a nuisance I am."

"Nearly," the Captain spun his chair around to the left and sighed, "And as hugely pissed off as I am, I can't avoid the fact that something is going on and you've just uncovered something of immense value."

"So you're letting us investigate?" Greg leaned forward a little in the squeaking, plastic chair.

"For now, I want you to have a faultless case file on this," the Captain turned back to Kayleigh, "You especially, you've already made a name, now prove your point."

"So we have your blessing to go after the dealers?"

"Yes, keep me posted if you need backup or anything to contain the situation. I want it off the streets, do you understand, Sergeant? Off the streets."

"Understood Cap!" Kayleigh jumped up and half saluted the Captain as she sped out of the office. Greg stood to attention to follow her.

"Greg, keep an eye on her, she's eager but I fear it might lead to something that I don't want to see or deal with."

Greg nodded and exited the office, heading to the armoury to gear up. When he arrived there, Kayleigh already had her Atlanta City Police Department jacket zipped up and was holstering her side arm. She was eager to solve this puzzle, knowing that there might be something further for her to see and that's what made the situation all the more exciting. Greg pulled the ACPD jacket from its hanger and drew it over his shoulders, the bullet proof vest jutting out from underneath the flimsy material. Taking his service side arm from its robotic holster, the beep released a clip of ammunition, one for patrol officers which hopefully the pair would not be needing to use today.

"So Greg, where and who do we start with?" Kayleigh asked with her hands on her hips.

"My next hit is a guy called Ray Ramirez. He's gone in to hiding recently, but he's the kind of man who will lead us to the big guy down the chain, so we need to find him first."

"Alright, any ideas on where?"

"I know the place to start," Greg holstered the side arm and headed out of the precinct doors with Kayleigh in tow.

"Wait, we're going by foot?"

"If you want the small-time guys you have to go old school, we'll go by foot, it'll be easy if he runs." Greg waved her on and the pair made their way into the bustling city scene of Atlanta, through the shopping district and into the less than appealing areas situated on its outskirts. The local police had managed to move the drug and gang activity out of the main city blocks and into the outer areas, this however provided a problem for the less fortunate who were left to bear the burden of the negative influence that followed.

As they squeezed their way through the mid-day shoppers, Greg moved to the side and pushed a four-digit code into a small fence panel which opened, leading to a small alleyway.

"Greg what are-"

"Just come here," Greg sighed pulling her in, "We can't go undercover flashing the ACPD on our backs, we won't even get close to these guys."

"So what do you suggest, I take my clothes off?" Kayleigh replied sarcastically.

"Jesus Christ, no. Look, take this," Greg lifted the lid of a small dustbin and pulled out two black jackets, "Put this on."

"What's this, your nighttime stash?"

"No, let's just say you're not the first to go undercover with me," he replied putting on the black leather jacket and pushing the sidearm into the holster.

"This really isn't your first undercover job is it?" she asked donning her own leather jacket.

"Less of that, we have a job to do. Let's go."

Greg led Kayleigh out of the alley way and back onto the streets, this time in less obvious clothing. As the pair wandered onwards down the bustling high street, the city slowly began to become quieter; people walked faster through the streets, a little on edge, the further they ventured. Finally, they hit the area they needed to be in. Gangs roamed the streets and the whole feel of the area changed dramatically. Reaching the end of the street, they stopped and Greg began to take in his surroundings.

"So who are we looking for? Some informant of yours?" Kayleigh asked with an edgy tone.

"A guy, PD, he knows the right stuff," he replied not even glancing at her. As he scoured the open area he noticed a man whose clothing choice made him stand out a little more than maybe he realised, "That's the guy," Greg pointed to allow Kayleigh a visual.

"He looks ridiculous."

"And yet a fountain of knowledge. Come on," Greg walked to the end of the pavement, looking both ways to avoid being run over by a speeding car, and continued across the street to meet the alleged informant. As they got closer the oddly dressed man turned and took a step back.

"Oh my days, is that you man!" he held out his hand to welcome Greg, who took it respectfully.

"Man, it's been a while since I've been down here. You well?" Greg asked politely.

"I am, you know keeping this place going and all that!" the man laughed before turning his attention to Kayleigh "And who might you be?"

"Ka–"

"Just a colleague," Greg butted in giving her a polite, but obvious, glare "We work together on some things. Speaking of which, I need some info."

"Anything for you man!"

"Do you know what this stuff is? " Greg pulled out a small vial of now mouldy blue liquid. The same liquid taken from the Hydroxii earlier.

"Woah man, put that stuff away," PD waved his arm down, looking around "That stuff be gold dust around here, man."

"How so? It looks disgusting."

"People say it makes you better.,"

"Better? How?"

"Makes you stronger, more powerful, bulks you up you know?"

"You ever taken it before?" Greg asked knowing the obvious answer but needing to act dumb.

"Na man, that stuff is whack and I mean, come on, its blue!" PD stepped back, "That stuff makes me gag, man. . ."

"So you know of it?" Greg asked curiously, stepping closer to him.

"Yeah man, but I don't do it, ya know. . . why? You want some?"

"Maybe, you know where I can find who has it? I heard Ramirez is the guy."

"Na man, you want a guy called Kenny Hays; he knows a guy, says he's navy or some shit."

Kayleigh's eyes widened a little as Greg turned to meet her shocked response, "Navy Intelligence?"

"Yeah man, some shady guy but that's all I know."

"You know where I can find this Hays guy?"

"He lives in an apartment block not far from here," PD indicated to his right, "Follow that road and you'll hit a crossroads, tallest block, that's what you want. Number 24."

"I knew I could count on you! Thanks a lot man, I owe you big time for this!" Greg shook PD's hand and gave Kayleigh a nod as they walked off.

"No problem man, you keep me posted on that job, yeah?"

"Oh I will!" Greg gave a small wave as he rounded the corner with Kayleigh in tow.

PD waved in return and smiled happily as he watched the pair leave. As they moved out of sight, his happy persona turned quickly into an altogether deeper, more serious tone. Pulling out a small earpiece he pushed it into his ear and pressed on the comms button.

"They know."

On the other end of the radio a low crackling split the pause before the reply came, "Confirmed."

The officers continued to walk the road PD had directed them to, the view far from pleasing but when you let criminals run the streets, it was hardly a surprise.

"So Greg, what's your history with that guy?" Kayleigh asked puzzled.

"I had to do some undercover work, I got to know him, gave him a lifeline. . ." Greg responded with little emotion in his voice.

"You don't sound too happy about that."

"No, I'm not."

"Come on, there isn't a lot I don't know about you is there?" she persisted.

"Listen, just don't. We're on a mission and we need to bring something solid back so. . ."

Kayleigh shook her head and sighed, disappointed not to get a response. Maybe her disappointment was a little to do with the fact that it felt like they had been walking much further than the end of the road, which just so happened to be more like a highway. In the distance, covering the skyline, were the tower blocks PD had mentioned, the tallest standing out a little more because of its shabby looks as much as its height.

After several more minutes of wandering, the pair got up to the apartment block and stepped underneath its large overpass which led to an abandoned car park, now in the use of squatters. Kayleigh eyed the apartment block and turned to Greg, "Thank god we don't have to climb to the top."

Greg checked the map, which was crudely drawn over but still partially understandable, "First floor, that's easy. Come on let's not hang outside here like lost tourists." Greg nodded to a small group across the road alerting Kayleigh to what was going on. Nodding in understanding, she followed Greg up the stairs trying to avoid the huge piles of rubbish and other objects that had been left lying around. As they reached the top the stench of the combination of body fluid and leftover food lingered in their noses. Pushing the door open the smell only got worse.

"Wow. How the hell do people live like this?" Kayleigh coughed trying not to breathe in too much.

"I would rather not know. Anyway here we go, room twenty-four," Greg leaned up against the door frame and knocked three times. Kayleigh placed her hand on the handle of her sidearm and readied herself for a confrontation. No answer. Greg knocked again, this time harder, "Hays you in there? Open up!" he called at the door. Still no answer. Greg pulled out his own sidearm, nodding at Kayleigh, who tried the door handle. It pushed back and the door swung open. Stepping inside they were hit with another smell, not quite as disgusting but certainly different. "Hays, you around?" he called once again hoping for a reply. The pair moved slowly and split up to search the apartment. The room was a mess, pizza boxes tossed aside, half of the food rotting inside.

"Wow this guy is quite the. . . guy," Kayleigh joked as she stepped over an unrecognisable pile of junk, weapon aimed forward. Moving into the next room, she slowly scanned it for anything that stood out. The mess made the view unpleasant and it was difficult to judge just what had been left behind. Glancing around, she eventually spotted something that she did recognise but it was not what she hoping to see. On the bedside cabinet sat a vial of the mysterious liquid, enough for one person. As she stepped forward she lowered her sidearm. Caught off guard, she suddenly felt a heavy whack across the back of her head which sent her scattering across the floor, her weapon bouncing across the room. By the time she had scrambled to recover her weapon, she found the attacker had gone along with the vial.

"Greg I think I found him, he's on his way out!" she shouted, jumping to her feet, and launching herself out of the door in pursuit.

Making her way back to the main room, she discovered Greg already had his sights on her assailant and was stepping closer, "Okay Hays, put your hands behind your back and step forward. I'm not here to take you in, I just have questions."

The man in question stood with the vial in his hand, his other raised in the air as a gesture of surrender. In a flash he darted to the side and vaulted the sofa; the officers followed him, giving chase as he leapt out of the window and onto an old, rusted fire escape.

"I take it he knows something!" Kayleigh shouted as she pushed herself out of the window and up the rickety steps in pursuit.

Hays pushed on through the apartment block, running through the clutter in the corridors on each floor in an attempt to lose the officers. The pursuit went on for a few floors before the structural integrity of the building become questionable and the chase slowed down. Hays pulled himself up onto the balcony section and spun around looking for a way out, the officers slowly stepped up with their sidearms raised.

"Alright Hays, enough running, end of the line," Greg eased

closer as he pulled the handcuffs from his back pocket. Hays continued to plan his next move despite the threat of arrest, his eyes flicking from left to right as he observed up the building across the way. The walls were cracked and showed signs of age, they could provide just enough of a grip if timed it right. Kayleigh leaned forward as Greg edged his way forwards, watching as Hays leapt from the balcony and wrestled to grip the wall of the building he had been eyeing up.

"Oh come on!" Greg pulled himself onto the balcony edge and glanced down, "Jesus. . ."

Kayleigh grabbed the ledge and leaned over, quickly pushing back wide-eyed, "Well, you first."

Greg watched as Hays hauled himself through an open window and made his escape, "Alright, don't miss!" Greg jumped and grappled, the wall slipping a little as he tried to find a footing. Shimmying across, he pulled himself to the window and crawled inside.

Watching on, Kayleigh stood both in fear and disbelief, jumping between buildings wasn't in her training and certainly wasn't on her to do list. She turned and tried to find something that would make the launch across easier. Frantically searching the surrounding area, she caught sight of a wooden board just above her through the metal grate above. Jogging up the stairs she tried to plan her way across. Picking the board up, she weighed it in her hands and leaned on it to see how much it would actually support her. The board bent with ease under the slightest weight as she pushed against it.

"Great," she sighed, pushing it against the balcony until it rested across an air conditioning unit, which squeaked under its weight. Kayleigh took a deep breath and pulled herself onto the board which creaked loudly beneath her as she shuffled herself across. Pressed against the air conditioning unit she prepared for the last hurdle. Abruptly, the board crumbled and fell away from her, the unit hanging on by the shoddy wiring it was installed with.

"Damn it, what is wrong with me?" Kayleigh shouted as she pulled herself up, the unit quickly coming away from the wall. As it finally gave way, she dived across and grabbed the window ledge leaving a cloud of dust behind her where the unit once sat. Hauling herself into the room, she rolled inside and leant against the wall, letting out a sigh of relief.

"Okay Kayleigh. . . no more heroics." As she sat down, she could hear the sounds of the chase taking place in the abandoned building.

Kayleigh hopped to her feet and tried to grab her sidearm, "Ah damn it!" Patting herself down she realised she had lost it in the action and was now defenceless. She couldn't let Greg take Hays on alone. If she could use the environment to her advantage, they could take this guy in for questioning and hopefully learn something that would give the Captain the chance to warrant more arrests.

Making her way, Kayleigh stepped out of the room slowly, glancing from left to right, eyeing up her surroundings and listening intently for any sign of Greg. In the clear, she crept against the dirty wall so she could slip away unnoticed if need be. The corridor was in a terrible state of decay, the walls a dark green and the carpets heavily stained. Continuing onward, she reached the end of the corridor and slowly pushed open the glass doors to the stairs leading to the upper apartments. Slipping through and quietly closing the door behind her, the stench from earlier lingered in the air as she climbed the stairs. She tried not to inhale too deeply as the sound of footsteps and creaking floors echoed loudly. Kayleigh darted up the stairs, following the noises. She glanced at the fire exit door which had just closed shut.

Slowly pushing through the door, she stuck her head around the corner. The distinct sound of running footsteps filled the staircase once more and she watched as Greg gave chase to Hays in the empty parking lot which connected the two apartments together. Kayleigh pushed the door open and joined in the chase. The huge holes in the roof where the night lights once lay let in the afternoon sunshine so that she cast a long shadow behind her.

Greg quickly came to a standstill as he watched Hays struggle with the fire exit door. Unable to push it open, he kicked at it in disappointment before turning to face the law, "Please man you gotta stop, let me go, please. I beg ya." Hays spoke with fear in his voice, glancing around as if he was expecting more officers in pursuit.

"Put your hands where I can see them, Hays," Greg called as he pulled his sidearm, "I have questions."

Hays stepped backwards, glancing more frantically, "Please just back off, you're gonna get me killed!"

"I have no sympathy. Now, you have one chance to stop and do as you're told," Greg offered as Kayleigh stepped up alongside him.

"We need you to answer some questions about a drug YOU have on the go," Kayleigh held her hands out in an attempt to cool the situation.

Hays stepped forward, his hands clasped together, "I'm begging you. If they see me with you they'll kill me!"

Kayleigh looked around puzzled, "We're in an abandoned apartment block, we can't possibly have a tail?"

"My employers are strict, they have me-," Hays staggered as the bullet blasted through his chest, dropping him onto his back.

"Shooter! Down now!" Greg shouted as he pushed Kayleigh aside and scanned the area for the gunman. Quickly, she stepped over to Hays, determining that he was definitely dead. She looked up to the huge gaps in the roof and stared in amazement at the figure before her. The shooter lowered their rifle slowly and stood staring in return. Their armour was a distinct match to what the Hydroxii usually wore in for battle, except the posture was all wrong - the assailant stood just like a human. The shooter lifted the sniper to their back and began jogging away.

"Greg go! The stairs, we have to get that shooter!" she pushed him onwards, back through the parking lot. The officers barged through the double-doors and sprinted up the stairs to the fire exit. Greg waved the sidearm from side to side trying to find the shooter.

"Greg left side!" Kayleigh pointed as she pushed past her partner to give chase. The shooter glanced over their shoulder and began sprinting across the rooftop towards the end of the building.

"They have nowhere to go, surely?" Greg shouted trying to keep up as Kayleigh pushed on. As they got close, the sound of jet engines blasted across the area and they exchanged confused glances as the shooter hopped onto the wall edge and gave a look down in an expectant manner.

"ACPD don't move!" Greg shouted over the jet engine sounds. The shooter turned towards them. To their shock and amazement, a Valkyrie dropship lifted up into view, its cargo hold open. Inside, another four soldiers, dressed in the same unusual Hydroxii-styled armour, stood with rifles in hand. The shooter hopped onto the doorway and took the arm of one of the soldiers who was hanging off the end of the walkway. Once aboard, the shooter gave the officers one last glance before the dropship fired up its engines and moved quickly away into the distance.

The officers stood and looked at each other in confusion, "What the hell just happened?" Greg shouted waving his sidearm in the air.

"I. . . don't know? They were wearing Hydroxii armour."

"What the hell are they doing here killing our leads?"

"I don't know but this just confirms my suspicions," Kayleigh stepped over to the gap in the roof and looked down at Hays' body, "Something is happening here. Either the Hydroxii really are involved or there is something going on with our intelligence friends that we need to learn all about. We should check Hays, see if he had anything on him, phone, or something to link him to them. If he was a supplier for that drug then we need to figure out who he was so terrified of."

Greg holstered his sidearm and shook his head, "You know I respect you but this is getting dangerous, I don't want to get put down."

"So you want to let whatever this is take hold of the city?"

"Of course not. . ."

"Then shut up and help me search the guy." Kayleigh moved away from the vantage point and back towards the doorway to head back. Greg followed, taken aback by the fact they had just watched a potential Hydroxii infiltrator squad take down a criminal, who was potentially linked to a dangerous drug, in broad daylight. Things were going to get stranger and more deadly if this case continued.

Kayleigh leant down and started searching Hays' body for anything that could help them link him to the drug which the informant had pointed them to. Probing his jacket, she produced a wallet with a phone crudely tucked inside it.

"Have you not considered the idea that maybe they were doing us a favour?" Greg asked.

"Have you not considered the fact that they now may be using Hydroxii labour to do their dirty work?" Greg looked on as Kayleigh stood with the wallet in hand, "The GIC are capable of a lot of things, and I have very big trust issues with an organisation that takes on city police cases, falsifies evidence to justify their ops and takes cases off local PD." She pulled the phone from its holder and pushed the power button, "There is something going on and I will find out what it is."

"Even if it kills you?" Greg asked giving her a protective stare, "Seriously, this is going to get us killed."

"Not if we put those snobs at GIC on their arses," she replied holding up the phone. The screen displayed the last logs on Hays phone, "We just need the right back up. Even the Captain believes we have something."

"Did you ever stop to think that maybe he is as terrified as I am of this becoming something more?"

Kayleigh shook her head and stuffed the wallet and phone into her jacket pocket as she began to walk away, "We have a duty to protect, Greg. Don't forget that."

Chapter 12

The pair stepped out of the elevator and headed toward the labs.

"If we get the techies to look over the phone we can see where the calls were made and who to, then we can pin someone for this and put this into the next gear," Kayleigh spoke quietly.

"Fine, you do that, I'll debrief with the Cap' and meet you later, okay?"

"Fine, but don't you want to be here when they do?"

"Not when I have a hot date with the wife, Kay, that takes priority. . . " He smiled as he put his hand on her shoulder, "Call me when you have something, okay?"

Kayleigh smiled back at him, "Okay, thanks for the assist." Greg stepped away towards the Captain's office. Kayleigh pushed open the door to the labs and looked around for any analysts she could coerce into helping her. After a quick glance, she spotted the perfect guy, conspiracy theorist master, Peter O'Reilly.

"Rai!" Kayleigh called with delight as she stepped over "I could do with some help!"

Peter turned, nearly falling off his chair from the quick swivel, "Kay-I didn't-what are you doing here?"

"Well, as my favourite technological marvel, I thought I would ask for your help," she casually sat at the end of his desk and grinned politely.

"Sure, I mean what can we-I-do for you?" O'Reilly stuttered as he tried to compose himself.

Kayleigh laughed, "I need you to scan this." She pulled Hays' phone from her pocket and held it up for him to see, "It's related to a case I'm working."

"Does the Captain know?" he asked reaching out for the phone.

"If I said no, would this be a problem?" Kayleigh placed the phone into his hand, "For now it's just between you and me, okay?"

"Ye-total-completely between me and you."

"Excellent! Call me when you're done." Kayleigh hopped off the desk.

"Yes ma'am-I mean Kay-I-"

"Okay O'Reilly, don't overheat, let me know how you get on."

O'Reilly nodded as Kayleigh smiled and wandered out of the labs and back to her desk.

Greg stepped out of the elevator and pushed the button on his keys, the car's lights flashed a dark yellow. Opening the door, he stepped inside. Before starting the engine he pulled out his phone and pushed speed dial, "Hey you! Just thought I would let you know I'm on my way to the restaurant," Greg called out happily, "So I'll see you in ten minutes, alright? Bye!" He felt like tried pinching himself to check that it hadn't all been a dream. He had been married only two years but the pair had been together for so long that it felt like they were married for much longer. As he pushed the engine start-up button the car whirred into life and Greg moved to push the handbrake down but something wasn't right.

"Greg Brack, it's so nice to meet you," a voice politely called from the back seat. In shock, Greg whipped around to see a man in the back seat of his car, "I think this has been long overdue, don't you officer?"

Who are you?" Greg asked in a puzzled tone.

"My name is irrelevant right now. What you should know is that I am the man you have been searching for!" The man held out his arms, presenting himself.

"So you're here to turn yourself in?"

The man laughed out loud in reply, "Oh no, Mr. Brack," he pulled out a pistol from his side pocket and pointed it at Greg, "I'm here to solve the second problem of today, personally."

Kayleigh stirred as her phone buzzed across her desk. Trying to wake herself up after falling asleep at her desk, she picked it up and answered the call, "Kayleigh here."

"Kayleigh hi, I-errr-need a word-now-in the lab," O'Reilly stuttered on the other end.

"On my way!" she clicked to end the call and jumped up from her chair, making her way to the labs. The precinct was dimly lit, it was late now and the night shift officers were sitting around waiting for something more active to do.

Arriving at the labs she waltzed in and sidled up to O'Reilly, "You have something for me?"

Startled, O'Reilly batted her hand away before realising who had spoken, "Oh it's you, thank god. I think you may have stumbled on something."

"Go on?"

"Look here," O'Reilly tapped on the computer in front of him and brought up data files, "Your phone is like my dream find except. . . it's a little too real."

"Explain?"

"Well, this guy you got the phone off has calls and contacts tracing back to major GIC operatives."

"And this is why I asked you to-"

"The data on this phone is a treasure trove, it is linked to a highly complex computer system; my biggest surprise is one of the contact's name - the Captain himself."

Kayleigh tensed a little and stared at the screen "So what have we picked up here?"

"I don't know fully yet but I thought you needed to know," O'Reilly leaned back and sighed, "Kay this could be a big deal."

"Exactly. The case I'm working is associated with the bodies that have appeared all over the city. Greg and I had an interesting meeting with a hit squad too."

"Well, you certainly found the holy grail," O'Reilly turned back and stared at the reems of data before him, "Give me a night and I'll have more for you."

"Knew I could count on you! I'll see you in the morning then?" Kayleigh asked leaning over the desk.

"Yep sure, definitely."

Kayleigh smiled and patted him on the back before heading out of the lab and to the elevator.

O'Reilly scrolled further through the data and began decrypting the data locked in the phone, making copies to back up for Kayleigh's case. As he sat entranced by the data, a noise echoed through the room catching him out. "Hello?" he called but there was no answer. Looking back, he found his screen blacked out and a shadowy silhouette covering it.

Turning to face the shadow everything quickly turned dark and O'Reilly found himself on the floor, the world slowly fading way, a needle dropping next to his head. Quickly, his fear was replaced with oblivion.

Kayleigh rolled over trying to avoid the blaring sound coming from the side of her head, groaning as she retreated further under the duvet, the noise still there. Sighing, she lifted her head and dragged herself across the bed, patting the glass counter-top until her hand finally grasped her phone. Picking it up, she put the phone to her ear as she rolled onto her back and pushed the answer button.

"What?" she groaned as she switched to speaker mode and laid it beside her.

"It's the Captain, get your arse out of bed. We have a situation."

Kayleigh pushed herself out of the comfort of her bed, "What's happened Cap?"

"It's Greg and O'Reilly, our analyst. They're missing. Get here ASAP."

"On it," Kayleigh pushed the end call button and stood up. Placing her bare feet on the soft carpet, she padded over to her wardrobe and dressed in her ACPD uniform. Stepping away from the wardrobe, she pulled out her standard issue police shoes. Ideas flooded her imagination as she wondered what had happened to them. One thought occupied her - she was next!

Kayleigh closed the door of her car; going to the back, she pulled open the rear door and took out her ACPD jacket. Putting it on, she walked quickly through the precinct car park until she reached the elevator; to her surprise, two armed guards from the military were on station.

"Are you Kayleigh Crow?" grunted the marine.

Kayleigh nodded and held up her ACPD ID badge. The marine leaned in, glancing across to the officer before nodding and pushing the elevator button to reveal an open lift. The marines stepped aside and Kayleigh entered, hesitating slightly before she pushed the main level button then turning to face outwards as the marines stepped back into position. Kayleigh stood with her head in her hands and sighed, she knew full well that O'Reilly either blabbed to somebody, or the GIC caught on, and that he would be awaiting trial for treason.

As the doors opened, the bustle of the station calmed as she slowly stepped out, the officers glancing over and muttering quietly before continuing with their work. Not a great sign. She carried on before the Captain appeared and hurried her into his office.

"Jesus Captain, what–"

"Shut up and answer my questions, Crow" the Captain growled as he slammed the door shut, "What in the hell did you and Greg get up to?"

"I thought Greg spoke–"

"He did but he clearly missed out some very important details!" He turned and glared at her, "Now talk!"

"Fine. Greg and I went into the outskirts, found a guy, he ran, we took his phone and found a number and I asked O'Reilly to look into it."

"Well, your little sidekick has got two officers in deep and they've been taken!"

"What do you mean taken? Have they arrested them?"

The Captain produced a tablet and played footage of

O'Reilly's lab. Kayleigh watched in horror as the footage showed a distorted silhouette injecting the analyst and dragging him off into the distance. It made for an uncomfortable watch.

"I have officers on lookout for anything suspicious but clearly these guys are good and don't leave any trails to follow."

"Sir, what about Greg, where did he go?" Kayleigh leaned in curiously.

"From what we can gather, he was taken from his car in one of the parking bays."

"Captain, come on, with all these marines and agents about how can you not know what happened?"

"Excuse me?" the Captain replied in shock.

"Come on, you have your own branch of the marine core here and navy intelligence raiding our equipment, how can nobody know anything yet?"

"We don't even know who we're up against, Officer-"

"Bullshit, we both warned you something wasn't right. You let us go after that guy in the districts so you clearly believe something is going on so don't even pretend that this is just on me. It's your fault as much as mine for laying back and doing nothing!"

"Enough."

Kayleigh breathed slowly as she took a moment to unwind. She watched as he sighed and ruffled his hair, accepting the situation, "Okay, I admit I lacked some interest but you cannot blame me for laying low on leads that head nowhere. Having the GIC monitoring my every move has made my job substantially harder."

"Then you admit there is a problem and the GIC are doing

their best to cover it up?"

"I don't know what I believe. I deal in concrete evidence and facts, something you haven't provided or proven yet, Crow."

"No, I won't stand for that," Kayleigh stood and opened the door.

"And where are you going?" he shouted rising from his chair.

"To do my job."

"Then at least take your new partner with you."

Kayleigh turned, gripping the doorknob tighter, "You've replaced Greg already?"

"That's not the case. She will be supporting you in the field and with your investigation. You know Greg would have been given the same support if the situation were reversed."

"Fine, but I'm having Greg back when we find him. Who am I stuck with?"

The Captain pulled the door further back and pointed at her new partner. She was small, slim-built, and nervous looking. A recipe for disaster. Kayleigh turned and sighed, "Seriously?"

"She will be valuable to you, give her some slack and do your job, Crow" he turned and ushered her out of the door, "Bring our guys home in one piece and show her why you're the best."

Kayleigh sighed, shaking her head, and waving her over. The woman jumped up in surprise and hurried towards her. "Umm it's nice to meet you," she muttered quietly, her gaze drawn to the officers muttering around them as the pair headed away from the main office.

"That's nice, you too I guess," Kayleigh replied, leaving the bumbling new recruit to stumble her way behind her. "Now I don't really care much for your back story, your past or the stuff in between. Just keep close and do as you're told."

The recruit ruffled her short, messy blonde hair, "Umm, my name's Amy by the way."

Kayleigh slowed and looked down a little. Amy was a little smaller than herself, her little hand held out in front of her, "That's wonderful, now follow me."

"Where to?"

"The tech labs, I had O'Reilly working on something before the bastards took him."

Amy looked away puzzled, it sounded as if Kayleigh knew who had taken the tech guy and her partner, "You know who they are?"

"Not right now. When we get close something happens, somebody gets shot. All I know is that there is something going on and that those idiots at the GIC know what it is."

Amy answered, "The intelligence command?"

"We have one of their top guys on site pulling orders; he's pulled me from more cases than I now care to recall. Last night me and Greg were confronted by someone dressed in what appeared to be custom Hydroxii armour. They didn't stand like them, they stood like a human."

"You think we're heading for another war?" Amy shrieked as she almost walked in to the tech lab door.

"No, not really. It looks like the figure we saw took O'Reilly. Look," Kayleigh pushed open the tech lab door, pulling the chair from the under the desk before sitting down. Tapping into the keyboard, she brought up the video file that the Captain showed her. Amy winced as she watched the scene unfold.

"You're right, they don't move like Hydroxii, they're too human."

"Exactly. And I think the GIC know something," Kayleigh

pushed back from the desk and spun the chair to face Amy, "If you're really my new partner you have to follow my exact orders, no ifs, no buts, got it?" Amy nodded. "Good now our best lead is to dig into this guy's phone, the one I gave to O'Reilly. If we can pinpoint where he is staying we can head there and find out who he is working for, and hopefully discover who took Greg."

"Okay, so where do we start?"

"Well," Kayleigh leaned back in the chair and looked around the room, "I was hoping to borrow one of these other techies."

"After what you've put one of their own through, nobody is willingly going to help you with this. No, move over," Amy urged Kayleigh from the chair, switching places with her partner as she began typing on the keyboard.

"Okay, so work before manners, so be it," Kayleigh stood with her hands on the back of the chair as Amy began bringing up all kinds of messages and blue prints from the phone, the kind of work she herself could never have done without some outside help, "So this is why the Captain assigned you to me."

"Hold on," Amy continued to work away, ignoring Kayleigh's remark. She indicated for Kayleigh to quieten her down as she tried to finish her work, "There," she pointed with a broad smile on her face, "That's your guy's most likely home address."

Kayleigh followed Amy's finger to the GPS location on screen, it was Hays' address. This was likely to bring up information on the guys who signed him up and those who put him down, probably for being caught out by the local police. Kayleigh tapped on the side of the desk, "Nice job, rookie. Now come on, we have a scruffy apartment to scour."

Amy smiled and the pair stepped out of the lab, "Does this

mean you're going to trust me a little?"

"Don't push it, this is a work in progress. We'll call it work experience," Kayleigh laughed pushing the elevator button, "But keep it up."

"Yes Ma'am."

The Captain watched through his office window as Kayleigh and Amy headed off into the elevator and onto the day's task. Recent events were taking a toll on the running of the station. Every officer was worried, not wanting to become intertwined in the web around their precinct, it was hard to stay focused. He stood and pushed the large button on the wall, allowing the glass in front of him to frost over. Confident he was safe from prying eyes, he walked back to his desk and sat down. Tapping on to his data pad, he pushed a menu and allowed it to run its program. Seconds later the program finished with a ping and he looked down.

>*GIC.Access.055.*

<*ACPD.351.*

>*Enter encryption command_*

Pushing the data pad aside he typed into his computer and entered the input it demanded, eventually dialing out to another user. Kato breathed in deeply, wondering how it all came back to this. Again. Those days should have been over but it's the friends you keep that keep you safe. Kato acknowledged the green light on the data pad, sat up straight in his chair and cleared his throat.

"Kato, you smug bastard, I think we need to talk."

Kayleigh anxiously patted the steering wheel as she tried to gently ease her way through the city. After the recent incident, she didn't want to run the risk of flashing the blues and reds to alert everyone nearby if she was indeed being targeted.

Eventually she turned to Amy. "So where exactly did you learn that hack you did back there?" she asked.

"I thought you weren't interested," Amy smiled smugly as she looked out of the window toward the stalled traffic.

"Well I'm passing time so come on."

"Alright. I was a data analyst for a big tech company. Actually worked for a weapons' company before I fell into police work."

Kayleigh flung the wheel to the right and pulled into the opposite lane to avoid the stand still, following the slow-moving traffic forward, "Why join the Atlanta PD though? Surely someone with your kind of experience and clear expertise would want to work for the intelligence guys. Deep cover, espionage. . ."

Amy turned to face Kayleigh in disgust, "And live in a basement till I retire? No thanks, I have friends."

Kayleigh laughed as she checked her mirrors before moving

across the junction, "Nice to know we have something in common."

"What about you? Why do you do it?"

Kayleigh paused for a moment and pondered the question. She bit her lower lip before glancing at Amy, "It's a long story. At the moment, the main objective is to get back at the GIC. They have been taking over our cases for months and I want to know what's going on."

"I won't ask too much. I just know everyone in that station thinks you're the best. Anyway, what exactly are we looking for in this place we're going to?" Amy asked.

"Well, Hays had a place in the outskirts, a real pit, so I think this address you managed to pinpoint is more of either a home address or a meeting point. . . either way we need to check it out."

"Didn't you and Greg find this guy's place anyway?"

Kayleigh frowned a little, "We thought we had."

"So?"

"Well it wasn't, so this is where fix this and save them."

Amy nodded as Kayleigh brought the car to a stop at the address. Pushing open the door, Kayleigh stepped out and rested her arms on the roof of the car. The address was far grander than the last address they had searched, it was in a more family-orientated area; children ran around the car as they played freely. Amy left the car and skipped to the pavement,

"So do we knock and ask or. . ?"

"Hays is dead, we go in." Kayleigh slammed the car door shut, squeezing past Amy, who glanced from side to side making sure the area was clear of lookouts of any sort.

The pair stepped up to the front door and Kayleigh gave it a tap, "ACPD, anyone there?"

"I thought we were just going in?"

"Just ticking a box," Kayleigh smiled as she pulled the handle down and opened the door before wandered inside, "Excellent, all ready for us."

Stepping inside the officers slowly began to search the office, moving documents and scouring cupboards in order to find the necessary information. Amy hesitated as she wandered through the office, lightly pushing aside the mess she encountered, barely lifting anything to really check the material. She felt under pressure, the officer in charge was looking for revenge and somebody to put down. She pushed aside a large pile of paper and revealed a small phone covered in a blue substance, "Hey Kayleigh, over here," she called out.

Kayleigh leaned against the wall divide and lifted an eyebrow, "Find anything?"

Amy held up the phone and shook it a little, "Think this might help?"

"Perfect, can you work your magic here?"

"Keep this between me and you," Amy held up a small data chip and smiled.

"Do what you must!"

Amy pushed the chip into the phone's connector port and plugged it into the monitor which sat on the reception desk. The pair watched as streams of data ran down the screen in a pile of menus and images as they swiped across. After a minute, the phone suddenly flickered and the pair looked at each other in surprise. A black and red line flashed across the screen before a voice began to speak.

"Officer Kayleigh Crow."

Kayleigh took a step back and looked over her shoulder,

"Officer Sergeant Kayleigh Crow."

Kayleigh stepped forward and cleared her voice, "That's my name? Who's this?"

"Your friends. . . you killed them," the voice stuttered, its constant fluctuating making it impossible to guess the real identity of the caller.

"If you've hurt them, I will find you and kill you-"

"Do you not care for those you work with. . . to keep the peace?"

"I do and I've done a damn good job till you, whoever you are, took that away!" Kayleigh stepped up to the monitor.

"Amy seems such a good replacement. Why don't you give up. . . give her the satisfaction of living?"

Amy glanced up at Kayleigh as she confronted the voice on the phone. Kayleigh was filling with rage as she listened to the voice. Maybe this was a bad move after all, they needed backup.

"Just tell me where O'Reilly and Greg are!" Kayleigh screeched at the monitor.

As if obeying the command, the monitor flickered and an arrangement of numbers appeared on screen.

"You'll find the co-ordinates here for you. Your world is changing, Officer and it's about to change even further than you could possibly comprehend." The voice cut out leaving the officers staring briefly at the co-ordinates on screen before slowly looking back to each other.

Kayleigh grabbed the phone and walked out of the door, Amy followed her, "Shouldn't we tell the Captain?"

Kayleigh swung round and put her hand on Amy's shoulder, "Not a chance, I'm not endangering any more officers. In fact you should head back. If I'm not back in 2 hours tell the Captain what happened and get backup."

"No way," Amy stopped and removed Kayleigh's hand from her shoulder, "You've clearly been through a lot and got yourself in some deep shit trying to stop it, so I'm coming to help you." She stormed past Kayleigh and wrenched open the car door, "So get your arse in here and let's get there".

Kayleigh rolled her eyes, secretly happy and impressed that somebody was willing to help her, someone as efficient as Greg even. Climbing into the car, she put the phone on the dashboard, "So what exactly are these co-ordinates?"

Amy tapped on the car's screen and pushed the data chip she had used earlier into its interface, "We'll find out in a sec."

"Where exactly did you get that?" Kayleigh asked confused.

"Work perk," Amy continued to push buttons until the screen revealed a location indicated by a red arrow.

Kayleigh acknowledged the location, "Well I like this perk. You armed?" Amy pulled her ACPD jacket aside to reveal a sidearm, "Excellent, let's go then, we won't have a lot of time." She floored the accelerator and the pair raced off to warehouse where they presumed the officers were being held.

After a short while, the pair reached the location given by the co-ordinates and parked the car close so as to be able to move in without being detected. Kayleigh indicated to her new partner to follow as she stepped quickly across the slightly overgrown greenery surrounding the dreary looking warehouse. Pressing themselves up against the aged metal that made up the walls of the warehouse, Kayleigh slid her hand to her hip and un-holstered her sidearm.

"It seems way too quiet," she whispered, "If this isn't a trap. . ."

Amy drew her pistol and pointed it down, the safety catch

disarmed, "There's absolutely nothing going on around the place, maybe it was just a pre-recorded message?"

"Yeah? And I'm a clown. . . come on," Kayleigh crept around to the back of the building with Amy following closely. Reaching a doorway, she slowly turned the handle which creaked as it loosened.

"You first, Amy," Amy looked at her blankly, "Come on, chop, chop, you want the action."

Amy sighed and raised her sidearm stepping inside and leaning against a large storage container before ushering in her partner.

Once inside, Kayleigh looked around, taking in the small surroundings and oddly placed barricades making up the long walls to both sides of the large container. "You see an opening down that side?" she asked pointing behind Amy.

Amy pushed herself up and peered along the wall, "No, just more badly placed containers."

"Well," Kayleigh said, noticing a large pull-lock sitting above the container door, "I guess we'll go right through the middle."

Amy closed her eyes and shook her head, "I should have stayed in the office. Alright, on three, I'll jump and pull okay?"

Kayleigh nodded and steadied herself.

"Three, two, one," Amy leapt up and grabbed onto the container lock, pulling it down. "Now!" she shouted over the loud click and thud of the heavy door. Landing on her feet she watched Kayleigh darted through.

"ACPD! Police, don't move!" Kayleigh and Amy called out as they stepped out of the container, pistols raised at eye level. As they emerged into the huge expanse that made up the floor of the warehouse, they spotted something sitting in the middle.

Kayleigh lowered her weapon and raised an eyebrow in confusion. Stepping forward she noticed what looked like a makeshift, emergency bed with a plastic screen surrounding it and the eerie beep on medical monitors, "Jesus Christ. Greg! O'Reilly!" she called out holstering her sidearm and sprinting towards them.

"Kayleigh, are you crazy? Oh, come on," Amy sighed as she joined her.

As Kayleigh stepped up to the cordon her mood changed from relief to disgust in a flash, "What the hell?"

Kayleigh pulled back the curtain to reveal a mess of what was once a human being, its body completely disfigured and almost unrecognisable. The figure on the table was broken, their skin torn from top to bottom and their body twisted beyond repair. The same blue liquid substance seemed to be pulsating from its body - a direct similarity to the previous cases. This time it was far worse. The victim was still breathing as it laid on the small emergency bed, the victim was alive. This could be the opportunity Kayleigh had been waiting for.

Kayleigh locked eyes with the still conscious being, quickly looking away when it shook pathetically. On the metal table opposite, its personal items were strewn. The I.D. badge gave away his identity - Officer Keith O'Reilly, Technology Analyst, Atlanta City Police Department.

Kayleigh turned slowly and met O'Reilly's lost, emotional gaze, "I am so, so sorry. . . I-" she leaned forward but O'Reilly twitched and the ping of a pin drop filled the warehouse with noise.

Amy's eyes widened as she saw the grenades, "Kayleigh!" she shrieked as she pulled her arm.

Amy threw herself and Kayleigh back through the container

as the grenades detonated and obliterated the warehouse around them. Both women landed hard on the ground outside and twitched slowly as the debris littered the ground around them.

Jack coughed heavily as he tried to clear his lungs of the black smoke that had engulfed the pair, "Spider. . ." he coughed as he rolled onto his back, wincing in pain from the fall, "You okay?"

"Oh just fantastic!" Spider groaned as he pushed himself off the ground.

"Good. Command you copy?"

"Clear Alpha, what the hell just happened?" Kato's tone identified him as the voice on the receiving end of the line.

"Sir, you were right, definitely something going on. That ACPD officer, Crow, is definitely onto something," Jack coughed again trying to clear his throat.

"Copy. Get yourself back to HQ to suit up, we can look at the next step on your way in, Command out."

"Copy. Wow did you see that guy?" Jack grimaced, climbing to his feet, "What the hell did they just stumble on? Human experimentation?"

"No idea, but whatever it is I do not want to see it again. Kato was right Jack. Something is off here. What the hell did those officers just step into?"

Jack brushed the debris from his civilian clothes and spied the women from his vantage point. What was the conspiracy that a police officer could have stumbled on, to be so necessary that they would openly give themselves up to catch her off guard? Jack tapped Spider on the shoulder and the pair moved from the site.

Chapter 14

Kayleigh gasped as she suddenly came to, her body aching and torn from the explosion. Groaning in pain, she pulled herself forwards and peered through the dust and debris. "Amy! Amy where are you?" she coughed loudly, trying to clear her throat of the smoke she had inhaled.

Amy's eyes flickered open briefly as she tried to move herself away from the painful position she found herself in. Waving her hands across her face, she flicked her blonde hair away and rubbed her eyes. "Kay-Kayleigh!" she groaned trying to call for help over the roar of the warehouse fire raging in front of her. Her ears were ringing from the explosion. As she looked to her left, vehicles of all kinds were pulling in, lights flickering on and off, only adding to her confusion. Through her blurred vision she could make out the silhouette of a body in front of her, their mouth moving but she only heard ringing.

The silhouette came into sharper focus and a human shape hovered in front of her, shouting for her attention, "Officer. . . Can you. . . Officer Gre-can you hear me. . ?"

"Wh-where's Kayleigh?" Amy as she tensed her hands due to the pain coursing through her upper body.

"Officer Green, can you hear me?" the man shouted again,

his voice clearer this time.

"Yes, I can. . . where am I?" she mumbled attempting to lift herself up once more but finding that her body only allowed so much movement.

"You're at the warehouse. . . what the hell happened?"

"We, we-were looking up a lead. . . on. . . that O'Reilly guy. . . found him in there, but it was a trap," she replied forcing her eyes open. As her vision cleared, she could see the Captain staring at her with a shocked expression on his face, "Jesus Captain, when did you -?"

"When I found out you two lunatics had gone off looking for a fight. . . Did you find O'Reilly? Or Greg?"

Amy closed her eyes and shook her head, "O'Reilly's dead, Sir. . . in there. They rigged the building. We walked right into it as well, damn it!" she pointed to the remains of the warehouse, "But something else was wrong, O'Reilly was different? Someone had done something to him, he was unrecognisable, Captain. He was barely human."

"What do you mean, not human?" the Captain quizzed sounding concerned.

"He was messed up," she lifted herself up and leaned back a little, "He was twisted, his body was battered and broken. They were pumping some kind of liquid into him. He looked in pain, Sir. . ."

"Damn it," he sighed getting to his feet, "We need this dealing with now."

"What do you have in mind, Sir, this group, they seem several steps ahead of us?"

"I have an idea, but Kayleigh won't like it," he turned and waved Kayleigh over.

She had finally got to her feet and moved slowly towards

them, "Sir?"

"I've called in a favour."

Jack pushed open the door, stepping aside to allow Spider to follow him through. The Atlanta Global Intelligence Command headquarters were very extravagant, its pristine varnished flooring lighting up the foyer despite its dark, black paint. As they walked through the foyer, the pair were met by General Kato who was joined by the remainder of the Viper One team.

"Welcome back, gentleman. It would appear you two had some fun?"

"As always, Sir," Spider half-heartedly saluted as he stepped forward.

"Sir, what's the plan, why are we meeting here?" Jack asked cutting the pleasantries short.

"As you're now aware the Atlanta police department have found themselves deep in something they are totally un-equipped for. Officers Kayleigh Crow and Greg Brack have spent the past few months trying to solve a mystery that has been affecting the people of this city."

Kato ushered the team in to a meeting room. Following them inside, he pushed a panel and lit up a large, white board, "Bodies have been turning up across the city. Disfigured. Torn. What you caught a glimpse of with the two officers just earlier, is what has been left, abandoned around the city." The team stopped shuffling and looked at each other warily.

"Sir, that liquid substance was what was coursing through that armour that almost killed us back in Kyreel. I don't get it; how and why is that stuff being pumped through humans like lab rats?" quizzed Venom, "What is this stuff?"

"Exactly," Kato brought up the police files that Kayleigh and

Greg had compiled and displayed the valuable information across the board, "These are all the reports, recent leads and so on. Everything links back to some kind of 'biological' weapon being tested. That's the guess here. Now if this is true, somebody, or some lunatic, is weaponising an unknown substance. Whether this is militia or Hydroxii, it doesn't matter. This stuff completely destroys the body of its host."

"Okay, I understand the complexities of what's happening in the city, but again, what are we doing here, Sir? We're a military strike team, not detectives," Jack asked uncomfortably.

"Your job is to work with Kayleigh, and her new partner Amy Green, to find Greg Brack before he becomes another victim. We have far more to offer the police in this operation and, with what we have had to endure in the past few days alone, I believe this is linked to our own operation."

"Surely it's safer to pursue this on our own, jurisdiction means nothing to us?" Venom questioned in a low tone.

"Normally yes, but one, I owe the local Captain a favour from days gone by and, two, this is becoming a problem for more than just us. Officer Crow and Brack were attacked by what they allege to be somebody wearing the same armour your unit are wearing, Jack."

The team glanced at each other as the Captain stopped for a moment, allowing that thought to sink in, "This shooter could well be the same one from the base attack who took the key for the orbital cannon. If so, they are operating in the city now. There are too many problems to leave this to one unit." The team nodded in acknowledgement, "Great, now Jack and Spider I had your suits brought in so gear up and meet us underground, your chariots await."

The team saluted and moved out of the briefing room. As

Jack let his team exit first, a flicker of purple light caught his eye. It was Harley.

"So, we get to play detective today? Excellent, always thought of myself as a finder of things," she shouted excitedly.

Jack turned and faced the AI, "Just try not to scare the new recruits, will you?"

Kayleigh winced again as the car lurched over another hole in the ground, "Seriously, will you slow down?"

"Sorry Ma'am, Captains orders, I'm to bring you in for briefing ASAP." The driver turned for a moment to look at Kayleigh who nursing her body, her police vest blood stained, "You sure you're safe for field work?"

Amy peered around the back of the driver and tapped on his shoulder, "She's fine, she's just grumpy." She slumped back into her seat smiling to herself.

"Easy for you to say. Just wish we could have got O'Reilly before they did whatever they did to him."

Amy watched as the driver brought the car back to the station. She brushed Kayleigh to get her attention, "Kayleigh. . . think we have a problem." Amy pointed to the front of the car and Kayleigh followed her finger to the blockade of four, black, heavily armoured vehicles parked in front of the ACPD station. The vehicles had no insignia on them, and Kayleigh knew just who had shown up.

"Wonderful, the return of the black tape," Kayleigh sighed as the car came to a halt.

Clambering out the pair headed inside, to their surprise there was very little activity above what normally went on, and this put Kayleigh on the defensive. Pushing open the door, she wandered past two GIC agents and, without a passing glance, pushed the elevator call button.

Watching the door slide open they stepped inside, and Kayleigh pushed for the main floor, "So what do we think? Demotion or just general bad news?"

"I'm hoping just general bad news. New recruits can't be demoted, can they?" Amy grumbled as she patted herself down, having partially forgotten she was still covered in dust from the explosion. The elevator pinged and the doors slid open. Kayleigh's eyes widened as she caught sight of five soldiers gathered around the Captain, the middle soldier resembling the one who had assaulted her and Greg.

Kayleigh painfully reached for her sidearm and confidently moved forward.

Seeing her reach for her weapon, Amy stared at her superior officer, "Kayleigh, what are you doing?"

Before she could get an answer, Kayleigh was already out of the elevator, sidearm aimed high. She turned to open the door with her back and spun into the room, pulling the pistol from its safety switch. The soldiers were altered by the sound of the door being swung open aggressively and immediately drew their own rifles, aiming them towards the pair of officers entering the briefing area.

"Whoa! Everyone hang on!" shouted one of the men in the briefing room, pushing aside the soldiers who were in the room.

"Weapons down!" Kayleigh shouted out, noticing Amy had also drawn her sidearm, she felt a little more in control.

One of the armoured soldiers stepped carefully forwards, aiming steadily at Kayleigh. The soldier glanced to the second officer who, despite being armed, seemed more confused than a threat, "I highly recommend lowering your weapon, Officer

Crow, and you Green. We're on the same team here. We're here to help you."

"Just who are you? And how do you know who I am?" she responded, swaying her pistol slowly from side to side as the remaining soldiers stood their ground.

"I presume this is the favour, Captain?" Amy asked lowering her sidearm slightly. Kayleigh gave Amy a hard stare before looking back to the door as it opened.

The Captain stepped back into the room and walked towards them, "Yes, Officer Green. Now lower your weapons everyone. I do not need a shootout here, not after I've already lost two of my best." He stepped up to Kayleigh and put his hand onto the pistol, lowering it steadily, "Please Kayleigh, I understand your frustration right now, but I need you to trust me. This is going to help us make sense of the situation and to find Greg." He indicated to the armoured soldiers to lower their weapons too.

Taking the hint, she slowly lowered the pistol, before holstering it and glancing over to Amy who did the same. She was extremely impressed that her new partner was ready to back her up, even in an unconventional situation like that, "So what's the plan?"

"Let's start by learning names, shall we? Kayleigh Crow, Amy Green, please welcome Navy General Brandon Kato, commander of this unit," the Captain gestured to the lead soldier, his darkened visor shimmering slightly in the changing light, "And this is Hunter, leader of this unit, Viper One."

"Nicknames, cute," Kayleigh gave a fake smile as she looked at the soldiers, noticing all the different traits and colours on their armour. Amy flicked her fringe from her face and gave a small awkward wave, which Dragon returned.

"Now if you please," the Captain pointed to the briefing room, "Today's objective."

Jack and his team stepped forward following Kato into the room, Draco giving Dragon a quick shove.

Harley buzzed into Jack's internal communications, "She does not seem to like you guys at all. Might need to make friends first," she joked, "This will make our circus all the more exciting!"

Jack sighed, "Be nice, please?"

Jack stepped up to the briefing room table. He admired the sleek design of the room in comparison to the lesser funded police force ones and wondered how the two had ever become so entwined. Everyone gathered round, Jack could already feel the deathly stare coming from Officer Kayleigh opposite him. This mission was going to be long and awkward.

With the two teams congregated round, Kato dimmed the lights and lit up the large table, "Jack," Kato nodded to him. He held out his hand, lighting the table up for a brief moment in a sea of purple before Harley materialised in front of everyone.

"Ah, well hello team! Glad to be here I–" she spun around noticing the two officers' stunned expressions. Holding her hands out wide, she stepped towards the two ACPD officers, "Oh I'm sorry, allow me to introduce myself. I'm an AI, my name's Harley and I'm highly unconventional." Harley held out her hand and then quickly retracted it, "Sorry, not so good with pleasantries."

Kayleigh took a step back allowing Amy to lean in, "What! A real AI?"

"Hey, a fan!" Harley gave the officer a thumbs-up before Kato tapped his hand on the table for her attention.

"Harley," Kato snapped his fingers, "the mission, please."

"Oh yeah," Harley cleared her throat and moved towards the middle of the table, "So, on topic. I've managed to use my powers of persuasion to piece together the events of the past few months, today and yesterday. To bring the ACPD officers up to date, the bodies you have uncovered in your city were pumped with an unknown substance that is linked to something we had a run-in with not long ago." Harley lifted her hand and poked the air placing a video behind her. The officers watched in awe of the firefight that was in front of them. "This helmet camera footage was taken from our fight with the object in question," Harley paused the video at the point where Venom was on the ground and Jack was fighting the armour, "This intelligent armour was full of the blue substance that was found inside the human remains of those littered around your city."

Kayleigh leaned in and raised her hand, "Sergeant? Yeah so, what is it?"

"Well, that's just it. We don't know. It isn't anything we've seen before. Current scans and so on don't give us any indication of its origin."

"Is it Hydroxii?" Kayleigh asked bluntly.

"No, the data recorded during the war have nothing linked back to this stuff. Whatever it is, is potentially homemade and volatile."

"But for what purpose?" Amy asked, "From your little movie, it was suggested the substance is more like a coolant."

"True, but the data recovered from the armour at Kyreel doesn't tell us that. In fact, I don't think it's coolant at all. But, as I said, I can't understand what it is right now which is why we need to work together to find out and why somebody is testing it on human subjects. Now Officer Crow, I am currently running through all the data you collected, and I agree with you. You're on the right track, so for heaven's sake girl, let us help you, there's still a bit to sift through yet. . ."

Kato pushed a button on the table and brought up a map, replacing the firefight video in the process, "So with that being said, Officers Crow and Green will team up with Hunter. The remainder of Viper One will split up into pairs and search the city at the co-ordinates Harley will give you. She believes they are likely locations given the data we recovered from the ACPD. Our missing officer could be in one of them, and they could be being used to house the substance in secret, out of the way." Kato voice echoed in the quietness of the room, "Now you two take these, these intercoms will keep you in the loop with Hunter and Harley."

The officers took the intercoms from Kato's open palm and pushed them into their ears, "Surprise, it's me, Harley, welcome to the team girls!" Harley boomed in their ears, making the women wince a little, "Oh, sorry. I'll slow down a bit. Anyway, down to business. I'll give each team their co-ordinates so watch on your HUDs for a location. Hunter and the ACPD will be Alpha, Spider and Venom will be Bravo, and Draco and Dragon will become Charlie team"

Jack stepped back and took the lead from Kato, "Alright, let's do this quietly and without trouble. We're all under Navy jurisdiction today so any problems, you know who to call out. Let's go bring back this guy in one piece." The team acknowledged Jack's orders and began to move out.

Jack watched as the rest of his team left and the ACPD officers turned and faced him.

"So, I guess you're the lead for us?" Kayleigh asked with a sigh.

"Yes. Now I don't know or care for whatever feud is brewing up here. I'm not the bad guy here. I'm here to support you so, please, help me to help you."

"Ditto that. I know things have been tough for you, Kayleigh, but we really are on your side," Harley stepped up to the pair and smiled, "I want to help you. And I can if you let me."

Kayleigh shrugged and ushered Amy out of the briefing room.

Jack shook his head and turned to Harley, "It's going to be a long day."

"Jack, you have to understand her position here. She's been through a lot. Cut her some slack."

"Well, wasn't expecting that but okay. Come on, we have a job to do."

Jack held out his hand and Harley hopped from the table. He was starting to enjoy her company, having a difference in attitudes kept them realistic, and this brief partnership required a more friendly touch.

In the station entrance, Jack watched as the two teams headed out in their respective GIC vehicles.

"Presume you're driving, hot shot," Kayleigh called as she swung the passenger door open.

"Yes, Harley can point me in the right direction, easier that way," Jack replied.

"So, how do you get an AI in your helmet? Is it not really strange?" Amy asked as she sat in the rear passenger side,

"Yes, now let's concentrate on the task ahead, okay?"

Amy grunted and swung the door closed. Jack shook his head and clambered inside, pushing the engine start up button, firing up the large vehicle, which took much of its design from its military equivalent which could traverse hostile combat zones. This one just had a lot more panels and windows.

As the teams headed into the city, Harley worked behind the scenes to sending each one to the desired co-ordinates. Her unique link to Jack's helmet allowed her to act like a navigational system and point him in the direction he needed to go, almost without words. But Harley wasn't good with staying quiet for long, "Alright Hunter, the first location isn't far. We should slow down a little. I'm going to tap into the building's maintenance and see if I can get a read on it."

Kayleigh shuffled in her seat, "Where exactly are we going?"

"Unluckily for you, another warehouse. It's not far from where you were ambushed. It's the last time an ACPD badge was last pinged. I presume you already knew that."

"Yeah, kinda like a safety-" Kayleigh mumbled in reply, "Hold on, if this is where he was last pinged, why are we split into three teams?"

"The guys we are chasing aren't morons. They're smart. I've got a lot of data to work with here and we're looking at an extremely organised organisation. They know how to hide the needle in the haystack. These locations are likely spots, not guaranteed. These three locations are the most likely for the geography of the area"

"How come we can't do this kind of thing on the job?" Amy leaned forward from the passenger seat, "Why do we need Naval support?"

"You don't have a super powerful AI and multi-sensory satellites," Harley replied was sarcasm in her voice.

"Fair enough then."

"Right, we're here. I'll park up in this alley and we can move on foot. Harley can ping the GIC network from above to give us an idea of what to expect, if anything at all," Jack ordered as he slowed the vehicle and opened the door, "Ready? Let's go."

Kayleigh and Amy nodded and exited the vehicle They slowly closed their doors and steadily followed the Augmented soldier across the quiet alleyway. Reaching the end of the alley, Jack peered around and checked over his shoulder. The officers were in place, keeping up at least. Pointing ahead, Jack led the trio out across the open parking spaces. Using an abandoned car as cover, he poked his assault rifle over the top of the bonnet and scanned the area, "Harley, anything?"

Jack's helmet buzzed a little before a green light flickered on and off in his helmet, "Nope. Clear."

"Okay you two, up front, let's move," Jack pointed ahead again and stepped out from the cover, his rifle aimed ahead. The two officers released their holsters and placed the pistols in their hands before following the soldier. He was adorned in an unusual armour and Amy found herself trying to figure out what it was.

Reaching the warehouse wall, the trio pinned their backs against it, Jack in the lead. Kayleigh's first reaction was to move ahead but, in this situation, she realised that in order to survive this mission and see it to its final outcome, she needed to give way to the super soldier. So, she would do what she needed to do, after all, she needed answers not just about her partner, but also about whatever the hell was going on in the super-secret war that seemed to be unravelling around her.

Jack looked ahead and aimed the rifle forwards. Holding up three fingers, and without looking back, he began to count down – three, two, one. On the clenched fist, Jack turned the handle and pushed himself against the door, taking aim and scanning the area. The three of them entered the warehouse and Jack stepped forwards glancing quickly from side to side. The ACPD officers crouched on their way in, hoping not to get caught out.

The warehouse itself was relatively large yet was only partially filled. It was covered in a mess of containers and crates of varying sizes, wrappers and packaging scattered across the floor, mostly damp. There was no sign of life at all, not even a mouse.

Jack stepped slowly, lowering his rifle in disappointment, "Nothing. Great. Crow, Green find anything?" he buzzed into the radio.

"Nothing from us two," replied Amy sharing in the disappointment, "Just a huge mess."

"Damn it! Harley what are we missing here?" Jack asked angrily, swinging his rifle by his side.

"Hey, hold on, we're not missing anything. The ACPD ping came past this point and stopped. It's an assumption. Something AI don't do but humans do. You wanted a start, and I gave you it. Jeez. . ."

Jack grunted before turning and stepping slowly toward the two officers, holding his hand to his helmet, "Bravo, Charlie, check in. Any luck? We came up empty."

"Nothing here, Sir, just a big, empty load of nothing," Spider crackled over the radio.

"Charlie, anything?"

"Nope, just disappointment and sadness much like this guy's heart," Draco chuckled.

"Hey! Beat it man-" Dragon scoffed over the radio.

Jack stopped By the two officers, "Right Harley, next plan."

"There are more blips, I'll relay them to Bravo and Charlie, but I have an idea for us."

"We're listening?"

"Well, having looked over more of the data, I figured out that Hays was working for a criminal gang, obvious info I know, but his links are intriguing. A long story short, I found his boss, or close to it, which I think could prove a good lead for us."

"Great where is he?" Kayleigh shouted in excitement, her voice echoing across the walls.

"Judging by the area and time of day, a night club."

Jack looked up to the broken window noticing the shift in brightness, "Okay, I have an idea then."

Chapter 15

Jack sat tapping his thumbs on the steering wheel, he flinched at the car doors opening. Stepping inside were the two officers, only this time all dressed up.

"Well, never did I think I would be going undercover less than twenty-four hours on the job," Amy smiled as she glanced in the wing mirror, "Seriously a bottomless cash pit, you intelligence boys have it easy, clearly!"

Jack didn't realise he had been staring at Kayleigh who had slipped into the passenger side. Her hair was loose, dangling just slightly over the shoulder of her red, velvet dress.

"Err Hunter? You okay?" Kayleigh asked waving a hand in front of the soldier's tinted visor, "You shut down or something? Need a reboot?"

"Erm no - anyway, you two look suitably dressed so let's go," Jack cleared his throat as he hit the accelerator, "Now I'll drop you two off just shy of the target. The night club is called 'The Palace'. You need to get in and find a guy named Keane, he's our man. From his biog, he's a bit of a big shot here on this scene - and he's dangerous."

"Okay, well," Kayleigh turned to Jack giving him an up and down glance, "I hope you're not coming in dressed like that?

Not exactly Hallowe'en yet, I'm afraid."

"No, I'll be climbing in through the upper fire exit and will provide an overwatch. Harley will scan the area with her remote access in order to get a good view of the building. I'll do my job once you two ID Keane and get him in the open."

Kayleigh laughed as she tilted the rearview mirror toward her slightly, pushing her hair out a little, "Good because that look is not good. Amy you ready?"

"Ready, just hoping I don't get a pat down. This pistol is a little-"

"Moving on," Harley butted in, "You both look beautiful, even if Hunter here won't admit it, his heart rate tells me-"

"Harley. The mission. Please," Jack peered into the mirror and Harley laughed, "Anyway. I'll be in the building to keep you ladies safe. You two get Keane. I've got you on the VIP list, so less to worry about. Kayleigh you're called Valerie Powell and Amy, you're the millionaire's assistant, Katie. Just go with it."

Amy folded her arms in disgust, blowing her now flat, blonde fringe away from her hair, "Assistant? Come on, I'm worth more-"

"It's cover. Now suck it up and get ready, you're up," Jack interrupted as he slowed the vehicle to let them out, "Remember I'll be on over watch, so if you need me, you call out."

"Roger, Captain," Kayleigh laughed, climbing out of the military vehicle, and slamming the door closed.

Jack glanced down before reversing the GIC vehicle into the alley, "I can't believe I'm doing this."

"What, the mission or worrying about your heart rate?" Harley giggled, "You can't hide-"

"I heard that," Kayleigh butted in over the radio.

"Can we stay on mission, please?" Jack cut back in as he exited the vehicle.

Jack walked slowly up the old fire escape and allowed Harley to use the suit's built in echo location to pinpoint where everyone in the vicinity was at that time. With his rifle tucked low into his shoulder, he moved forwards before finding an entry point highlighted by the AI. The door was slightly ajar to let out the smoke from the room it led to.

"One contact, centre of the room," Harley whispered in the radio.

Jack quietly stepped inside, placing his rifle to the caught-out guard's head, "Clear." He continued to step forward until the music from the night club suddenly became very loud, the door ahead opening to reveal a blaze of strobe lighting as two men stepped inside. Jack stepped forward, putting the rifle on his back, he threw an uppercut to the nearest man who reeled backwards, leaving the second man unsure of what to do before he soon found himself headfirst against the door frame.

"What the hell was that?" called out Kayleigh as she flinched, holding her ear. She glanced to her left and took notice of a few party attendees pointing and muttering about her, "Sounded like you fell down some stairs, Hunter."

"It's sorted, keep going," Jack whispered as he dragged the two men to the corner of the room. Stepping to the door, he had an almost perfect view of the whole night club and the hundreds of other partygoers who were also on show.

"Harley, I'm going to need some help."

"On it, bringing up face rec now."

Jack's HUD inside his helmet flickered to a new screen,

picking out faces in the crowd, it brought up data on everyone – names, addresses, lifestyles, everything on record. The GIC had an extensive database on the people it protected and on its worst enemies, nobody was missed in the intelligence division, it was deemed acceptable in the fight against the rising militia terrorist attacks and to prevent future fights.

Glancing from dancer to dancer, awkward shuffler to confident drunk, Jack scanned each of them, "Where are you two at?"

Kayleigh squeezed between two dancers as she dragged Amy behind her, "Main floor, forward entrance, so far nothing obvious, guys," she replied as she smoothly, half-grooved her way.

Amy tried to join in with the dancing as she followed, "Wow, I haven't done this since I was in college. . . still can't dance," she stepped forwards trying to keep pace with Kayleigh.

"Remember why you're here, Green. Just keep your eyes open," Jack replied.

"Hmm, good call big brother."

Half an hour passed, and the officers still hadn't got any closer to their target. Amy tugged on Kayleigh's long dress and pointed to the bar, making a drinking motion with her hand. Nodding in approval, the pair stepped aside and sat down by the bar. Sitting on the slightly off-centre chairs, Amy ordered a drink as Kayleigh took a look around. The club was alive with energy, it was a bit overwhelming. The barman placed two cocktails on the counter and strode away. The women picked up their drinks and clinked their glasses, downing them in one go. Kayleigh began to loosen up, maybe more than her overbearing overwatch would have liked, but at this moment in time, she didn't care.

"You know what, coming here was a great idea," Kayleigh put her hand on Amy's and smiled, "We absolutely should do this again!"

"Oh yes!" Amy waved to the bartender once more and held up two fingers, "I need another after the hell we've been endured so far, I call it pain relief!"

"Cheers!" The women toasted once again and finished another round swiftly.

Jack emerged from his vantage point and glanced at the women, "You two having fun?"

"Yes, there is nothing happening, and I am washing down my emotions. The party is boring but the drinking–" Kayleigh paused as a tall man, dressed in a sharp black suit, sat down beside her.

"Excuse me, Miss," he said calmly over the music, "My employer has taken an interest in you." He pointed over to a small VIP section, just underneath Jack's vantage point, "He was wondering if he could enjoy your company and buy you a drink?"

Kayleigh blushed.

"Does her beautiful assistant get a meeting too?" Amy shouted over the music.

"Of course, I'm sure he wouldn't mind meeting the two of you," he smiled making Amy cringe a little. He ushered the pair towards the VIP section.

"Think we're about to meet our man," she whispered into her earpiece, glancing briefly up at Jack. She couldn't quite make out the unusual helmet design but knew he was situated nearby, "We're directly below you."

Jack let out a sigh of relief. They almost had their man, "Brush your earpiece to confirm it's him, we'll do our bit from then on."

The area was far quieter than the club itself. As they wandered through the heavily guarded VIP entrance, the women strode confidently down the corridor. Kayleigh clenched her fist, finally a genuine lead was about to present itself and, with her riled up on the last two cocktails, she felt ready to get some answers. Amy however was feeling the opposite. As they wandered into the new, quieter area she felt isolated, more aware of her darker surroundings. The people she was rubbing shoulders with were usually the ones she and Kayleigh arrested regularly. The few people on the VIP floor, were in pairs, dressed in high value clothes and wearing high value jewellery.

The man pushed open a door and swung around to hold it for the pair of them. As he led them in, the little info they had been given about Keane, appeared to be correct. On a standout seat, dressed more like a throne, he sat dressed in a dark suit, his hair slicked back imitating long-forgotten crime bosses.

"Ladies, welcome!" he ushered the two ladies sitting on his knee away, calling over Kayleigh and Amy, "Please, I would like to make your acquaintance." He bowed slightly from his chair glancing up at the officers with a sinister leer.

"And whose company do we have the pleasure of?" Kayleigh asked smiling as she held her dress a little.

"Ah, my manners. You can call me Keane! I run business around here."

At the mention of his name, Kayleigh drew her finger across her fringe and tucked her hair neatly behind her ear, trailing her palm across her almost invisible earpiece.

"Copy. Standby," Jack acknowledged and adjusted his position.

"So, who are these lovely ladies before me, please do tell me?" Keane quizzed.

"I'm Valerie Powell," Kayleigh curtsied a little as she smiled.

Keane leaned across forward, pointing to Amy, "Your friend?"

Amy leaned forward and waved, "Ermm. . . Katie." She suddenly felt incredibly uncomfortable. All eyes in the room were now firmly fixed on them. She avoided making eye contact with Keane who was looking for her direct attention.

"Just. . . Katie?" Keane asked puzzled.

"Assistants, no need to know any more than that," Kayleigh jumped in to deflect any doubt about their identities. She stood forwards to take centre stage and to keep Keane's full attention.

"Crow, you need to keep him to the back of the room," Jack ordered.

"Ha! So, what's a girl to do in here, hmm?" Kayleigh asked, advancing slightly.

"First," Keane pointed toward the officers as two, bulky guard-types stepped forwards, "just a check. Don't want to be in dirty company, you understand."

Kayleigh twitched a little trying to think of a plan, she had hoped that the big bad wolf would have strode into the room by now.

"Crow, play the flirt. . . sure it'll help," Harley suggested helpfully.

Kayleigh sighed; she hadn't planned on this. Ruffling her dress, she stepped forward and brushed past the first guard, before leaning on the second, "So why don't you do it for them...", she smiled coquettishly, striding past the two guards who, despite their build, seemed to move out of her way. The guards followed Kayleigh as she moved towards Keane who was becoming very distracted by her now.

"Hmm, if you insist. . ." Keane called, jumping from his desk, and ushering the pair to move aside.

Jack sprinted to the back of the room and climbed out of the window, jumping the fire exit banister in a single swift movement. Harley brought up a highly detailed visual on his visor's HUD and friend of foe colours appeared around the five in the room. Jack stepped back and lifted his armoured boot, kicking the door open. With the door splintering on impact, he entered the room to everyone's surprise. Stepping forward as the first guard moved towards him, Jack dodged quickly to avoid a punch before landing his own, dropping the first guard to the floor. The second unholstered his firearm and aimed as Jack made a grab for it, managing to land a punch to the guard's nose and relieving him of his weapon. Throwing it over his shoulder, Jack stepped up to the final guard and landed a punch to his head, knocking him out cold.

Keane shook as the soldier effortlessly took control the room, "Holy shit man, who's that?"

"My big brother," Kayleigh replied as Jack stepped up to Keane, hitting the crime boss in the face, knocking him to the ground instantly.

Chapter 16

Keane's head rang with an ear-splitting screech as he slowly came to once again. Attempting to rub it, to alleviate the noise and headache, he found himself bound to his 'throne', at the mercy of the soldier and the women he was attempting to get to know.

"What? Come on, let me go!" he shrieked in panic, "Who the hell are you?"

Kayleigh stepped forward out of the shadows, the nearby lamp illuminating Keane, "You're in your throne room, Keane."

"Jesus, you two are crazy. When I get out of here I'm going to put a god damn bullet in your heads!"

Kayleigh smiled and flicked her fringe away from the face, "I highly doubt that. Now, where shall I start? Oh yeah, your man Hays. He's been supplying a very unusual drug around Atlanta, where did you get it?"

Keane laughed a little, "I'm not telling you anything!"

"So be it," Kayleigh turned on her heels and waved her hand to summon the next level of the interrogation.

Keane wriggled in his chair staring at Kayleigh as she stepped away, unaware that Jack had been standing behind.

As he stepped into the light, his jet-black armour barely illuminated by the lamp, he placed his hand on the back of Keane's and slammed it down hard onto the desk in front of him. Jack held Keane's head in place, allowing him to breathe to the side, the blood from his nose dripping down his cheek.

Jack slowly leaned down to Keane's ear, "I think it's my turn," he growled as he steadily applied more pressure to Keane's skull.

"Fuck! What are you man?" Keane's bold, confident demeanour was waning as he squealed under Jack's heavy hand.

"Your nightmare. Now answer the nice lady's question." Jack lifted his hand and sidled back. Keane breathed in hard and shook his head, panic-stricken as he locked eyes with Kayleigh.

"So, shall we start again? The drug. Where did you get it?" she asked calmly.

"Ah! Some guy, I don't know names he just offered me a hell of a lot of money to supply it. I didn't care!" Keane shouted with fear in his voice.

"I need more than a guy. Who was it?"

"Ha! I'm not telling you more than that, those guys are freaking scary, man."

"And the armoured soldier in the corner here doesn't give you that vibe?"

"They'll kill me if I say anything; I'm not scared of you or your friend!"

Kayleigh lunged forward and slammed her high-heeled boot into Keane's foot, leaving him screaming in pain. She reached down to her thigh, grabbed her pistol from its holster and pulled the drawback, slamming it onto the table, "How about we try this again? Answer the god damn question."

"You're all shout and no action aren't you?"

She slammed her fist into the table before placing the pistol firmly against Keane's forehead. Keane squirmed in his throne as he felt everything quickly slip out of control.

"No action?" she leaned the pistol harder into Keane's forehead, running her finger along the trigger, considering whether just to pull it and be done with it.

Jack stood as Harley buzzed into his ear, "Jack she's going to kill this guy if we don't do something. She is heavily intoxicated."

"I can see that but I think Keane needs this."

"But we need the intel Jack, don't let her pent-up anger jeopardise the mission."

Jack twitched as Kayleigh pointed the pistol to her right and fired a single shot.

"Jack. . ."

Jack stepped towards Kayleigh as she slammed the pistol back onto the table, "How about that? Talk!"

"Holy-fine, fine, fine. I got them from some army type dressed in a suit! He had some weird guards, lots of firepower, talked about taking the city! We took a cop too; I worked the op for him! Gave him the muscle!" Keane squirmed, retracting his hand.

"Better, so let's get to the target. Was his name Greg Brack?" Kayleigh snapped.

"I don't know, I don't ask questions!"

Kayleigh leapt forward and grabbed Keane's head, slamming it into the table once again. Jack pulled her back. He pointed back to Amy, who hadn't moved an inch through the ordeal.

"Okay Keane, let's do things my way. Answer the question.

Was the officer's name Greg Brack of the ACPD?" Jack asked calmly as he took centre stage.

"I didn't ask the name; they didn't tell us that just where to go!"

"And where was that?"

"I can't remember!"

Jack pushed Keane's head down onto the table, "Remember, Keane, that smug smile will be wiped from you face by the time we're done here."

"He was intelligence!"

The two women looked at each other with wide eyes as they both stepped back towards Keane.

"What do you mean, he was intelligence?"

"He had a pair of guards like you. . . had GIC on their arms."

Jack turned back to the ACPD officers as they all had the same thought, "Like me?"

"Yes! Now what the hell else do you want from me?"

"I want some intel. The ACPD officer, where did they take him?"

"Fuck you!" Keane shouted, spitting at the soldier.

Jack grabbed Keane's head and slammed it into the table, "Where is he?"

"Ex-Navy site! East of here!" Keane cried out as Jack let go and backed away to face the two officers.

"Harley, have you got a location?" he asked calmly,

"Yep, old naval yard, target located and. . . set. We need to go now!" Harley.

"Alright you two, let's go. Bravo, Charlie, we have a solid lead. ETA to the following co-ordinates?"

"Ten minutes, Sir, we're out of the way," Venom replied panting a little as the sound of crunching dirt echoed through the communications channel, "Finally we can stop looting the place!"

"Same Hunter, lot of traffic to contend with too," Dragon responded with a loud buzz.

"Not close enough, all teams meet at the Navy site. We're on our way, we don't have time to wait!" Jack ushered the officers out of the door, "Come on, we have to move now!"

The trio pulled on the doors and threw themselves inside as Jack fired up the vehicle, hitting the accelerator hard, throwing up dirt as they sped off. As they reached the main road, the traffic was heavy, probably the nighttime party animals. Frustrated, Jack slammed on the brakes. Amy crept forward and pushed the switch activating the blaring the sirens and blue lights of the police.

"That might help, Hunter!" she threw herself back as Jack made another quick turn.

Several minutes later Jack brought the vehicle to the old perimeter fence and brought the car to a halt. The trio clambered out and all unholstered their weapons.

"Bravo, Charlie, ETA?"

"Five minutes, Sir. Picked up the stragglers on route," Draco replied.

"Not close enough" Jack flicked back to the officers, "You two on me, we're going in. Ready?" The pair nodded, "Alright follow me."

Jack brought the rifle to his chest and jogged across the long, damp grass, the cover of the slowly approaching storm proving helpful, allowing him to get close without too much hassle. Pulling his wet, already heavy, boots out of the mud, Jack pushed up against the base wall; the two officers joined him, far from happy.

"I did not intend to get wet tonight, Hunter! Seriously, how can I be expected to do this is in god damned high heels?" Kayleigh whispered over the light rain.

"We can't wait! Okay, we move on three. I'll shout Navy and if they turn round with assault rifles in hands, you're cleared to shoot, got it?" The officers nodded and Jack turned around. He held out three fingers and counted down. Three. Two. One. On the clenched fist, Jack pushed open the door and the trio threw themselves inside the old base. The open hangar bay was covered in an assortment of containers and weapons' lockers, providing enough cover on their entry.

"Navy! Everyone weapons down, hands in the air!" Jack commanded. His order was met with the raising of firearms, "Or not then!".

Jack fired, his assault rifle lightly tipping as it let out the first shot, followed by the officers behind taking down a small handful of the armed guards on site. Slowly finding cover, the remaining guards fired back in a wild barrage of bullets but they couldn't hide from the precision of Jack's aim.

"Clear!" he shouted as he wiped them out.

On his signal the trio ran forwards, weapons raised, into the guarded area and came across a collection of weapons' lockers of various sizes. Amy began opening them. Inside the first lay an assortment of infantry weaponry - assault rifles, light machine guns, precision rifles - enough for a small army, enough to cause a lot of devastation in a populated city.

Closing the lockers, Kayleigh moved to a large table in the middle of the room and pushed aside a pile of documents to reveal a computer screen, "Hunter, you might want to have a look?" she stepped aside to allow him to stand beside her.

"Jack, pull me, plug me in and I'll see what these guys have on this drive," Harley shouted excitedly as she projected her image and began pushing and pulling data visually. Kayleigh stared patiently as the AI worked her way through the data drive. Finally, she found something.

"Okay, I've got a location."

"Point the way, we don't have time," Jack pulled the chip from the computer and Harley dematerialised again.

"Copy. Head east and there's a corridor, follow it to the end."

Kayleigh acknowledged the information and ushered Amy to follow her. Jack stood in front of the computer, glancing down at the fallen guard. He paid particular attention to the badge on the shoulder. It was unfamiliar to him as belonging to any locals or militia groups.

"Harley, recognise this badge?"

"Not really, you think it's the militia we took on at the fort? Seems a lot of guns on show for a crime lord," Harley buzzed, "I've called Kato and alerted him to the find."

"Whatever is going on, we can do more digging later, let's get this officer home."

The three of them entered the room, weapons raised and spread out. The room wasn't big, enough for a handful of personnel and the solitary cryo pod which stood in the centre of the room. Jack pushed on the release panel and the pod hissed, releasing a layer of fog around their feet. Unsure of what to expect, Jack sighed as the pod revealed nothing and looked to Kayleigh who slumped to the floor.

"Where the hell is he?" she shouted, "I don't understand. . . why did they take him? What's going on?"

"Harley?"

"I-I don't know. The last log-" Harley stuttered as Kayleigh threw down the weapon.

Jack peered into the tube to find an ACPD badge and a small patch of blue liquid, "His badge is here, but no body."

"Damn it," she responded disheartened, "I have nothing else to ping off, Jack, we've hit a dead end. I feel bad for her."

Jack got down on one knee and put his hand on Kayleigh's shoulder to try to reassure her, "We'll find him soon, you have a good partner in Amy, and we can help-"

Kayleigh turned and glared directly into Jack's mirrored visor, "And what good that has done so far."

Jack leaned back feeling a little hurt, but it was the truth. They had been completely unaware of the situation in Atlanta. Something big was moving through the city and those who should know, had no idea what was going on. Jack rose to his feet and Harley buzzed in his ear.

"Jack?"

"Harley?"

"I've been doing a little more digging through that data and well, intriguingly, I've found a co-ordinate."

"In the city?" Jack asked stepping to the doorway to give Kayleigh a little privacy.

"No, it's a space co-ordinate, just on the edge of the milky way. I've linked in Kato; we can discuss it back at the base."

"Copy that," Jack turned and wandered back into the room, "Come on you two, time to finish up."

He held out a hand to Kayleigh. Looking up at the soldier, she took it and clambered to her feet. She slowly stepped toward Amy and held out her own hand, "Think I need to thank you."

"Excuse me?" Amy replied a little confused.

"For today. We've been partners for less than a few hours and you've been my most trusted ally. Takes a lot to do that."

Amy gave a wide smile and took her hand, "No problem Kay, I've got your back." She turned to Jack, "Alright big guy, show us out."

Jack smiled behind his visor, despite all the heartache, something good had come out of the whole thing and he knew just how much a strong partnership meant to any team. Before leaving, Kayleigh leaned in to the cryo pod and took the ACPD badge, there may not be anybody to rescue but it was something to give back in any case, MIA or otherwise.

Back at the Atlanta Police Station, the two units stood in the briefing room, the officers and their Captain on the left, Kato and his super soldiers on the right, Jack taking the lead as Dragon laid half across the briefing table with Draco at his side.

"Well, it's been eventful working with cops!" he shouted, waving a bit.

"We haven't had the pleasure of working with Navy intelligence before. We've had a lot of trouble in recent months from our city division, so I think I speak for the precinct and these two especially, when I say thank you and I hope we can both work together again soon."

Jack stepped forward and offered his hand, "I agree, you have two great officers on your books, Sir."

The Captain took the hand and shook it as hard as he could, "Sadly, I presume this means our favour has now been served, Brandon?"

The General laughed and placed his hands on his hips, "I think we can call it a long-term favour for now. We'll be in touch, nice to see you again." Turning to the door, the General waved the Viper team on, waving back as they left.

Jack stood firm, "Officer Crow, walk me out?" he asked calmly.

Kayleigh, still in her messed-up undercover clothes, nodded and followed them out. Pushing open the door, the rain was considerably harder than before, and the bustle of midnight city-goers was a lot quieter this time around.

"I just wanted to give you my own thanks for today, it's been different, but for all the right reasons."

Kayleigh laughed and put her hand to her face, "And there I was thinking you were going to ask me on a date!"

Jack let out a small cough of laughter, "That's the alcohol talking, Crow."

"You soldier types aren't all black tape and boring are you?" she smiled.

"We try, part of the job though I'm afraid," he replied but the tone of his voice lowered a little, "On that subject, what did your Captain mean by trouble with the local agents?"

Her pleasant mood changed almost instantly as she lowered her hand, "This guy, Falaney, has been taking all our intel and reports, using his jurisdiction to take everything off us. I don't trust the guy. They even seized the Hydroxii we took in."

"Me and Harley can look into that. We need to discuss this agent with Kato and look at taking on this case or supporting you where we can."

"I could look into that mixture more thoroughly too if I could get my hands on the data records, and look at bringing in that Hydroxii to talk to," Harley butted in.

"Thank you, I just - Greg?" Kayleigh froze up on the spot.

Jack turned sharply to the sound of screaming and panic, his eyes firmly fixed on the man stumbling towards them, "Stop right there!" Jack shouted releasing the rifle from his back, "Don't move!"

At the sound of shouting, the rest of Viper squad stepped out of their vehicles and took up positions behind the open doors.

"Wait no, that's Greg, don't shoot!" Kayleigh screeched as she ran down the steps towards him.

Swaying towards Jack and the panic-stricken Kayleigh, the extremely fragile officer creaked down the street, his body battered and bruised, his ACPD vest seeped in blood which ran down his legs as he forced himself onwards.

"Ka-Kayle-" before he could call out to her, a single sniper shot tore through his body-vest, breaking the brittle body almost in half.

"Shots fired, shots fired!" Jack swivelled around, surveying the skyline, trying to find the shooter, "Viper on me-Kayleigh wait!" he called as she sprinted past him, not to her fallen friend, but to the metal fire exit in front of them.

Scanning upward, the silhouette of the unbelievable stood out once again - the completely immaculate silhouette of another soldier wearing the same armour as Jack and his team, "Augment shooter up top! Viper, lock down the area, Harley scan it, ping that copycat now!"

"On it. Everyone back, get back, Navy, get back!" Spider shouted ushering the gathering crowd back.

Orders given out; Jack sprinted off after Kayleigh who had already managed to get halfway up the stairs. Reaching the top, Kayleigh drew her side arm and pointed it at the shooter, "ACPD drop the sniper now, this your only warning!" she growled, standing firm in front of the heavily armoured soldier. The enemy augment snapped the sniper in half and clipped it to their back before turning to face the approaching officer.

"Do you really think you could kill me, officer? " the soldier mocked. The voice from inside the helmet surprised Kayleigh. The accent was Spanish, and, at a guess, she was no older than Kayleigh herself.

"Don't make me try, you little bitch," Kayleigh snapped as she steadily strode forward, "I will put you down without hesitation."

"You've already hesitated. . . " the soldier flicked her sidearm from her belt and, holding her pistol in one hand, fired at Kayleigh with perfect precision, the shots hitting an overhang which came crashing down blocking Kayleigh's eye line and pushing her back. Jack reacted to the shots, pushing himself over the gap, and fired his rifle at the enemy augment who stood triumphantly over the blocked officer. Pushing her sidearm back into its holster, the soldier spun backwards and darted for the buildings edge.

"Stop!" Jack called out as Kayleigh joined in and tried to give chase. The soldier turned allowing their shots to hit her chest, the bullets sparking on her personal energy shield. The fleeing soldier's visor cleared from its darkened tint to reveal a young, female Spaniard who smiled. Bringing up a canister from her utility belt, she clicked the trigger, fizzing away in a ball of yellow light.

Kayleigh stood and let her shoulders drop, loosening her grip on her pistol which slid slowly out of her hands and bounced onto the floor. Her entire mood turned from blind rage to disappointment.

Jack lowered his rifle, the rain splashing lightly across his visor, "Harley where'd she go?"

"I-I can't pinpoint her. She's disappeared."

Jack turned to Kayleigh, "Kayleigh..." he called out taking gentle steps forward, "Kayleigh, are you alright?"

She slowly turned her head, glancing over her shoulder, "Leave me alone. . ."

"Kayleigh, please, we can find-"

"No! You've done enough damage already," she snapped turning and walking away, "For the best and brightest, you guys don't know anything about what's really going on, do you?"

Jack glanced towards her but looked away, he felt disappointed too. The whole operation was generally a success, in terms of high value data they recovered, but he couldn't help feeling a little uneasy around Kayleigh as he was learning more and more about her struggles with the intelligence agent and her failure to protect the citizens she had sworn to protect. Jack's train of thought was interrupted by a small buzz in his ear.

"Jack, we need to keep an eye on her."

"That's not my job," he replied striding away from the rooftop toward the exit.

"Maybe so, but she's going to do something drastic if this situation isn't calmed down."

"Harley, we have a whole host of problems right now, the emotional well-being of one person isn't my priority, it's stopping whoever is threatening to cause a war."

"Alright, I was just being nice. Anyway, good news, I've managed to run through the list you found and along with those co-ordinates I've pinpointed some information that might be worth noting."

As he stepped down from the fire exit, Jack's HUD lit up, "Jack, it's Kato, sorry to bring you in so soon but those space co-ordinates, well they aren't just of any old location, it's the location of a cruiser's SOS."

"Is it an attack?"

"We don't know. There was a cruiser heading that way. Anyhow, move it, you and your squad are jumping on the nearest available ship, the Chicago, and investigating."

"Sir, what about the situation here?" Jack asked anxiously.

"One problem at a time. We need to get back into the fight, we're three steps behind already."

"Okay, on my way," Jack buzzed the radio and began to jog to the vehicle he had used all day. Pulling open the door he had partially stepped before he glanced at Kayleigh who had finally reached the station entrance. Watching as she stepped over to her fallen partner, he looked away, closing the door, and starting the car up. He hit the accelerator and headed off to the naval yard.

Chapter 17

Jack slammed on the brakes as he closed in quickly on the guard post of the naval yard. Its distance from the entry road was slightly less than he anticipated, probably no thanks to the twenty-four hours of flat-out fighting he had endured, even super soldiers got tired. At the push of a button on the dashboard of his vehicle, the window slowly wound down revealing the black helmet and the dark visor. The guard, dressed in a warm, large raincoat pushed the intercom.

"ID, Sir," the voice distorted slightly in the rain.

Jack pulled his Navy key card from his belt and plugged it into the data reader. The machine whirred in a strange fashion, the guard stumbling slightly as he pushed keys on his control pad. Leaning back in his seat, Jack turned to the protective fence, huge Lancer Antiair and Ground Tanks were lining the perimeter fence in a two-by-two formation. He watched, slightly in awe, as the newest Lancer to join the line slowly parked on the inner, right corner post and released its huge four-pronged missile launchers into an active stance. It was a little boy's robot overlord dream. The machine eventually flashed green, and he collected the key card, but he wasn't set just yet.

"Sorry Major, as a precaution I'm going to need you to look into the retinal scanner," the guard informed him calmly.

Sighing, Jack accepted the precaution and pressed two buttons on the neck of the helmet, squinting slightly as he lifted it from his head, the protective armour retracting up back into the helmet. Placing it down, Jack stared into the scanner, it gave a quick reflection of its user, his hair a complete shambles and his eyes not exactly combat ready. The machine pinged, and the guard saluted, the fence splitting allowing the soldier access. Starting the car up once more and slowly trundling down the entrance road, it wasn't the hordes of GMTF marines, or even the collection of armour on display that caught his eye, it was further beyond the infantry line.

Slowly driving out of the forward section of the base, the vast naval yard lit up in an array of blue lights, illuminating the way for all kinds of aircraft and, most noticeably, the various classes of ships that lay docked, refuelling and re-supplying, their vast shapes, and sizes an incredible sight for any ground officer. Although Jack had worked in space operations, seeing them on 'dry land' was impressive. Jack was still new to the battlefields, at the age of twenty-three he was relatively new but highly regarded. Five years of operational combat came fast, his skills deployed across space and ground work to stop the Hydroxii assault. Despite all of that madness, the incredible planets, and the 'becoming a man' process, his inner child still gave him that butterfly feeling as he turned the vehicle to face the carrier he was to board, the Chicago.

Bringing the car to a halt, Jack pushed open the door and stood; he looked up through the rain at the huge carrier. On its forward section, the immense cannons and the Global Military emblem painted across its front.

"Jack, nice of you to join us," turning with a little smile, Jack met a man, smaller than himself, his uniform of navy decoration, "I see you like her then?" It was the Captain of the ship, his Chicago badge across his cap.

"Just reliving some childhood dreams, Sir," Jack held his smile as he glanced back to the ship.

"Ah, I get that feeling all the time! Captain Horatio Clay, nice to meet you in person Major," he held out his hand which Jack grasped firmly.

"A pleasure, Sir, so what do we know?" Jack returned to the problem at hand.

"Let's talk on the way shall we?" Horatio held out his hand, gesturing to Jack.

Jack leaned back into the vehicle to pick up his helmet and tucked it under his arm. He stepped to the side of the Captain.

"A carrier, Watchtower, was leaving on route to drop supplies off, I won't bore you with little details, basically they left the Milky Way and, no more than fifteen minutes after leaving, an SOS signal was broadcast."

"Couldn't it have been an engine issue? Seems odd to send a cruiser and a black ops team to investigate something simple?"

"True. But what you-"

"Hey! We sir! We!" Harley squealed loudly from Jack's helmet intercom.

"Sorry, you and Harley, uncovered from that militia holding is the exact same location that SOS is sitting in now. So from that, we have to presume it was a deliberate attack, outside of our system, quick disable and raid job," The Captain glared a little.

"Sir, I imagine you're aware of the fight at Kyreel?" Jack asked, stepping aside to avoid being mowed down by a speeding forklift.

"I am and that's what frightens me. If the militia are getting this strong we have a massive problem, and I want it fixed before I, or anyone else, is hit next."

The pair stepped onto the docking bay; its extended arms dug into the bulk head of the cruiser. Horatio twirled his finger and the naval yard officer nodded, yelling commands. Streams of other officers nimbly moved from the scene as the pair joined the last remaining supplies being loaded into the belly of the ship.

Stepping inside the command centre of the Chicago, both the crew and Jack's team stood to attention.

"Captain on deck!" The crew saluted in unison.

"As you were," Horatio nodded, accepting the salute. The crew returned to their posts.

"Jack, you move like a rock, seriously we've been here for ages. Suppose I should ask what happened back there?" Spider enquired, stepping forward to greet his team leader.

"Bluntly, potentially our copycat from Kyreel took that shot and our relations with the police isn't peachy," Jack sighed thinking of the officer and the hell she was being put through.

"Again! Hell this isn't good, I thought we were the good guys?"

"Did you get a look at them?" Venom asked stepping towards Jack.

"Actually yes," Jack spoke a little louder, "The shooter was a woman, Spanish. She was toying with us, easily had a good shot at Kayleigh yet just blocked her off to make a show of things."

"Hmm, smug show girl, Spanish though," Draco sighed.

Horatio turned to his crew, "Alright, get us off the ground,

Ensign, we have a busy morning ahead. Once we're clear, I want us in, we have to get there quickly."

"Copy Captain, disengaging ground locks," the Ensign replied pushing a few keys and pulling forward a lever.

Horatio turned to Viper One and ushered them to the command table, clearing the map of Earth in the process, "Did I hear you say you had an encounter with a Spaniard?" he asked, his eyebrow raised.

"Yes, why?" Jack replied, placing his helmet on the edge of the table.

The Captain brought up a 3D model of a woman's face, "Recognise her?"

Jack's eyes widened a bit, "Yeah, that's her. Who is she exactly? And why is she dressed in AO armour?"

"Her name is Katarina Lorenzo. Born in Barcelona, Spain. Jumped from Spanish marine to Spanish secret service very quickly. She was good, incredible in fact. We worked together on a joint op even during the Hydroxii fight over Earth. She vanished for a little while after being offered a position as the first in the Augment Operation from day one. Till three years ago. . . ." The screen changed to a new model, a 3D environment, an augmented soldier in the centre of the screen, Hydroxii and Human forces surrounding them, "She eventually sprang back into the limelight when she stormed a heavily fortified facility under siege from both sides. Single-handedly took on both sides and robbed the facility of its tech. And it gets worse. From then on she soon turned her full attention fully to the GMTF. One by one, garrisons in the outer systems with high value information, technology and personnel were attacked, destroyed, killed and all without a trace of forced entry. High Command has dubbed her the Conquistador." Horatio pushed the middle key on the command table and a simulation played out. The soldier in the centre moved incredibly quickly, showing no remorse as she carved through what would be considered dangerous conditions, eliminating the Hydroxii. The human forces stepped in to the simulation, but to everyone's horror, were cut down in the same dominating matter, the soldier eventually clicking a canister and teleporting away.

"Wait, that energy ball, what is that, a personal teleporter?" Jack asked pointing at the simulation.

"We think it's homemade, something she put together herself. Problem is she can use it anywhere, even to jump through walls into buildings. No one has got close to finding out how, either."

Spider placed his rifle on the table and tapped it, "Then we need bigger guns if we see her again, that'll stop the little bit-"

"Or we could be tactical. Anyway don't we have a ship to rescue?" Harley interrupted from Jack's helmet once more.

Spider grunted and pushed off from his rifle, "She has a point, we will deal with that when the time comes, for now you guys and girls need to gear up. You'll be happy to know we picked up a few goodies for you in the armoury. We have a good few hours before we can get close so grab some shut eye ... I heard it's been a busy day."

The soldiers saluted and strolled out of the room talking amongst themselves. Jack stayed behind, he intended to make the most of the opportunity for a rest. Taking his helmet from the table, he wandered off down the corridor and entered the first dorm he came to, not particularly caring who it belonged to, after all, the crew were busy preparing for a rescue. Placing his helmet on the desk, he sat on the bed.

Harley stuttered into her digital body and sat down as if resting herself, "I'll shout loudly in five if you want, don't let the bed bugs bite, little one," she mocked.

Jack grunted, waving a hand in the air and slipped backwards on the bed, the heavy battle armour providing adequate comfort. Really, he didn't care. He just wanted to close his eyes.

Chapter 18

Jack jumped up from the bed, slamming his head on the low overhang, "Harley, seriously?"

"What? Don't you like animals?" she laughed over the barrage of animal sounds. Jack threw a paperweight at the helmet. "Okay grumpy, come on, you're ten minutes out!"

Jack slid across the small, firm mattress and clambered out, rubbing his eyes and shaking his head. Picking up the helmet, Jack wandered down the corridor pushing the helmet back onto his head, the armour wrapping itself around his body once more, "Any more info?" he asked pushing the button to the armoury.

"Apart from the-" before she could finish the armoury was lit up with flashing dark, red lighting "Okay, apparently I missed something?"

The loud speakers boomed across the entire ship, "All hands to battle stations, pilots move to standby, this is not a drill, all hands battle stations!" It was the Captain, his voice loud and commanding.

Jack stepped in to the armoury and began to pick up his weaponry, "Captain what's going on?" he asked pushing the communicator on his helmet.

"A problem. Grab your gear and meet your team in the command centre ASAP," he ordered.

"Copy, on it," Jack replied, accepting the severity of the situation. He pulled an assault rifle from the rack, placing it on his back. He then selected a shotgun, surely a valuable weapon in a close quarters fight, again placing it onto his back. As he stepped back, Jack's eyes were drawn to an unusually designed pistol. It's bright LED light ran along the frame; its muzzle was longer than usual. He opted to attach one of the new pistols to his belt. Armed, Jack sprinted out in the direction of the command centre.

Reaching it, he found the dumbstruck crew staring in disbelief. He quickly found out why. Stepping alongside Venom, Jack gazed out of the window with the same reaction. It wasn't what they expected at all. On an enlarged control screen, the vast darkness of space was filled with debris from two ships. An Hydroxii battle cruiser lay at a ninety-degree angle, its forward section barely connected to its hull. Large chunks of its underside were spread across space. Stuffed into the forward section of the Hydroxii ship, was the Watchtower, the vehicle they had been sent to save. It was buried inside, its once huge forward cannons, capable of obliterating ships at distance, sat snugly inside of the huge gap under the ship. It too had plenty of damage, huge panels of armour plating lay wrapped across the Hydroxii ship and in the surrounding space. Ground and air vehicles from both sides were floating away from their respective hangar bays.

"Christ, what happened here?" Draco asked in bewilderment, "Am I seeing this?"

Spider turned to his teammate, "You are, it must have been one hell of a duel. How did they ram its nose section inside?"

"Ensign, FOF tags?" Horatio asked, his eyes not leaving the screen.

"None, Sir, nothing. No heat signatures either," the Ensign mumbled a little timidly.

"Bastards. I'm really hoping this isn't what it looks like, but I want everyone holding in their firing positions and all pilots on standby incase the Hydroxii come back and squabble with us. I want to be the bigger ship here."

"Sir what's the plan?" Jack asked glancing at his team.

"This is now a search and rescue op. We're here to rescue any survivors, even though the prospect of finding anyone left alive are slim. I want you to take your squad aboard the Watchtower, scout the place out and check on the cargo, perhaps it wasn't just supplies they were carrying. When you're done, board that battle cruiser, find the black box, we can try to piece together some evidence of what happened and hopefully. . . hell, I don't know, just get out there. We'll pull alongside the Watchtower and dock from there. We'll steady the wreck as much as we can to make things easier, just watch out for holes in the ships."

"Understood, Viper on me," Jack ordered as he wandered out of the command centre, his team followed closely as they headed down the corridor towards the docking bay. Reaching the door, Jack turned and pushed the intercom, "Sir, we're ready."

Draco placed his hands on the shoulders of both Venom and Spider, "So have you guys heard the rumours about the ghost ship?" Draco leaned back, his hands outstretched, making an oohing sound.

Venom swung her arm backwards, slamming her fist into Draco's thigh, "Idiot!"

Spider laughed smugly as the ship shuddered, the huge

docking clamp locks cutting the mood short, the thud focusing the team back onto the job.

"Okay Viper, we're locked in, keep us in the loop," Horatio buzzed in to the team's intercoms, "Stay safe, the ship probably won't be airtight, keep it slow and steady please."

"Copy that, moving in," Jack replied, pulling his rifle from his back, the team drawing their own rifles in response. Pushing the door lock, the large metal doors swung open to reveal a long bridge leading towards the derelict ship.

The team stepped inside; their rifles aimed low. Jack noted the severity of the damage, whilst also being slightly in awe now he was so close to the Hydroxii battleship, the huge domed nose section looming menacingly outside of the bridge. Reaching the end, Jack pushed the door panel, the bridge hissed as the air was vented. After a few seconds, the panel flashed green and the doors swung open. As they took their first steps inside, the aftereffects of the battle could be seen by the entire team. Pieces of debris, of varying sizes, floated around and slammed against each other, infantry weaponry spun aimlessly in the mess. However, it was the dead crew man which left the biggest impression.

Jack held his arm out, ordering the team to follow him through. The team carefully trod through the chaos, stepping lightly, so as not to knock the dead who were floating by. The burning question on everyone's mind was what exactly a Hydroxii ship was doing at the same co-ordinates as a human ship. The whole situation was very strange. There seemed little to confirm they came looking for each other.

Continuing further into the ship, the team scanned their flashlights into the rooms they passed searching for some kind of answer, or survivors, yet there was nothing – just debris and the dead. The ship was eerie, the corridors creaking from the force of the impact, making the ship seem alive in a strange way. Any control panels the team came across remained inactive, no power pulsed through the ship, not even an ounce of emergency power. Jack wondered if perhaps the ships had been hit by something which had rendered them both 'dead in the water', that would explain the crew's inability to avoid the collision. Maybe the Hydroxii fell to the same problem. Jack's head spun with more and more questions; the fluttering of the radar pulse every so often bringing him back to reality.

"Viper checking in. No sign of life so far, a ton of debris and zero power, not even emergency power."

"Alright Viper, get to the hangar and find those supplies, maybe something was important in there. Also get to the Watchtower's command centre, get the black box. Chicago out," Horatio buzzed in before falling silent once again as Jack ushered his team in to the next corridor.

The corridor was a mess of cables, from the console hanging delicately on the wall, sparking across the floor. The five flashlights continued to illuminate the corridor as they stepped through, pulling open the exit door. The extent of the crash hit home again as they stepped inside. The entire right-hand side of the corridor had been completely ripped off, any poor soul in the vicinity would have had zero chance of fleeing in time. Jack kept his head firmly forward; he had seen terrible sights in battle but it never made it easier.

Spider glanced to his right, his flashlight flickering off something in the darkness of space.

"Hold!"

The team came to a halt, scanning the area slowly.

Spider stepped to the end of the corridor, his boot hanging slightly over the ship's wall, he held his flashlight out for a few seconds. Squinting slightly as he peered into the darkness, his eyes widened dramatically as he discerned an outline, "Contact!" Spider fired his assault rifle out into space.

Spinning round the team faced the enemy. The enemy fighter decloaked, its red armour glinted darkly as it fired its plasma cannons into the corridor at the team. Taking cover behind various tiny pieces of, still moving, debris the team returned fire; the shots from both sides making barely a small thud in the silence of space, the plasma, though, booming loudly against the inner hull.

"Spider, move!" Jack called out as he shot at the enemy fighter as it stared down his teammate.

Spider dodged behind a moving piece of hull plating, which took the brunt of the fire.

The pilot faced Jack, bombarding him with a barrage of plasma.

"Chicago, this is Viper. We need some help, enemy fighter on the East side, over!" Jack shouted into his intercom, firing another few shots but missing entirely.

"Copy, assistance on route," Horatio replied, the bustle of movement could be heard clearly in the background.

Jack swung round to find Venom who had taken cover behind a tiny door panel, luckily her slender body frame allowed for it to be adequate protection, "Venom, push that door panel out!"

"What!" she replied, glaring behind her visor, "Are you mad?"

"Trust me, push it out. We can use it to distract the fighter, they're weak at the back, the panel will force it to move!"

Venom withdrew her rifle, positioning her back against the door, she placed her hands on the corridor wall. Breathing in, she pushed against the panel. As it opened out, she grabbed hold of some loose piping and swung back into the safety of the corridor, watching as the panel flew towards the fighter. The pilot faced towards the oncoming debris, firing cannons at it, causing it to rotate and spin, cutting a thick scar into the cockpit section of the fighter.

"Even better! Viper shoot the scar!" Jack ordered aiming at the front of the fighter, blasting three short bursts into the gouge made by the panel.

Angered by the damage, the fighter began to lean inward, frustratingly shooting almost pointblank cannon fire into the corridor, the tiny shards of debris proving pathetic protection against its onslaught. As Jack began to panic a little, the Valkyrie dropship loomed into view. The Hydroxii pilot sensed the dropship nearby. The Valkyrie's two forward miniguns rotated wildly, destroying the fighter which spun wildly away before exploding in a blue ball of energy.

The team emerged. Jack stuck his hand in the air, "Nice job there pilot!"

"You're welcome Hunter. Captain wants us to cover the area in case more try the same thing," the Valkyrie pilot replied.

"No complaints here, keep us posted," Jack turned to his team once more, "Come on, we're close to the hangar now."

"Just need to drop down an elevator shaft. Anyone scared of heights?" Harley added jokingly.

The soldiers stepped out of the corridor and into a large room. Four shafts lay ahead, of which only one was missing an actual elevator.

Jack leaned into the dark abyss inside the shaft. Poking his rifle inside, the tiny flashlight only just bright enough to give him a view, "Hmm, not much distance. Alright, the lack of gravity will make it easier for us to get in, we'll just hop in and out."

Dragon peered down into the gap, "Sweet darkness. Let's hope there's a bottom. Don't fancy floating out to the void."

Draco patted him on the back, "Or a monster..."

"You two quit it. I'll lead, Spider and Venom you two move second once I give the all clear. Draco and Dragon, you two move in after they've hit the bottom," Jack turned as he gave the order, the team nodding in acknowledgement. "Alright, in we go," Jack pushed the rifle on to his back and leapt inside, pushing off from the back of the elevator shaft and springing from side to side, the darkness becoming increasingly encompassing. "Harley, do something, please."

"What's up Jack, scared of the dark?" she asked.

"More scared of dropping out of the ship, Harley"

"That's a good reason. Hold on," Harley buzzed as she flicked on the night vision built into his helmet as he descended further, reaching the floor far more quickly than he had expected. Turning to face the elevator, he pushed his fingers into the gap and began pulling the doors apart, the light a little blinding with the night vision on.

Picking up on his discomfort, Harley switched back to the normal visor HUD, "Alright team. Jack's safe. Time to jump."

Pulling the assault rifle from his back, Jack shone the light around the dark, abandoned hangar bay. Valkyrie dropships, bombers and an assortment of military vehicles hovered around, suspended in mid-air. Jack stepped from side to side through the assortment of crates hanging motionless. Slowly, two-by-two, the remainder of his team joined him in his search.

"Jack, north-west corner. I'm picking up a faint energy reading, stands out like a sore thumb."

Jack moved towards the energy source as did the other soldiers, a tiny blue light flashed on the top of the small crate.

"And there is your mystery," Harley announced, the disappointment clear in her voice.

Jack placed the rifle onto his back again and grabbed the crate, flicking the metal locks away and pushing the lid open. As it slowly fell back, the energy radiated out, heated up Jack's heavily armoured chest and slightly blinding him.

"Woah, what is that?" Spider asked.

Harley scanned the device, "Well, I don't know. It's not human. By the looks of it, it's a source of power. . . but not one I'm aware of."

"Could it be a prototype of some kind?" Jack asked grabbing the device.

"Not that I know of, but it's radiating an enormous energy signature."

Venom joined the conversation as she leant inwards, "Is it a beacon?"

"Doubt it, it's not the source of the SOS anyway, it was too weak."

"Hmm, Viper to the Chicago, do you read?" Jack buzzed into his intercom, rotating the device in his hand.

"We read you Viper," Horatio answered, clearly enjoying the thrill a little.

"We've found an energy source, not one we, or Harley, have come across before. Permission to bring it aboard at the end of our run?"

"Harley, is it safe onboard?" he asked quietly.

"Besides the strange light show, perfectly by my standards."

"Then keep hold of it, safely, carry on Viper."

"Will do, Sir," Jack pushed the device into his utility belt, the light emitting like a very large, personal beacon. "Okay Viper, back up. Next stop the command centre, we need the black box. Once we pick it up, we should head straight to the Hydroxii ship. We can grab their black box, save us a trip, and the data can be uploaded at the same time." The team nodded. Jack ushered them back up the elevator shaft to continue their search for a route to the command centre of the ship.

The black box could provide key information on anything from a power surge to an attack, everything the ship and its crew experienced would have been recorded. The team picked up the pace a little as they neared the command centre. The dark and gloomy mood would have been enough to give normal soldiers nightmares, even the hardened veterans would have had trouble on board the ship.

"You know. . . it's weird. Despite two potentially aggressive species coming together, there's no bullet or plasma scarring on any of them, or on the ship itself," Draco spoke in a hushed tone as he scanned a nearby corner, "Am I the only one wondering about that?"

"Probably not, but the crew of the Chicago probably don't want to imply anything without actual evidence," Harley replied, "And anyway, we don't want to be pointing our guns at the Hydroxii, especially if it wasn't them."

Draco quietened down once more as the team reached the command centre door. Jack tapped the door panel with his palm and grabbed the rifle, taking aim as the doors slowly edged open. Stepping inside the scene was similar to that of the rest of the ship, only this time the crewman were more recognisable.

"Jack, head to the Captain's chair. On the back, under the backrest is a panel, pull it off. The black box should be there." Jack stepped forward and reached down to the chair as Harley had instructed. The panel was weak, as quickly gave way.

"Alright, now push me into the port and wait a sec." Jack accepted the request once more, pulling the data chip, he plugged it into the port, "Excellent, lots of space. Right. Thumbs at the ready. . ." Two small circular thumb prints lit up on either side of a box outline, "Thumbs on the readers, please." Pushing his thumbs on the readers, the box outline flickered blue and dropped down to reveal a bulky box, ironically, it was black. "And we have a box! Courtesy of me, now get me out please?" Jack pulled the data chip from the panel and pushed it back into his data pad.

Grabbing the black box, Jack allowed it to magnetise to his utility belt, "Okay Chicago, this is Viper. We have the black box and are now on route to the Hydroxii ship."

"Copy that Viper, I'm sending your Overwatch to you. I don't suppose you guys fancy jumping across ships now do you?" Horatio laughed down the radio.

"Hey, sounds–" Spider punched Dragon before he could continue the joke.

"Copy, thanks for that, tell our eye-in-space to pick us up where the Hydroxii fighter was waiting," Jack requested.

"Copy that Viper, keep me updated. Chicago out."

Jack squeezed past his team, pushing the door panel and ushering them out back through the ship for another trek, back to the same spot where they were attacked. The tedious task of wandering through the desolate decks of the Watchtower was starting to bug the black ops team, who if they could have, would happily have let the EVA crew deal with this problem. Unluckily, they found themselves involved in a large conspiracy.

Several decks later, the team reached their exit, the Valkyrie hovering almost in mute flight over the side of the wrecked hull.

"Your taxi awaits you," the pilot called out in their radios. Hopping over the gap, one by one the team boarded. Firing up the thrusters, the dropship tilted around the debris field, the pilot leaving the door open, giving the soldiers an even grander view of the wreckage they were threading themselves through. "Okay, I'm going to drop you off on the top of the carrier. On our run around we clocked the outer hull was cracked so should be easy access 'specially with the zero G."

"Copy Overwatch, give us the green light when we're there."

"Will do, Major".

Leaning the rifle on its side, Jack flicked the firing rate to automatic, the idea of boarding an enemy ship unprepared, despite the war's end, would be stupid.

As the dropship came to a gradual stop, Jack glanced over his shoulder, the thumb of the pilot appeared in the tiny window slit, "Okay, one at a time. We'll enter through the same access point, the northern one. Once inside, check every corner. It might be a derelict ship but in current conditions, I'm not sure we can be as lax. I imagine, if there are any Hydroxii survivors, they're bound to be pissed off. Let's try being diplomatic. Call out before opening fire."

Spider faced Jack, "What if they shoot first?"

"Shoot back and don't miss," Jack replied bluntly.

Spider smiled behind his visor as he watched Jack hop out onto the hull. Steadily walking forwards, Jack reached the point they would use to gain access to the huge ship. Leaning over, he took a look at the distance between the gap and the floor within. Incredibly, a pile of debris was neatly arranged in such a way that the drop wouldn't be so severe, although zero gravity would solve the dangerous effects of falling. As his team appeared, Jack took a leap of faith and floated down into the ship, landing awkwardly on top of a heap of miscellaneous items.

Wobbling down, he stepped off the debris pile and flicked his rifle upward, aiming down its sights, scouring every corner with his weak flashlight. The ship was incredibly dark, the sunlight only just penetrating inside this section. Again, no power, even emergency power wasn't in effect. Coincidence? Jack asked himself.

"Wow a real Hydroxii battlecruiser! Now this is a treat," Harley shrieked excitedly.

"Jeez Harley, all that big talk and you've never seen a real cruiser? Where have you been, in a hole?" Spider mocked as he moved ahead of Jack flashing his light across the next set of corners.

"Well theoret…. – Hey. . ."

"Harley, back on the job please. Which way do we need to go?" Jack butted in, snapping his rifle around and continuing to examine the area.

"Hmph. Well, looking at these schematics, we need to head to the forward section, they use the same setup we have for black boxes."

"Alright, Viper on me. Harley light the way if you please."

Jack's HUD blipped to the sound of a way point mapping out, on his radar, the route to follow. Pointing forwards, Jack led the team to the first door. Prying it open, flashlights illuminated the corridor in a strange lightshow as they stepped in and followed its long winding route.

As the Viper One team pushed on through the ship, jumping whole sections, prying doors open and nudging past the dead, Harley soon picked something up on the radar.

"Oh. Hold up. . . "

Jack slowed to a stop, the team following suit, the group flailing their flashlights around, "Problem?"

"I'm picking up some movement ahead, not debris, definitely living."

"Alright, on me, tight formation."

Jack crouched slightly, pointing the rifle forward, stepping cautiously towards the red markers on his radar. One. Two. Three. Three red markers were now clearly illuminated on the team's radars. Jack slowed, almost tiptoeing, before lowering the rifle a little, "Naval intelligence, identify yourself!" he called out. A mysterious blue glow emitted from around a corner. Jack tried again, "Nava-"

His question was answered with bursts of blue plasma fire, lighting up the dark corridor considerably, "Everyone take cover!"

"Hmm, clearly they don't like us!" Harley added sarcastically.

Returning fire, the team pinned themselves against the walls to avoid the barrage being flung down the corridor.

Venom glanced at the floor, kicking a piece of rectangular debris, possibly an inner panel, with her boot, "Jack, I have an idea!" she shouted over the radio. Dragging the debris toward her, Venom then grabbed it and crouched, "Get behind me, we can use this as a shield to get close."

"Copy," Jack replied, patting Venom on the shoulder as she

began to step forward. Jack's assault rifle rested against the side of the panel, allowing him to fire without fear of being melted by the plasma barrage. The remainder of the squad continued to shoot as the pair moved forward, pushing the attackers back into their corners.

"Okay. . . close quarters in. . . One. Two. Three!" Venom shouted pushing the panel forward, catching the lead Hydroxii soldier off guard and knocking it back. Venom pulled her rifle from her back and fired pointblank at the alien's chest, the shots easily piercing the alien's protective armour.

Jack stood tall once again, firing a full clip into the nearest Hydroxii soldier. Too close to the next target, he dropped the rifle at the feet of his enemy and threw a fist at the alien, knocking it back. Jack landed a second punch, knocking it to the floor. Pulling his pistol from his belt, he fired two shots and the alien slumped to the ground in defeat.

"Clearly the Hydroxii blame us. Typical" Harley buzzed as Jack stepped over the dead body.

"Which is why we need that black box; we have to produce the evidence to prove otherwise. We have to keep moving," Jack waved, ordering the team forwards, their pace increasing.

Clearing more corridors, with zero resistance, the team soon reached the ship's hangar bay.

"Okay troopers, the hangar. We'll need to cross this; carefully does it please," Harley explained to the team.

Jack stepped through the partially broken door and began to poke around. Just like their own ship, its armour wasn't dealing with the lack of gravity well; Hydroxii armoured vehicles were hovering in the air, clattering the infantry carriers which bumped lightly into, and out of, position. He glanced at the Hydroxii dropship. Jack wondered if they had tried to get out, but for some reason were cut short. Pushing aside a weapons cache, Jack leant over another hole and hopped across it, his radar blipping for a short moment, "Woah, you guys see that?" he asked.

"I did," Harley replied, "Obviously."

"I did too, more Hydroxii? Their camo system affects radar slightly," Spider added as he raised his rifle.

Jack watched as the blip pinged once more, "We should confront them, we don't want them sneaking up on us further into the ship, this is their territory, they know all the tricks. Let's try this again, shall we? Maybe these guys won't be so trigger happy." The team nodded and followed Jack, their rifles aimed forward, clambering over small crates on their way to the exit door.

The doorway was open, the radar pinging again, four more times. Jack slowed up, holding his hand up and counting down, not wanting to risk a radio transmission so close to the enemy. Five, four, three, two, one. On the clench of his fist, the team launched forward and out of the doorway, fanning out as they pointed their rifles outwards.

"Navy, hold fire!" Jack called out, his eyes widening a little as their flashlights flickered across a team of five Hydroxii soldiers, who twisted in response.

Jack glanced at the lead soldier; his armour was that of one of a Hydroxii's special forces team. The Hydroxii soldiers held their rifles high, their blue LED lit helmets lighting up the corridor as much as their flashlights did. Both teams stood, rifles aimed; the Viper team flicking theirs from side to side, the Hydroxii a little more relaxed in the situation, the home turf advantage proving useful. Jack eyed the lead soldier again, the Hydroxii's helmet marked lightly across the scalp section in gold trim which flickered slightly in the light. Although the helmets hid their emotions, the mood was extremely tense, neither side wanting to be the first to shoot. The situation would become all the more explosive if somebody made a wrong move.

Jack dared to step out, one hand holding his rifle high, the other by his side as he walked towards, who he presumed to be, the leader of the unit. In response, the remaining Hydroxii special forces aimed directly at the approaching human, causing him to stop abruptly; his own team, though, took a tougher stance and stepped forward slightly. The lead soldier, quickly held his huge arm in the air, glancing aggressively to his right, then to his left. The silent command was obeyed as the unit gradually lowered the plasma rifles they were wielding. Relieved, the humans lowered their rifles in response. However, neither side lowered their weapons fully, both wanting to be prepared for a quick firefight.

The lead Hydroxii lowered his arm, holding its plasma rifle comfortably in one hand, and stepped forward, closer to Jack, "What is it you want, human?" he spoke in perfect English as his voice thundered through its helmet.

"Answers," Jack replied bluntly, his finger twitching lightly on his rifle's trigger.

"Then we have the same goal. You are not of the fallen vessel?" the special forces leader asked tilting his huge head slightly.

"No. We're answering its distress call. We arrived to the scene just now."

"Then maybe we can work together. After all, our races are united, are they not?"

"We are," Jack loosened his grip on the trigger.

The Hydroxii team leader stretched out his huge hand and leant forward, "I think you should begin by telling me how you escaped the foundry, Human Halliday."

Jack took the huge hand and the two gave each other a hug, like the one two brothers would give each other after a long time away. Both teams looked at each other, partly in confusion, partly in concern.

"Jack, you fancy telling me what's going on?" Spider asked, anger in his voice.

The Hydroxii leader stepped around Jack and up to Spider, who had to look up slightly at the towering alien, "I do not need a human to speak on my behalf, I will answer. I am the master of this ship. This. . shell, was my vessel."

"Then what happened?" Venom interrupted, "If you were at the helm, you should know?"

The Hydroxii leader turned to face the female human, "We were pursuing a tip off, as you humans call them, it led us to your vessel. Moments after our paths crossed, a cloaked vessel entered the situation, firing some kind of weapon, rendering both vessels dead in the water. . . did I use that term correctly?" the alien asked turning to Jack.

"You did," Jack smiled under his helmet, memories of previous missions flooding back.

"Excellent. Before we could respond to the attack, our vessels were hit heavily and colliding, as if we were drawn together by a powerful magnet."

"What did the enemy ship look like?" Jack asked turning to the Hydroxii.

"It was of human design."

"Any distinct markings? Ship names?" Harley buzzed through.

"None, completely black. You serve with a construct?" the alien asked turning to Jack.

"I do, not by choice, but she gets the job done. She's good for me."

"I am indeed! No need to be rude," Harley jumped in with a grumpy tone of voice.

"Apologies construct. How did you arrive here?" the Hydroxii glanced behind Jack as if trying to find the source of the sound, "Are you, too, a ship master?"

Draco stumbled in and laughed loudly, "Oh, he's no ship master!"

The alien turned sharply to Draco, who stepped back a little in fear.

Jack stepped between the pair, "No, we came via the Chicago, a human naval cruiser. We were hoping to find your ship's black box, but you're the perfect fountain of knowledge. Would you return to my ship, help us fix this?"

"I—"

Before the alien soldier could reply, Horatio buzzed in through the intercom, "Viper, this is the Chicago. We – two - situation? -report!" the transmission jumped and echoed before completely fading out.

"Chicago, this is Hunter, repeat?" but no reply came back.

"Jack, we have two Hydroxii frigate class cruisers on radar, they've just exited slip space now!" Harley relayed.

"Mjuyr, your ships?"

"I'm afraid not," Mjuyr replied shaking his head, "And by the sounds of the sudden transmission failure, there is a jammer in the area."

"Damn it. Harley, ping that jammer now!" Jack turned away slightly.

"I have something, it's coming from the Watchtower, in the loading bay!"

"Great, another back track–"

"Worse still, I don't think those cruisers like what they see, " Harley added, "They are about to come along side. If they suspect we took out their ship, we have big problems!"

"Can you hail your friends?" Jack asked turning back to Mjuyr.

"Not from here," Mjuyr responded bluntly,

"Great, new plan. We get you back to the Chicago, use the comms tower there to talk down this stand off before it escalates!" Jack turned to his own team, "You guys head back aboard the Watchtower and find that jammer. Harley can walk you in. I'll escort Mjuyr back, he'd be imprisoned rather than put to good use without an escort"

"Copy. Right you three, on me, let's go!" Spider took the opportunity to lead the team and pressed on back through the ship.

"Well Mjuyr, follow me, we need you to save the day."

Heading back towards the Watchtower, Jack felt an odd leading a band of Hydroxii soldiers, it wasn't often possible. The heavy footsteps of the large Hydroxii soldiers resounded in the silence of space as they darted down the corridor. Reaching a closed door, Mjuyr punched the panel, bracing himself against the door to allow his squad inside. Upon entering, a barrage of blue plasma sprayed the lead soldier, the squad quickly taking cover.

Jack grimaced as plasma blasted off the door, "Mjuyr," Jack called down the radio, "Cover me, I'll move them around."

Mjuyr grumbled into his mouthpiece in his mother tongue, grunting a command the others understood. A spray of blue plasma skimmed Jack's shoulder as he rushed forwards, firing shot after shot until the clip clicked, before twisting a grenade from his belt. Using his left fist, Jack knocked down the nearest Hydroxii soldier before releasing the frag grenade, gently rolling it across the curved corridor floor. Heavy bodies thudded against the walls, a single Hydroxii managing to scramble behind him. Expecting a hard hit, Jack braced, but found only a stroke as the attacking soldier limped beside him.

"We must go, Jack. Move!" Mjuyr shouted as he grabbed the smaller, human team leader by the back of the neck and pushed him forward.

"Moving, moving!" Jack stumbled as he struggled to keep pace with the immense power of the Hydroxii.

Spider held up his arm to signal a halt, glancing up, the familiar human surroundings were welcoming, "Alright guys, quick hop, skip and jump."

Pushing hard from the deck of the battered Hydroxii ship, Spider led the way, hauling the augment suit into the hull of the human ship once more and sweeping the flashlight around. The ship's emergency lights had gone out, leaving it in complete darkness. One by one, Viper One jumped back into the ship, the welcoming feel deteriorating in the darkness and moving shadows.

"Spider, did you see that?" Draco whispered waving his arm in front of Spider's helmet.

Taking aim, Spider tried to follow his teammate's gestures but found himself on edge, "Nothing, Draco stop-" staring into the dark abyss a heavy calibre round forced the pair apart. Eyes wide, Spider watched as the shadow dived in between the team, firing more shots.

"Shadow's attacking, what ne-" Looking up, Spider realised it wasn't a shadow, but a jet-black suit of human augmented armour.

The attacker turned, the visor flickering from its tinted glare to clear, inside was a female face.

"Lorenzo! " Spider rolled onto his front and fired a barrage towards the soldier, the bullets grazing her armour's personal energy shield as she darted for cover, "Stay still!"

Kneeling, Venom scanned the area, the torchlight only revealing so much. She tried to take everything in, any detail worth imprinting into her head in the hunt for their evil alter ego. Getting to her feet, she glanced from side to side, her finger itching on the trigger of her weapon. Stepping forward, her torch revealed Spider who snapped to attention before pointing his rifle upward. Before Venom could follow she was dropped to the ground by a heavy weight. Bullets pinged around her. Attempting to grab her pistol, she found nothing but a rifle in her back. Draco and Dragon rounded the large crate and released Venom with a few shots at Lorenzo. As the shots ricocheted off her, Lorenzo pulled out her teleporter and pushed it, fizzing out of the fight. Viper One followed the female soldier further into the ship.

"Follow her, don't let her go!" screamed Spider as he rushed into the corridor with his team in tow. As he took aim once more, Lorenzo disappeared in a blaze of yellow lights, before appearing behind him, bringing her rifle across his back and knocking him to the ground. Bringing her sidearm out, she aimed as Spider rolled over, a barrage of bullets forcing her to escape once more in a shroud of teleportation light. The remainder of Viper One regrouped and stood back-to-back in the corridor awaiting the next attack.

"Stay close, she's out there," Spider ordered in a low voice.

The team edged further into the corridor. Returning in a ball of light, Lorenzo flicked on a wrist shield used by Hydroxii close-quarters combatants, placing her sidearm against its plasma sides and pushed forward, pounding the team with high impact bullets, forcing them to disband and seek cover. The specially designed pistol left arcs of orange energy scorched across the corridor.

Edging backwards, Dragon leaned on a control panel releasing it from its hold, "Guys," he shouted over the barrage, "Get behind me, I have an idea!"

Dragging the panel in front of him, Dragon hobbled slowly as he emerged out of his cover, using both arms to push against the powerful shots.

"Everyone on Dragon, move forward we need to get that teleporter!" Spider ordered.

Leaning their rifles around the panel, the team created enough stopping power to destroy Lorenzo's shield, leaving her vulnerable as she suffered from the blowback. As she sidled back, a device caught Spider's eye.

"She's the jammer!" Pushing past the team, he aimed and fired slow, controlled bursts at the soldier, piercing the jammer strapped to her back. As it short circuited, the team's optics returned to normal. Pulling on the nearest grab handle, Lorenzo pushed her teleporter one last time and disappeared for good.

Spider tapped his helmet, "Jack, it's down, I repeat, the jammer is down!"

Captain Horatio stood, the dim lights of the battle station code red made this current situation all the more tense, "I know what this looks like but please-" Horatio spluttered as the Hydroxii ship master growled in reply.

"It looks to me like an act of aggression, human!"

"You're not listening, we came to answer a distress call from our ship, why would we-"

"Why would you not? Retaliation for the countless dead humans. Why don't we settle this," the Hydroxii ship master nodded, "ship master to ship master?"

Horatio winced. He wasn't prepared for a firefight and honestly didn't know if his ship was up for the task of taking on two heavily armed Hydroxii frigates.

"Sir, they're powering weapons," the Ensign shouted, fear obvious in his voice.

Horatio stepped forward, "Give me time to recall my team. We can discuss this proper-"

"Do not test me. I will relish this fight," the ship master leaned forwards in his chair as the sight on screen puzzled him.

"You will not dare attack an ally, ship master X'yum, unless you want to answer to my burning wrath," Mjuyr pushed Horatio aside and leaned his huge hands on the tiny human console, "I suggest you power down or I personally will answer the battle cry."

X'yum grunted and the screen reverted back to the view outside. The two Hydroxii frigates floated freely in space, ready for a close-quarters fight. Mjuyr didn't seem concerned, but Jack and Horatio stepped up in awe as they watched the opposing ships hovering over the wreckage.

"Bit more than I expected Jack, " Horatio shook his head, "Ensign get us moving, I don't want to hang around, we have what we need."

Mjuyr stepped up to Jack and put his hand on his shoulder, "My apologies for this, we shall go aboard my brother's ship and understand what has happened today."

"Thanks, but watch out, I don't think this is as clear cut as it seems," Jack patted the huge Hydroxii team leader as he passed by, ushering his squad to move out.

"Jack, can we come home now?" buzzed Spider.

"I'll get a Valkyrie to you now, we have some work to do back at base, hopefully it'll give us a clue to where we're off next." Jack slumped in the officer's chair and breathed a sigh of relief. Disaster had narrowly been averted. Every mission moved them closer to an elusive and deadly enemy.

Chapter 19

Kayleigh slid slowly into a slouched position, trying to stay out of sight. She found herself glancing higher and higher over her computer, finding it hard not to stare at the officers clearing her partner's desk of personal objects. Her current mood made her highly likely to do something stupid. Kayleigh stood and slowly stepped up to the kitchen. Drawn to the coffee machine, she pushed the button and quickly positioned the cup under the tap. As it filled, Kayleigh leaned against the counter and sighed.

"Sergeant?"

Startled, Kayleigh turned to face the Captain, "Oh hi, Cap, what brings you to this trusty machine?"

He turned and calmly closed the door, keeping an eye out to make sure nobody was about to enter the room, "Are you okay Kayleigh?"

She froze for a moment, unsure what to say, "Absolutely fine, just need my coffee," she half laughed picking the cup up, fumbling as she did so and spilling some on the floor.

"No Kayleigh, you're not, take some leave. Please."

"Sir I'm-"

"Go home Sergeant, you're going to do something you'll

live to regret," the Captain grabbed her arm.

She knew what was wrong, it was natural, but being at home might just lead her to break down. However, she knew she wasn't being given a choice.

The Captain glanced down and released Kayleigh's arm, sensing the unease, "Please for now, at least for a few days, you won't work properly keeping it all inside."

"Fine, but I want to know if that Navy team find or do anything."

"Kay–"

"I mean it, that's my only lead to uncovering the truth."

The Captain sighed and pulled open the door, "Go home Kayleigh. Read a book. Just, stop. Please."

Kayleigh sipped her coffee and considered her choice of words. Deep down she knew that, realistically, it was over. She had crossed so many boundaries, it was becoming difficult, not only for herself, but the Captain too. She had finally reached the end of the road. She placed the cup down and stepped back, "Okay. Okay I will Captain, promise I'll binge some TV."

As she left the room, Kayleigh sighed before unzipping her bulletproof vest and placing it on her desk. Pulling her coat over her shoulders, she pushed her hands into her pockets and hid her tightened fists. She knew that once she left the station she had given up, but maybe it was a lost fight. She just had to accept her fate. Grabbing her backpack, she wandered towards the elevator. She slid her ACPD tablet into her bag, gave the Captain a salute and pushed the call button.

Exiting the elevator, Kayleigh was greeted by awkward glances from two officers who fumbled past. As she stepped forward, she overheard the officers mumbling behind her; she knew they were probably talking about her but didn't much care. Pulling her car door open, Kayleigh climbed in and prepared for the painful trip home. Twisting the key, the car rumbled to life and Kayleigh lowered the handbrake, allowing it to steadily roll free. She slowly worked her way through the relatively quiet traffic. Most people were on their way into the city not heading for the outskirts, and it made the drive home faster which allowed less time for her to dwell on her own twisted thoughts.

Reaching her home, Kayleigh drew the car to the side of the road and pulled on the handbrake. That act cemented her personal failure with the mission; her mission to protect and ultimately to find out just what was happening, why Greg, and everyone close to her on the case, was now dead. She leaned slowly forward and rested her head on the top of the steering wheel. As her eyes filled with tears, she rubbed them with her sleeve and climbed out of her car. Her emotional outburst would have to wait. Fighting with the front door, she forced her way inside and slammed it behind her, sliding down to the floor and finally, releasing all the pent-up energy she had been holding inside for so long. Kayleigh screamed as she slammed her fist into the floor before flinging her jacket across the hallway. For a moment she felt better. She slowly lifted her head and stared at the framed picture of Greg and herself. They had been a real pair, successful officers and incredible friends. She was always invited to Greg's family parties, she really felt connected and always had their support. Now she wondered what they thought of her.

She used her sleeve again to wipe away the uncharacteristic tears and wandered toward the frame. Picking it up, she twisted the back and carefully pulled the picture free, smiling as she rotated it in her hands. Above the table, hung Kayleigh's commendation from her heroic moment during the closing stages of the Human-Hydroxii war. She placed the picture into the commendation frame and stepped back, "I will find out who killed you, Greg. I promise."

Kayleigh knocked her fingers against the table and walked away into her house, kicking her shoes from her feet she slumped onto the sofa. As she sat there, the digital monitor that hung on the wall flickered to life. Kayleigh tilted her head and leaned forward. She watched her monitor flicker intensely, it eventually stopped and a faint purple line rippled across its screen. Kayleigh slowly stood and glanced from side to side. Was she being spied on? Should she be concerned? Her answer came, but not in the form she truly expected. A message appeared on the monitor - *Tap here.*

Standing in bewilderment, Kayleigh moved gradually forward, spinning around the room looking for someone to jump out and scream 'Surprise'. The monitor pinged softly, the purple button rippling in the background. Hesitantly, Kayleigh held her hand to the screen and pressed the button. As she did so, the screen flashed wildly as thousands of files flickered across it like a piece of art. Images of people, vehicles and blueprints scrolled across before finally coming to a stop. Kayleigh stepped back in complete confusion. What the hell had just happened? As if answering her thoughts, an envelope appeared on screen and shook before opening revealing a single letter. The letter H.

"Harley?"

The letter shook again and vanished. Kayleigh began to pull various images to the centre of the screen. Her heart began to beat faster as she realised what the unusual AI had just given her - a dossier on everything the intelligence division had on the entire situation; bio-analytical reports, arrest warrants and blueprints for various buildings, including the club she had entered to make her arrest with the navy special forces soldier, Hunter. It was just there, all for her to finally view. As she brought up another picture, the images parted by themselves and Kayleigh pulled her hand away. She stared as the images sifted themselves and revealed a blueprint of a high-rise building, a crude purple arrow projected on to the image. The image was of the Herta Banking Building in downtown Atlanta.

"Harley, what are you trying to tell me?" Kayleigh ran her hand along the blueprint and the image became 3D, allowing her to view a unique route inside which led her to a computer-generated server room. "A server room? What are you-" Kayleigh placed her hand on the wall as a purple circle indicated a particular set of servers within the room. The image was frozen and titled '*Evidence*'. Before she could ask more questions, her data pad buzzed in her backpack. Kayleigh slowly stepped backward and spun round to unzip it. Pulling out the data pad, she read an objective -

The truth.

Chapter 20

Jack tapped his helmet as he stared deep into the tinted visor.

"Jack, come on. I can't scour all this myself," Harley tutted as she steadily swiped virtual recreations of the data from side to side.

"You really can, Harley. You're literally an AI," Jack turned to Harley with his hand raised.

"Well yeah, true. But it's not as fun without dragging you in - oh wait, there we go."

"What did you find Harley? Why did you get us all in a room to watch you comb through mountains of data?" General Kato stood with his arms folded.

"Sir, I have uncovered our snake in the grass. I present to you Agent Frank Falaney, the official pain in the arse of the Atlanta City Police Department."

"Falaney?" Kato leaned in, "There's no way it's him."

"The data doesn't lie, Sir. He-"

"Is dead," Kato stared at the 3D image of the dead man, unable to move.

"You mean our problem is a dead guy?" Spider asked.

"He's not dead, he's alive, and I guarantee one hundred percent this is our man," Harley responded, not impressed with the team's questioning of her analysis.

Jack stepped forward and glanced to the image, "If he's dead, then we need to figure out who he is."

"The man is dead, Jack. I watched him die." The team turned to Kato who slowly retreated from the table, "He was with me during the early days of the war. Our base was attacked by a Paladin raiding party. He died that day. I buried him."

"Well, we're hunting a ghost, Sir. I promise you; this man is the source of all our issues," Harley pointed to the 3D model and turned back to Kato.

"There is only one way to answer this one. I want you to ID him."

"Sir?" Jack stepped towards Kato, "You want us to just. . . ID him?"

"Yes, I want a visual made of this man. If he is Falaney, Harley will be able to register him via facial recognition. I'm certain you won't match him, it's just impossible."

"Seems a waste–"

"Don't question my actions, Captain Young."

Spider stood to attention for the first time in Jack's presence. Jack watched as he shuffled on the spot. Kato was completely lost in thought as Jack stared at the image of his dead comrade.

Jack moved forward and banged on the table, "Okay, you heard the man. Let's make a move for this."

"Jack, I want you in vests and pistols only. This is an opportunity to tell whoever this is that we know there's something wrong. I want you in and out without making a scene. No suits. No press. Do you understand me, Major?"

Jack nodded, "I do, Sir. Let's go Vipers."

Jack rested against the sleek, black Naval truck and adjusted his vest. It felt wrong to be dressed in a standard issue, bulletproof vest. Not wearing an incredible powerful, body-moulding, Hydroxii-Human hybrid armour made Jack feel completely unprotected. He could almost understand the General's decision, but to go out unprotected, after being attacked a number of times by an attacker in their own top-secret armour, felt like a problem.

Spider slammed his fist twice against the door panel. Jack jumped, pistol half unclipped, "Woah, easy gunslinger," he laughed prising open the driver's door, "Kato said no heroics didn't he?"

The rest of the team arrived and climbed into the navy vehicle, the tinted glass revealing nothing inside. Having been so heavily active on the field, it made a change to see his team out of their suits and looking human for a brief moment. Jack started the car and weaved his way out into the streets of Atlanta. The team were silent, preparing themselves for a different kind of mission. This one was more recon than anything - ID the agent, assess the situation. If this agent was who Kato was so shaken up about, that would present its own problems. The battlefield had shifted once more and Jack wondered just where it was going to take him next.

As they made their way into the city, it was clear things had changed. Police checkpoints had sprung up and people were being searched; this rogue super soldier had really thrown everything in the air and the general population feared what might happen next. Tensions were rising. The team began to realise just how important their mission was in making sure the city didn't boil over into a frenzied riot.

Arriving at the scene, the unique design of the Banking

Tower made it stand out from the average city high-rise.

"Okay team, remember we're not here to spook Falaney, we just need a positive ID," Jack turned to the Viper team, "Dragon, Draco, you stay here with the car while we head inside," the pair nodded, "Our job is to not tick him off, let's go."

Jack, Venom and Spider strode confidently towards the building's grand, glass entrance. Once inside, Venom and Spider turned and surveyed the room. Jack took in the concerned glances of the civilians.

"Hello officers, how can I help you?" a man asked calmly, he was well dressed and potentially the manager.

"We're looking for someone—"

"Me," Jack turned and stared at the man before him, "I believe they are looking for me."

He stepped forwards and held his hands to his side, "Are you Mr. Falaney?"

"I am. And to what do I owe the pleasure?" Falaney stood, eyeing up the officers. There was a large scar wrapped across his face.

As the two men made small talk, Harley buzzed in to Jack's ear, "Give me two seconds, Jack."

"We've had a call suggesting you had a potential data breach and wanted to offer our serv—"

"I'm already on-site, officers," Falaney moved for his back pocket, Spider and Venom swiftly reached for their pistols. Falaney laughed, "No need to be so aggressive, officers. Are we not on the same team?"

Jack waved his hand to the side, indicating to the officers to stand down. They both let go of their sidearms and watched as Falaney produced an ID badge.

"See. I'm one of you Navy types. I'm already here and so I think you can go back and tell your superiors."

"Why don't-" Venom stepped forward before Jack held out his arm to stop her.

"If that's the case, then we will go back to base and report in. Seems admin haven't picked up on your appointment to the case."

"It would seem so," Falaney watched with a large smile, filling Jack with a high level of discomfort. Jack ushered his team to the door, almost pulling Spider out of the building.

"Oh, and Major?" Jack paused. He hadn't revealed anything about himself in the conversation, yet somehow Falaney knew his rank, "Give my regards to General Kato will you?"

Spider pivoted and pulled his pistol, before the click of three more loaded pistols echoed through the hall. Fearing a face off, Jack pulled his teammate from the building and waved his hand to Dragon and Draco, ushering them into the van.

As the team climbed in, Spider leaned forward from the back seat and knocked Jack with his arm, "What the hell was that? How did he know who you were?"

"I don't know, Spider, but that's not important right now. Harley?"

"Positive ID for Frank Falaney. Our ghost has been identi-fied."

"Kato will not be pleased," Jack pushed the radio button on the dashboard, "General, we have a positive ID. Advise on how to proceed." Jack and the team sat patiently, awaiting a response.

"Bring him in, I want to talk to our ghost."

"Sir, he's protected right now. An arrest would cause a scene."

"Copy, then I think we go back for a night raid."

"Copy that, Sir. Returning home."

Jack stopped and pushed himself against the concrete wall, holding steady in position. Feeling the tap on his shoulder, Jack swiftly moved around the corner, swinging his assault rifle from side to side and scouring the skyline as he did so. The silencer which had been twisted onto the rifle made the rifle just marginally longer than normal.

Jack stopped and held his fist in the air, "Okay Harley, give us a sweep."

"On it, Jack. 3D visual scan is go." Jack stood as a 3D mockup of the building spun in front of his visor and indicated their target, "Okay so our target is on the thirtieth floor. Either he's been kicked out of his home or he's working late."

"Whatever the reason, we take him in tonight." Jack moved around the corner and placed a small device on the door, just beside the locking mechanism.

"Jack, you know I–"

"Harley, just let it go, okay?"

"Fine, fine. . . " Harley sighed, disappointed not to get to do her thing.

The device flashed green, and Jack pulled it from the door, pushing it open and entering the room. Staying to the outer walls, the team briskly made their way into the entrance hall once again.

"Jack, I've cut the security feed. You're welcome," Harley announced sarcastically.

"You do your thing, and I will do mine, Harley."

Reaching the buildings staircase, Jack turned to his team, "Ready?"

Spider shuffled forward and glanced to his right, "Why are we taking the stairs?"

"I don't fancy taking a plunge thirty floors should this guy decide to drop us out of the sky."

"Fair," Spider shuffled back into position and watched as Jack waved his hand forward and they began to swiftly climb the banking tower's grand staircase. Steadily the soldiers ascended, with Harley running in the background, keeping the security under control, it meant they could move quietly through the building without interruption and without a fight. The last thing the Viper team needed was a firefight in a public building, though they were prepared for combat, this time they needed a quick win.

Kayleigh moved quietly through the dark alleyway, pushing her back against the wall, she glanced over her shoulder before preparing to enter the banking tower. To her surprise the door had already been opened. She leaned closer and brushed her finger along the lock. It was warm to the touch, not a usual temperature on a cold night. Kayleigh pushed her questions to the back of her mind and gently pushed open the door, shuffling herself inside and closing it behind her. Brushing her body along the wall, she slithered through the darkness, surprised by the lack of security in the tower.

Kayleigh pushed herself against the door of the security office and placed a magnetic device against the lock. The device hummed and she smiled as it worked its magic. Kayleigh wondered if she would ever get an opportunity to thank Harley for the treasure trove of information and the location of this unique piece of evidence. As the machine flashed a green light, she sidled inside and jogged to the computer panel hooked to the main wall. She pushed the device against the computer and stepped back to allow it to work once more. Kayleigh's feeling of unease increased as she stepped further inside. She shook her fears from her current train of thought and pulled the magnet from the computer as it flashed green once again and the low dim lights shut down. Kayleigh unholstered her sidearm and switched on her weapon's flashlight.

Stepping out of the room, she reached the elevator and pushed the call button. As it was already at ground level, Kayleigh slowly stepped inside. So far so good, but it felt too easy. Every fibre of her body was yelling for her to stop now and save herself, but she put all that behind her as she pushed the button for the thirtieth floor. Kayleigh fidgeted as she waited to exit the elevator. She had to be prepared in case there was somebody watching or waiting for her.

As the elevator slowed and gradually stopped, Kayleigh raised her weapon and held her finger tight against the trigger. With a ping, the doors slowly opened, and Kayleigh stepped out in a determined manner, glancing from side to side to ensure her safety. Satisfied she was alone, she pulled her data pad from her pocket and held it in front of her, the dimly lit screen acting like a map to her prize. Stepping down the corridor, she branched off into the outer reaches of the thirtieth floor and followed her beacon onward. She shone her flashlight at every door she passed, reading, and sighing when it was not the one she sought.

After a few long minutes, Kayleigh finally reached the cross on her map and peered up from her data pad. The sign on the door read *Server Room*. Excitedly, she pulled the magnetic device from her pocket once more and attached it. Smiling gleefully as the door clicked open, she stepped inside and slowly closed it behind her. As she entered, the visual on her data pad enlarged the image and gave her a complete view of the room in real time, pointing her to the exact location she needed.

Stepping through the cold of the server room, she reached the final cross on her map and a command appeared on the screen. It was a server number. Kayleigh left the data pad on the floor and hurriedly shone her pistol against the server numbers. Finding her prize, she closed her eyes and whispered a triumphant 'yes' to herself before uncoupling the drive. Pausing for a moment, she held it in her hand and finally put it in to her bag, "I've got you now you bastard!"

Kayleigh jogged out of the room, ignoring the data pad and the additional message that flashed onto its display. Sidearm in hand, she reached the corridor, freezing as she heard the sound of movement and doors opening. Pulling back into the darkness, she held the flashlight in her hand to hide the beam as a door swung open. Hurriedly, Kayleigh moved for the adjacent room and pushed her back against the door.

Jack held his hand in the air for the team to stop and braced against the wall, "This is it Vipers. Let's get our answers."

The team nodded and Jack pushed open the door, the team pouring in and spreading out as they all took aim at the man causing so much trouble, Frank Falaney. As the door closed behind them, the team stood, their rifles aimed at the agent who sat facing away from them.

"Well, if it isn't my favourite band of the intelligence division," Falaney rose from his chair and turned to face the soldiers, "The honour is mine, I think?"

Jack stood firm with his rifle, "Frank Falaney, you're under arrest and we will be taking you in under Article two one four of the Naval Intelligence order."

As Falaney began to step away from his desk, the team took a step forward, prompting the agent to pause for a moment, "Hunter. . . or do you prefer Jack? I don't think you really understand the problem you face do you?"

Jack hesitated for a moment as he pondered just how this man knew his identity. The project team he was in was, so far, under wraps, barely anyone knew who was connected to it. Before he could counter, the door adjacent to them swung open and the team found themselves unsure of where to aim.

Jack lowered his rifle as he recognised the person entering the room, "Kayleigh? What the hell are you doing here?"

"I may have given her some intel," Harley called out into the team's intercom.

"You did what?"

Kayleigh stepped calmly out of the doorway and towards Falaney, "So, you are a dirty agent?"

"I see you brought back up?" Falaney laughed as he steadily moved behind his office chair.

"Officer Crow, you need to leave. Now!"

"No! I want to watch you take this scumbag in myself," Kayleigh smiled as Jack turned back to the rogue agent.

Jack put down his rifle and produced a pair of handcuffs. Stepping towards Falaney, Jack's stride slowed as he got closer, something was wrong.

As he tried to grab Falaney, his hand passed through him and Falaney turned, with his villainous smile and laughed, "Did you really think I would be so easy to track, so easy to bring down? Now Jack, I am so many steps ahead of you, you really have no idea what's in store for humanity."

Falaney's virtual image flickered briefly as he phased through the table and stood proudly in the centre of the room, "But the best part is. . . none of you will live to see that." Falaney's image disappeared, and everyone stood in confusion.

"Harley, track that signal, he has to be-"

"Jack - Look out!" Harley shouted as the glass shattered and Lorenzo stormed into the room. Before anybody could stop her, she had already charged at Jack and had disarmed him.

Everyone had their rifles aimed at Lorenzo, but she stood firm with a highly modified plasma pistol placed against Jack's head.

"Weapon's down," she called out confidently.

As the team watched Jack struggle in Lorenzo's grip, Venom slowly stepped forward. Turning, Venom held her rifle firmly aimed at her teammates.

"Venom, what the fu-"

"Enough. Just. . . don't," Venom spoke with a tinge of uncertainty as she stepped to Lorenzo's side.

"No way-"

"Just do it," Jack groaned trying to shuffle out of her iron grip. Everyone lowered their weapons; Spider slowly lowered his.

"I said. . . weapon's down," Lorenzo ordered again, pushing the pistol closer to Jack's helmet. Spider slammed the rifle down and slowly stepped back. Lorenzo pulled Jack further from his team until she was confident she had enough time to react to any movement, "Retract the armour."

Jack squirmed a little and obeyed the Spaniard. Reaching for his helmet, Jack pushed the command button and allowed the hybrid armour to release his body.

"Helmet off."

Jack slowly pulled the helmet from his head and placed it down on the desk and turned to face her, "Now what?"

"Now we leave," Lorenzo darted forward and before the Viper team could reach out, Lorenzo, Venom and Jack disappeared in a ball of light.

Spider slammed his fist on the desk and screamed, "What the hell just happened!"

"I–" Harley stopped briefly as she thought, "Everyone you need to get out now. There's a bomb on the–" Before Harley could warn the team, an explosion shook the building and the beams groaned from the sudden detonation. Everyone rocked as the building quickly became unsafe. Kayleigh fell forward into the desk and stared back at the Viper team.

"Kayleigh, put the helmet on. Now!" Harley shouted loudly through Jack's empty helmet. Hesitantly, she pulled the helmet over her head as the building heaved and began to collapse. Harley activated the suit's armour. Kayleigh closed her eyes, allowing the unique armour to cover her body as gravity began to take effect and she began to fall.

Chapter 21

Jack grimaced as he slowly regained consciousness, feeling disorientated and confused about where he was. As he shuffled, he began to remember what had just happened. He tried to stand up but found himself tied to a chair. Scanning his surroundings, he found he was being held in some kind of interrogation room without any support. Struggling, Jack then sat back in his chair as the adjacent door swung open and a number of people came into the room. Jack observed those entering with a feeling of dismay and disappointment.

"So Venom, what did it cost to betray-" Jack paused as a man threw a fist against his head. Jack spat blood before shaking his head from side to side.

"Eyes on me, Viper," the man commanded as he pulled up a chair and sat opposite him, "I have questions."

"And I have no answers for you," Jack glared up toward Venom, who, without her helmet, couldn't help but glance away from her now ex-team leader, "Especially not her. In fact, it's me who should be asking you the questions."

"Yes, well. . . Major Jack Halliday, unfortunately you are in my custody. So, let's start with where the AI, codenamed Harley, is hmm?"

Jack glanced down at the table and peered at the naval gear displayed neatly across the table, the items positioned precisely, "And why would you need to know that, Mr. . ."

"Consider me your alter ego, Jack. Now I'm going to ask again. . . codename Harley?"

"You're going to have to work harder than that. Come on. . . " Jack slumped back in his chair and shook his head as he looked to the ceiling. The man leading the interrogation looked behind Jack and nodded. Before Jack could get a visual, a large hand had grabbed his head and forced it down on to the cold, iron table, the objects swept from it clattered to the floor. As Jack was released he flung himself backwards and watched as the Hydroxii's camouflage revealed its ship master class armour.

"I believe you two are already acquainted?"

"We've met but I know who he fears," Jack smiled as the ship master grunted, held back by another in the room. The Hydroxii soldier slumped against the wall, mimicking the other humans in the room.

"But this time the field is even, and your team cannot protect you now, Jack."

"What's that supposed to mean?"

"Have you not heard?" the man brushed a broken data pad from the table and placed his own down for Jack to see. Pushing the screen, the data pad began to play an audio recording:

"What the hell just-"

Audible shuffling.

"I-"

"Everyone you-out now. There's a bomb on the-"

Jack's eyes widened as the sound of the explosion and of concrete collapsing suddenly quietened, the screaming of his team, of police officer Kayleigh, playing in his mind.

"Jack you are alone. No one is coming to save you. You have nothing to hope for. We are going to destroy you. . . piece by piece."

Chapter 22

Kayleigh shuffled as she slowly regained consciousness, her senses completely overloaded as her body adjusted. Realising she was still alive, she pulled herself forward before screaming in pain as her body demanded she lay herself back down. Breathing heavily, she slumped back into the hospital bed and began to glance around the room. Everything was quiet and she was alone. Kayleigh wondered if she was literally in purgatory, until another human appeared to greet her.

"Officer Crow, you're awake?" the nurse stepped up to the officer and reached towards her. Kayleigh winced and threw her arm up to block the nurse's touch, flinching in agony as she did so.

"Where the hell am I? What happened?"

As she began to become uneasy, a friendly face appeared from behind the nurse.

"I've got this Doc. . ."

"Understood General."

Kayleigh watched as the nurse smiled and wandered out of the small room. She looked at the man and recognised him as the General who was friends with their police captain, General Kato.

"I'll ask you. . . What the hell is going on?"

Kato carefully pulled a chair from beside her bed and sat down, "First off, how are you Crow?"

Kayleigh twitched in response, "In god damn agony. Where am I? Where's Jack?"

"Kayleigh, you're currently in a medical bay in the Naval Intelligence headquarters. You were brought in with the rest of the Viper team." Kato titled his head, "What's the last thing you remember?"

She lay for a moment and recalled the final moments from the banking tower. The confrontation, the betrayal. . . and the building crashing around her, smothering her. Kayleigh's heart raced as she began to remember the incident. She turned to Kato who held her shoulder,

"Kayleigh, you and Viper were pulled from the rubble of that banking tower–"

"How did I survive?"

"The armour you were wearing, Jack's, is a hybrid armour. It's a military breakthrough in merging human and Hydroxii technology. Jack leads a unique team as the only non-augmented soldier in the squad. The others were medically. . . adjusted. . . to wear the armour. The armour has a built-in survival cell. In extreme situations it will lock, or harden, keeping the occupier inside alive long enough for help to arrive."

Kayleigh held out her arms and admired the bruising, "Suppose I'll take a few bruises over death. But where are the others?"

"Alive and debriefing. My–"

"Where's Jack? Where did Lorenzo–" Kayleigh shook as she recalled the moment she had realised Venom had betrayed them all, "Where's Venom! She–"

"We know about Venom. I caught that much from my operative, Spider. We're working on a plan of action now."

"So, what becomes of me? Patch me up and throw me under the bus like your friend, Falaney?"

"Not a chance!" a familiar voice echoed in the room, causing Kayleigh to jump as Harley appeared beside her, using the data pad as a conduit, "No you're coming with us!"

Kayleigh raised an eyebrow and turned back to Kato. As she looked towards him, the remainder of the Viper One team, battered and scarred, appeared in the room.

"We're inducting you into the team, Crow. Think it's time we scored a win for a change," Spider stood with his arms folded, "I think Jack would have wanted that."

Kayleigh smiled widely, unable to hold back in her joy and surprise, "Well. . . when do I start?"

Kayleigh fidgeted in her new navy uniform, feeling the discomfort from the tightly bound bandages beneath it. She was still smiling despite everything. She had never expected she would be wearing a naval intelligence officer's uniform, but desperate times called for desperate measures. She could already hear Greg's sharp remarks.

General Kato entered the briefing room and she rose to attention, watching as the others followed,

"At ease, Officer."

Kayleigh lowered her hand and sat back down. The remainder of Viper One surrounded the table and Harley appeared at its centre.

"A full house, perfect. Welcome to the team, Crow, I knew

we would make a naval woman of you. You look good."

Kayleigh smiled as Harley started to wander the large digital screen on the top.

"Okay Vipers, welcome to Harley's War Table." As she spoke, data steadily scrolled and images rotated as she controlled them with her hand, "Today's mission is a rescue op for our own Jack 'Hunter' Halliday. We have credible intelligence that he is being held in an old military bunker on the abandoned planet of Keller."

Harley moved her hand and replaced the images swiftly with that of a revolving planet.

"The area surrounding the base is extremely dangerous. Volcanic activity makes this place a ticking time bomb, hence the abandonment. The attempt by someone to mount a full-scale war against Earth's governments has reached a point of escalation; we cannot afford to let it go any further. This ends today, Vipers. I need you all to suit up, arm up and neutralise this threat. Falaney is not winning this one." Kato swiped the monitor beneath his hands and switched the planet model for that of a large space-faring ship, "You will board the Chicago with our friend, Captain Horatio, aboard his light cruiser and land on the planet, using experimental Hydroxii camo technology to get on the ground undetected. From there, well, I trust your judgement, Vipers."

Spider leaned forward and slammed his fist on the table, "Let's end this now!"

"Agreed, Spider. I want you to take the lead on this. Harley, link up with Spider and get them in and out alive, you hear me?"

Harley raised her hand and saluted, "Understood Sir!" She turned to face Spider, whose amber- tinted visor glowed menacingly in the low lighting, "Let's do this Spider!" Spider held out his hand and Harley appeared to take it, disappearing from the table, and lighting up his data pad on his shoulder plate.

"Okay Vipers, arm up. Come back in one piece please." The team saluted and left the room. Dragon and Draco fist bumped and patted each other on their way out.

Kayleigh rose from her spot and stopped as Kato held her for a moment, "Sir?"

"I know you're probably not happy to be here, but I think you're going to fit right in with the team. They admire your tenacity, Crow. You're loyal. That's important, especially with recent events."

"Thank you, Sir, it's been. . . strange. But I won't let you down. I've come too far and lost too much to do so now."

"Good luck, Crow."

Kayleigh saluted and stepped out of the room, filled with a sense of pride that she felt compelled to act on. She was about to jump into the hornets' nest, and she was going to be fully prepared having been given the right equipment for the first time. They were taking the fight to those who had done so much to her over the past few days.

Today was the day she was going to get that win for everyone she had lost.

Climbing the gantry, Kayleigh's eyes were drawn skyward almost by instinct as she found herself surveying the ship that sat, cradled in the giant robot arms, above the facility. The large, emblazoned name of the ship, 'Chicago', was battle scarred but could still proudly be seen written on its side. The large turrets, which sat alongside its hull, swivelled in cycles as the crew worked through the system before takeoff. Kayleigh could almost imagine the combat those weapons had seen in the last year before the end of the war. She paused for a moment as the team split around her, already mission-ready, planning their strategy in their heads. Kayleigh had been further removed, not as aware of the way everyone else had been protecting the people of Earth, protecting humanity. It felt strange to finally see the interstellar side of the war up to now she had only had a moment's engagement in. This ship held so many memories inside of itself that she was now to be a part of.

Re-focusing on her objective, Kayleigh stepped forward and headed towards the rear, the large ramp already in use by the personnel setting up for the insane task of breaching an old military facility to free one man. There were so many unanswered questions.

Kayleigh wandered through the crew like a ghost, everyone had their own job, their mission. She admired their dedication as everyone smiled and engaged with each other in order to prep one ship for flight. Kayleigh stood to attention as a call came out across the ship.

"Viper One, report to the command deck. All members of Viper One on deck."

Kayleigh smoothed her hair, pulled her ears, and smiled as she gathered her thoughts and strode down the corridor to answer the call. Arriving on the command deck, the crew nearby turned to attention and saluted her as she entered. For a moment she was taken aback. The rest of the team arrived.

"Kayleigh, welcome about the Chicago. The finest light cruiser in the fleet," Horatio tipped his hat briefly.

"Thank you, Captain, it is quite the moment for me. Never thought I would be on a ship, let alone about to go off planet," Kayleigh steadily wandered the deck, continuing to admire the consoles and crew at work.

"Ah, you never forget your first time in space, especially off planet. I hear you've had quite the promotion, Detective?"

"Yeah, you could say that."

Horatio turned and faced the command crew, "Are we ready for launch, Ensign?"

"We are green to go, Sir."

"Excellent, get us off the ground, we have a busy day ahead of us."

"Aye, Sir. Disengaging ground locks now."

The ship shuddered as its large engines steadily pushed it up and out of reach of the naval base. Kayleigh wandered to the main viewing window and stood, watching as the view changed and the sky's colour twisted and turned as the ship began to climb.

"Thirty seconds till orbit, Captain."

"Understood. Once we make orbit, engage the main drive and set the waypoint for Keller."

"Sir? The-"

"The Keller, Ensign."

"Understood. . . Sir. Inputting co-ordinates now."

Kayleigh turned back, "Captain, what happened on Keller?"

Horatio sighed as he removed his hat, "Keller was the home of a substantial human strike force. They were on mission to hit a high value target in the Hydroxii fleet-"

"And my people had discovered it." Everyone turned as Mjuyr entered the room, "We put an end to an almost flawless strategy."

An awkward silence filled the room and Kayleigh couldn't help but glance around at everyone's reaction to the Hydroxii soldier wandering onto the command deck. No one raised a weapon in response.

"That loss dug a hole so deep it rallied everyone to make a desperate move," Horatio stepped forward to meet the Hydroxii face to face.

"And that desperate move led me to come face to face with your Hunter, Halliday. It changed the face of battle when my people realised that we had no war to fight with your kind. We were the aggressor. And so the war ended. Just about."

"Correct. And this operation is to continue this thin alliance. We can't go back to war. There is no need and we would have very little answer for it. Honestly."

Mjuyr stepped up to Kayleigh who stood, unsure of how to react, "Jack speaks highly of you. I hope I will get to see you in action today."

Kayleigh smiled and glanced to the side, desperate to avoid further conversation as Mjuyr wandered to the centre monitor. As she walked away, Kayleigh wondered just how Jack and such an alien could work together, drop their fear and anger and engage in a combined fight for good. The man was unreadable, and Kayleigh hoped she would get one last chance to ask him. Stepping back, she placed her hands on the monitor and jumped as Harley materialised.

"Crow!"

Kayleigh nodded as she watched the AI step towards everyone.

"Okay Vipers. . . plus one, let's get mission ready. Our mission is to infiltrate an old military installation on Keller. The facility hasn't been active in some time, I can provide the original plans but it's safe to assume whoever we are fighting will have modified the base and will be more than ready for us." Harley lifted her hand to provide a new image of another variation of a ship, "We will get to field test a new experimental dropship, armed with a Hydroxii cloaking device, courtesy of Jack's favourite ally, Mjuyr."

Mjuyr stood unmoved as he listened intently, avoiding the deadly stares and chatter from the command deck crew.

"The Chicago will exit hyper space and we will arrive on site, literally on top of them. We will go in on pure momentum to avoid a heat trace. Then we will breach the facility, slowly making our way to where I will enter the base's system and find our team leader, hopefully alive. Are we ready?"

Everyone nodded and Harley clicked her fingers, "Perfect, Captain."

"Vipers your mission is high priority, we need Jack back alive, and, with our raid, we intend to destroy the facility and, hopefully, with it, the militia movement. We arrive in five, so gear up and be ready for a fight."

"Understood Sir," the room echoed, and the team began to filter out of the command deck.

Harley clapped her hands to get Kayleigh's attention, "Crow."

Kayleigh leaned back towards the table and rested her head on her hands, as if she was talking to a child, "Yeah?"

"I want you to keep Jack's armour warm for him. I know it fits; seems right for you do the honours."

"Oh, okay. . . "

"I would get you your own but it's bit short notice. Go get geared up and I will talk you through the mission."

Kayleigh patted the table and left the room, heading for

the Chicago's armoury as instructed. Upon entry, she slowly stepped inside as she observed the team pull rifles and pistols from weapons' caches. She watched as the team huddled and prepared with each other.

Kayleigh stepped up and Spider met her glare. "Crow, your armour," Spider stood holding out Jack's helmet and placed it into her hands. Kayleigh rotated it and faced the helmet's visor. She admired the battle scars etched into the unusual material. Glancing to the ally Hydroxii, she noticed it bore a close resemblance to his. It was the armour of a super soldier.

"Go on Kayleigh, put it on. We're all set."

Kayleigh gulped as she pulled on the helmet, this time she was able to feel the armour as it warped around her body, carefully surrounding her. The armour, though, wasn't noticeable, it felt like an outer layer of skin rather than something clunky. Kayleigh began to understand how the team were able to move, engage and fight with such ease.

Harley buzzed in Kayleigh's ear, "Hey, fits you nicely."

"I'm surprised, I didn't think I had a man's body shape."

Harley laughed, "Best thing about this armour is it moulds itself to its wearer. Makes it easier to pass along should that need to happen."

"What is it made of?"

"That's a subject for another day, right now we are at our destination. Time to head for our chariot."

"Understood."

Kayleigh boarded the Valkyrie dropship and smiled as Dragon saluted her arrival.

"Pleasure to see you in combat, Crow. Was a bit bad ass when you tried to take on Lorenzo. Can't wait to see round two."

Kayleigh paused as she took a seat opposite Dragon, considering whether she would have another go at Lorenzo. The mission had so many possibilities, taking down Lorenzo would be a personal win and one would relish.

The team turned to Horatio who stood at the landing ramp of the dropship, "Okay Vipers, get in and get our man. I want you all accounted for, understood? No heroics."

The team saluted and Spider stepped into the Valkyrie's cockpit and began to cycle the dropship's engines. As the ramp was raised, Horatio stood and saluted one last time. Kayleigh slowly turned to face the rest of the team.

Horatio watched as the dropship took flight, shimmering as the camouflage hid the ship from prying eyes. The Captain turned and closed the landing bay door behind him, there was so much riding on the outcome of this mission and he knew he would soon have a much larger fight on his hands. He just didn't know who it was to be with.

Chapter 23

The team rocked as the dropship landed as planned. The mission was on. They lined either side of the interior, Dragon and Draco stood opposite Kayleigh, the pair unusually ready, but in sync as expected. Kayleigh stood awkwardly behind Mjuyr's giant body as he twisted his plasma rifle in his hands.

Spider stepped from the cockpit and patted her on the back, "Okay team, first port of call, we get Harley into the mainframe early, we find our glorious leader and get him the hell out, in one piece, then we blow this place to pieces."

"Hoorah Spider!" Dragon patted Draco in excitement.

"Alright Vipers. . . on me, let's move."

Spider aimed his rifle high and stepped out first, Mjuyr and Draco followed his lead and Kayleigh and Dragon followed. The team steadily stepped across the facility's crumbled airfield and made their way to an access hatch.

Spider leaned against the door and patted the console with his hand, "Kay, you're up."

Kayleigh lowered her pistol and stood glumly at the console, "What–"

"Just hold your hand over it, I'll do my thing."

Kayleigh obeyed the command and held her free hand over

the console screen. The screen shimmered a dark purple, Kayleigh had a brief flashback to the moment Harley snuck into her house and gave her all the data on Falaney. Back on mission, Kayleigh jumped as the access door unlocked. She stepped back, allowing Spider to step forward to lead the team inside. They moved quickly through the facility, the outer area was easy to cross for the Viper team as they walked without incident between the cracked walls, broken from the combat of previous years. Kayleigh clung closely to Spider as he confidently moved through the labyrinth-like corridors, she listened to her breath against the inside of the helmet, pinching herself as a reminder that she was wearing such incredible armour. The mission, though, was one of the most important of her life. The outcome would have huge repercussions for both sides.

Spider held his hand up for the team to come to a stop. Spider ushered Kayleigh forwards, "Kay."

Kayleigh obliged and placed her hand over the panel again, watching the small screen shimmer purple before flashing, the colour dissipating as if running up her hand to her arm. The door clunked and Spider pushed it open, swinging from side to side on the lookout for enemies. Satisfied it was safe, Spider lowered his rifle, "Okay, Kay and Harley get to work on spotting our man. Once you've done that disable any defences and find us a way to blow this place sky high. You three on me, we're gonna move ahead."

The two soldiers saluted and shook hands as Spider stepped between them, the pair fist bumped and followed their man out of the room. Mjuyr didn't make a sound as he followed his human team leader.

"Kayleigh, head to the main console, I'll start looking for

Jack."

Kayleigh did as she was asked. Holding out her hand, she watched this time, as the purple shimmer rolled down her arm and Harley appeared as an image this time.

"Excellent, right let's get to it then, shall we?"

Kayleigh watched as Harley worked, rolling data and information across the screen.

"Harley? How do you, like, interact with computers?"

"What do you mean, Crow? I'm an AI, I just hook myself in, so to speak!"

"Yeah but. . . how? You don't even need to be plugged in. Like now, you've interacted with three panels without contact?"

"I-I just apply myself to the technology. Do you feel uncomfortable?" Harley turned to face Kayleigh, who stood in the armour she had borrowed from Jack to survive the building collapse. Harley hesitated as she felt something, "I can make myself invisible-"

"No. . . no it's fine. Keep working, I'm just being curious."

"Copy that."

Kayleigh leaned back and rotated the pistol in her hand. She shook her head as she began to think. Something felt wrong. They had managed to arrive on site undetected and without even a shot fired. If Jack was here, somebody of his position should be heavily guarded? She turned to Harley who worked away on the monitor screen, almost dancing as she happily dug through the data. Surely she wasn't the only one thinking that? Or was that the difference between her and the Viper team? A career of life saving decisions, against the career of military operations.

Kayleigh jolted as Harley shouted inside her helmet, "Vipers,

I've got our man. Spider I've adjusted your HUD, Kayleigh and I will meet you there."

"Copy that Harley. Let's start our sabotage now. Kill the power. Time to strike."

Harley turned to Kayleigh, placing her hands on her hips, "Kay, come on, we have to go girl, come on!"

"Sorry, hold on."

Kayleigh moved up to the console. As she reached the AI, Harley shimmered and, as Kayleigh held out her hand, the purple glow glistened from the console, flowing up her arm once again.

"Less of the awe, Crow, we have to go!"

"Right–sorry."

Kayleigh held her pistol and left the main console room, preparing herself for the prison rescue op.

Jack flicked his head up, spitting to his side a huge clump of phlegm and blood that had built up in his mouth. He watched as his interrogator pushed himself back and shook his left hand, flexing his fingers.

"I'm impressed Halliday, you can handle yourself."

"Take these cuffs off and I'll show you."

The interrogator laughed aloud before turning to the others in the room, "I think you underestimate your company Jack. You're quite the decorated soldier though, shame nobody will know when we kill you."

"Then why don't you?"

"Apparently we need you alive, for a little while. But . . ." the man threw the chair opposite across the room, shattering the plastic all around, "You're going to be our punch bag."

The man ushered the large Hydroxii soldier forward. As the soldier laughed before falling silent as the power went out and the room fell into darkness.

The Hydroxii soldier's helmet lit up the room in a cool cyan glow, "What's happening?"

"I don't know. Command do you read?" the interrogator called.

"Command copy? We've lost all power."

"I can see that, what's happening?"

"We have a breach, Sir."

The man hesitated before smiling, "Is it them?"

"Yes Sir."

"Excellent, send teams to meet them on route, we will gear up and face them head on. Team, you know what to do."

The enemy team nodded and activated their own helmet lights. Jack watched as the room dimmed to almost complete darkness as they left one by one.

"We will be back, Jack. I'm not done with you," the man slapped Jack on the back before leaving, allowing the door to slowly close shut.

Jack struggled in his restraints as he was left alone, but there was no escaping them without help. The darkness left him uneasy, he half expected something to take a cheap shot at him or fire a shot, just to make him suffer. Though he couldn't quite understand his current situation, despite the theatrics and physical torment, he didn't feel like a complete prisoner of war. They seemed to be waiting for something. Were they waiting to take on Viper as a team? Questions ran through Jack's head as the door swung open and he squinted as lights illuminated the room and he found himself surrounded once more.

"Jack? Wow you've looked worse."

"Spider?" Jack winced as he glanced up as the soldier in front of him.

"The one and only."

Spider placed his rifle on to the floor before pulling his combat knife from his chest and cutting the restraints from Jack's wrists. Jack sighed as he carefully pulled his hands in front and flexed his fingers.

"Thank you, guys," Jack turned in surprise as he watched his own armour enter the room. As he stared, the wearer placed their hands against the dual buttons on the helmet and the armour retracted to reveal a familiar body. Pulling the helmet from her head, Jack was met with Kayleigh's smile.

"Hi Hunter, or should I call you Jack?"

"Well, I didn't expect that. You're finally living the enemy's life, huh?"

"Something like that. Your team saved me, Jack. Your armour. . . I'm lucky to be here."

Dragon stepped up to Jack and patted his shoulder, "She's one of us now!"

"As much as I'm enjoying this reunion, isn't it time we made our escape?"

Jack turned and faced his Hydroxii friend, glancing up to the alien's armoured helmet, "Well, look at you? This is quite the rescue squad. It's good to see you, Mjuyr."

"Kayleigh, hand Jack his armour, it's time we blew this place and got out of here. Harley did you find a way to destroy it?"

"I did–"

"Do it, we're not hanging around to watch, let's go!"

Kayleigh stepped towards Jack, who took the helmet in his hands and rotated it to face him briefly. He glanced at the scratches and indents in the armour and looked up at Kayleigh, wondering just what she thought of it all.

Jack's moment of thought was cut abruptly by Harley's voice demanding his attention, "Come on Jack, let's go lover boy."

Jack pulled the helmet over his head, allowing the armour to coat his body once again. He felt at home again in the suit as it wrapped itself comfortingly around his battered body. Jack activated the headlamp on his helmet and turned to face his team, "Pleasantries aside, we need to leave. These guys are. . . dangerous."

"Who are they?" Kayleigh asked.

"I don't know exactly, but there is a lot going on. We need to get back to Earth and warn Kato, now."

"Understood, come on let's move," Spider pushed the rifle into his shoulder and led the way, "You don't mind if I lead, Jack?"

Jack laughed as he pushed himself on through the corridor, "No, I'll let you take this one, this time. We should be careful; they were waiting for you to come."

"Why not attack us on route-"

"Because where is the fun in revenge, if you don't make it last?"

They all stopped abruptly as they reached the end of the corridor. The group that had interrogated Jack had used their active camouflage on their armour to surround the Viper team.

"About time we all got together, I think revenge sounds fair," Spider rocked his head side to side aiming directly at Venom.

"You wanted a fair fight, Jack," The man who had led the interrogation held out his arms, his armour flickering, "Let's see if you're really what they say you are." Pulling a compact rifle from his back, the man quickly fired a barrage of bullets which ricocheted off Jack's armour as he stumbled backwards. The corridor lit up in a ball of flashing light as weapons were drawn and both sides went to war.

Spider launched forwards firing his assault rifle at Venom, who knelt down to return the fire. Spider swung his rifle hard against Venom's armour. It bounced across the floor as Spider tackled her to the ground and began to hit her armour with his fists. Venom held her arms up to deflect the blows. As Spider pulled his arm back, Venom pushed a panel on her shoulder and a blast of energy knocked him over. This gave her a chance to jump forward, unclipping her sidearm to fire at the man who had previously been her teammate. He twisted to allow the armour to take the hit.

Spider turned, "Was it worth it?"

Venom twitched waiting for the shot, "Was what worth it?"

"All this? The betrayal? What exactly is your game here?"

"You wouldn't understand."

"You're right. How could I understand someone who would betray their friends and species for a bunch of terrorists," Spider unclipped his pistol from his utility belt and, like a cowboy, fired until the magazine clicked empty. Releasing the empty magazine, he lunged forward as Venom pushed another button on her armour. In front of Spider an orange energy shield split the feuding pair.

Venom lowered her pistol and slowly stepped forward, "I'm sorry, really I am-"

"Save it," Spider glanced to his right and held his pistol towards the open doorway beside him, "You truly earned your nickname, Venom. I hope you have a plan because I'm going to find you."

Venom held her hand to her helmet and clicked her intercom,

"Finish your fights, it's nearly time."

Spider turned behind him and watched as a further two energy shields blocked the path, his teammates caught in their own conflict. He could only watch as Venom slunk into the darkness.

"I don't think so. . ."

Dragon and Draco leaned on each other as the energy shield buzzed just behind them, heating their armour. Lorenzo spun her pistols in her hand as the three of them stood at a standstill.

"A little outnumbered here, Lorenzo?"

"Might want to count again. . ."

The pair glanced to their side. As they looked back to the Spaniard, a shimmering figure revealed itself and the large Hydroxii soldier appeared, shoving Dragon. His armour sparked as the alien forced him against the energy shield, Dragon screamed out loud as it superheated behind him. Draco switched fired his assault rifle as the alien threw out it's huge arm and knocked his teammate to the ground. Lorenzo pounced, firing her pistols as she stepped forward, hitting Draco's armour over and over again. Rolling onto his back, Draco fired the assault rifle at Lorenzo's legs knocking her off balance. Switching quickly, he fired at the Hydroxii soldier's back, causing enough of a distraction to allow Dragon to fire blindly from his position, plastering the alien's armour and releasing his grip.

As the Hydroxii soldier stumbled back to Lorenzo, the duo moved in unison and stood their ground.

"Is that it? Come on, I expected a proper fight!" Dragon mocked as he stood confidently.

Lorenzo laughed and stood beside her Hydroxii teammate,

"We're just getting started." She clicked her canister teleportation device and the pair vanished.

"Damn it. Harley, give us a ping on their location," Dragon shouted into his helmet as he swivelled to watch Jack and his equivalent locked in their own fight. An incredibly one-sided fight.

Jack held his arms in front of his face as the man quickly jabbed at him, eventually forcing him against the energy shield. Jack screamed as he pushed his hands against the shield, it quickly heated his armour from the inside. Jack used his foot to kick himself away from the shield and knock back his attacker, reaching for the man's sidearm, and quickly firing every bullet it had in the magazine, as he lunged forwards and the pair crashed through an open door and landed on the floor. Jack twisted and tried to pull himself but found himself being hit again and again by the man's relentless punches.

"Not quite the fighter I imagined, Jack!" The man kicked Jack who, at this point, was starting to feel the effects of his interrogation, "Do you not have that fight in you? Come on!" Again he kicked Jack, who screamed inside his helmet. The man shook his head and stepped aside, "You have no idea what I've had to endure because of your pathetic government!" He stepped to a locker, opening it to reveal a stock of weapons, "The loss I have suffered. But today, has given me my chance at redemption. . . in the form of revenge." He pulled a pistol from the locker and fired it towards Jack, enjoying the thrill of watching his enemy squirm on the floor.

Eventually, throwing it aside, he continued to goad Jack who was slowly scrabbling across the floor, "To have this opportunity is quite something. Shame I had to make it a little easy." The man twisted and pulled a shotgun from the locker and fired, the impact pushing Jack into the floor, his armour beginning to crack

"Jack your armour–"

"I know. . . Harley."

"You have to get up!"

Jack pushed himself up off the floor as another blast rocked his armour and pushed him back to the floor.

"Jack. . ."

"Harley, if–"

"No. I have an idea. Hold your hand over that control panel."

"Are you–"

"Now!"

Jack pushed himself from the ground and glanced behind him as the man rocked the weapon in his hands, pumping the empty cartridge from it.

"I hope it's worth it, Harley," Jack held his hand over the console and watched as a purple glow flowed from his peripheral vision, through his arm and out of his hand. His bewilderment was met with another blast from the shotgun, and he slumped back on to the ground.

The man grabbed Jack's leg and pulled him from the crumpled position he had fallen into. He pushed another cartridge from the shotgun and held the weapon almost directly in front of Jack's helmet. Jack breathed in heavily, his body screaming in pain from all the bruises and broken bones, this time he had no fight left in him. His head fell and he lay there waiting for the final shot.

"Goodbye, Jack. . ."

As the man moved to pull the trigger, the room erupted in a ball of light and Harley's voice echoed round the room, "Wait!"

The pair of fighters looked round in confusion as the room shimmered and began to take on a new form.

"What is this?"

As if to answer him, the room stabilised and began to show something new, but familiar to him. The man released the weapon from his hands in shock and walked away from Jack, towards the recreation of a moment in his life. The moment he learned the truth, or so he thought.

Chapter 24

Standing in the middle of the room, the man lowered his weapon slowly as he steadily glanced around. In his head, he could hear the scene playing out.

"Get down, kid!"

The man watched as a uniformed soldier pulled a young teenager to the floor, bullets tearing up the ground beside them. The teenager shook as they sprayed the ground close to his legs.

As the firing stopped, the soldier glanced over the small barricade, "Okay kid, listen, get out of here!"

"W-w-where?"

"Anywhere, just pick a direction and you run, do you understand me?" the soldier grabbed the thin youngster, almost touching his nose with his own, "Understand?"

The teenager nodded wildly, and the soldier let go of him.

"Okay. . . on three. One. . two. . th-"

The soldier fell back as a stream of bullets tore through their barricade and the teenager flung himself to the ground, holding his hands over his head as he screamed. His breath quickened as the sounds of plasma engines roared all around him, firing echoing across the area.

The man stood, mesmorised by the memory recreation, completely unphased by Jack who grunted as he pushed himself off the floor to take it all in himself.

The teenager carefully pulled himself off the ground and came face to face with a Hydroxii soldier, seething under their helmet as he vented the hot gas from his rifle. He grunted and waved his arm as a man, covered in dust, walked steadily up to the teenager. Confused he slid back, and the man held his hands out, "Hey, it's okay. It's over now I promise." the man smiled slightly as he stepped forward, "I'm here to take you away from this."

The teenager scrambled backwards. His hand bumped against the fallen soldier's assault rifle. As he picked it up and slung it across his body, he shook like a leaf.

"Go away!" He fired the rifle and the attention of the Hydroxii soldier turned to him as it aimed its own rifle squarely at him.

The man held out his hand, "Wait!" He turned back to the teenager, "Suppose I would be trigger happy after of all this, but, what if I showed you how to use that properly? Use it for good?"

The teenager shook as he lowered the heavy weapon.

"My name is DeMarko," the man smiled as he held out his hand.

Jack's eyes widened as he started to piece the recreation together.

The teenager whimpered as he lowered the rifle, "M-m-my name is William."

"It's nice to meet you William. Why don't you throw that aside and we'll talk?"

The man watched as the conversation ended and the

teenager, his younger self, slowly walked away.

The recreation ran on as the truth slowly came to light.

"Commander, the boy?" the Hydroxii soldier questioned.

"Set him up for Project Vanguard. I think we have our trials. And start excavating immediately," DeMarko pulled a Velcro badge from his armour and revealed an unusual emblem as he walked away. On the ground, the logo of the Global Military Task Force blew in the wind.

Jack slowly turned his attention to the centre of the room as the recreation disappeared and the dark utility room the pair had fought in was revealed again. He stared at William, who stood, unmoving.

Harley materialised on the console, "It's William, is it?" she asked.

"It's William. . . Castle."

"Will, I found this moment, deep in the archives here–"

"He talked to me about what happened. His story. He talked about the global government, how they were to blame for the death of my family, my friends. But. . . he instigated the whole thing. He brought the Hydroxii to my home," William turned to Jack and Harley, even behind a visor, the emotion was easy to sense, "He killed them for a god damn dig site?"

"Do you know what he was looking for?"

"I didn't even know they stayed. . ." William clenched his fist, his confusion changing to anger.

The room shook and debris tumbled as the entire base rocked.

"Harley?" Jack called out, pulling himself painfully to his feet.

"Jack. . . we have to go right now! Someone's detonated a plasma core. . . and the lovely mountainside. . . is a volcano!

Need I say more?"

The base shook again and the room became distinctly warmer in the few moments after the second quake.

"Time to go!" Jack shouted as he made a move for Harley.

"Wait! Give me ten seconds."

"Are you kidding me?" The room shook again, and large chunks of the ceiling began to fall. Jack watched on as Will stood, lost in the centre of the chamber.

"Jack, that dig-site he mentioned, that could be what this is all about. All this fighting, DeMarko is after something worth killing anybody for. Please. . . just a moment."

Jack moaned as he pushed off from the console and limped to Will, "Come on, we have to go."

Will turned and stared at the once enemy combatant, "Why would you help me?"

"There's more to me than you can understand. Come on, we can make things right."

Will pondered for a moment before Harley jumped back in, "Got it! They found something. . . And we have co-ordinates. Jack pull me!"

Jack stepped back and placed his hand over the console, watching as the purple aura glided up his arm, "We really need to talk about that Harley."

"Later. Viper One, we have to get to the Valkyrie right now before the lava-"

"Did she just say lava?" Dragon butted in.

"Head for the Valkyrie, me, Jack and our special guest are on route."

"Copy that!"

Jack and Will stepped out of the room as the base continued to collapse and began to follow the path back towards the others. The quakes became more frequent and suddenly the problem was literally following them as lava began to filter in between the corridors. Blocked by the river of lava, the two soldiers took a step backwards and dived through an open doorway. As they hobbled along, they were met by the large body of a Hydroxii soldier. He drew his plasma rifle and fired wildly down at them. Splitting up, the pair pressed their backs against the walls as they waited for the rifle to overheat, allowing them a chance to retreat.

"Jack, follow me we can get out through the service tunnel," Will pulled Jack's arm and ushered him to follow as the huge alien soldier walk steadily towards them. The pair ran into the large, open service area, Will sprinted through as a quake rocked the room and the concrete ceiling cracked. Jack hesitated as the chunk fell from the sky, moving forwards, Will turned and ushered him on, "Come on, we're so-" Will stepped back in surprise as an orange energy shield split the pair up, "No, no, no! Jack, behind you!"

Jack spun round and watched as the Hydroxii soldier stepped into the room and closed the large bulkhead down.

"Jack Halliday. . . You think you can escape me?"

"I certainly made a good go of it."

"Still full of that infuriating human humour. . . I can't wait to finally get my chance to kill you."

"I think you guys have been trying that a lot."

The alien soldier laughed beneath its helmet as the base shook again and the floor cracked, lava slowly oozing through it.

"Jack, we don't have time-"

"Your AI is right, human. Time has finally run out for you," the alien reached down to its hip, gripping the handle of a weapon and rotating it in its huge hands, "Do you know how many of your kind I have had the pleasure of killing, Jack? You humans cling to your weapons, rifles in hand. My people are a more resilient species." The alien activated the hilt of the weapon to reveal a slightly curved plasma blade, "How many of your kind I have slain, up close. . . the smell of fear."

"Same can be said for us, think I've got a fair Hydroxii kill count."

The alien laughed and reached for another hilt attached to its belt, "Come human, I will give you an honourable death." The alien threw the hilt at Jack who caught it, ignoring the ache now coursing through his wrist. The Hydroxii roared and lunged at Jack, who activated the alien weapon and held up his own plasma blade to deflect the opening blow. The blades met each other with a sharp bang as Jack jumped back.

"Jack you can't-"

"Harley-" Jack stepped forward to meet the attack, swinging the weapon down to the ground trying to hit the alien, who quickly twisted and knocked Jack back.

"Do you even know how to blade fight?" Harley questioned as the alien pushed forward relentlessly.

"I'm learning!" Jack stumbled backwards and fell, groaning as he landed flat on his back, the energy weapon de-activating in his hand.

"Jack!" Harley screamed as the Hydroxii brought the plasma blade down hard. Jack placed his hands over his face and braced for the impact. With his arms crossed, the blade slammed against the armour but was met with a purple spark. Opening his eyes Jack rolled away from the second hit and stumbled to his feet as he re-activated his weapon.

"Harley?"

"You're welcome. Can't do that too many times though. Remember last time?"

"I do. Won't come to that."

Weapon in hand, Jack stood waiting for the next attack. The alien moved quickly, powerfully lashing out again and again. Each attack was blocked by Jack's parry before the alien eventually got the upper hand and batted the blade away. The Hydroxii used it's free hand to grab Jack by the throat and lift him off the ground. Trying to catch his breath, Jack struggled to break free.

"Enough of this fight" the alien slammed Jack into the orange shield, the armour shimmering as the unique material sparked off it. The alien glanced down at the purple glow, "Your AI can't protect you now human!" It pulled its hand back and held the blade straight.

"No!" Harley screamed as the shield she had created flared brightly around Jack.

Jack shook as something impacted the alien's helmet. He watched as the Hydroxii slowly twisted, revealing it's scarred face. The soldier turned, Jack still squirming in its firm grasp. It bared its teeth and let out a deep growl; its glare was met with the returning stare of a human soldier. Jack glanced towards the balcony and watched as Spider lowered his sniper rifle slowly and gave the alien a typical, human finger gesture.

"Miss me?" Spider mocked as he adjusted his stance.

The Hydroxii slowly smiled through the crack in its helmet as Jack shouted out a warning, "Spider. . . Behind-"

Spider turned on his heels as a barrage of plasma fire lit up his armour. Caught out, he swung back to return the shot and found the attacker bearing down, already laying punches into him.

Jack writhed and placed his feet against the plasma shield, pushing as hard as his body would allow, throwing a fist in to the alien's chest and knocking it back briefly. It released Jack, dropping him on to his knees. Scrabbling across the floor, Jack grabbed the plasma blade and stumbled to his feet. The pair launched forward and Jack pushed himself, as hard as he could, to hit the alien again and again; but his body wasn't keeping up and the alien had a significant advantage. Kicking Jack back, the alien rotated the blade in its hands and swung its blade down hard. As the blade descended, a single shot echoed around the room and the alien's hand shattered, sending the plasma blade hilt skittering across the floor. Confused, the alien gave Jack the opportunity he needed. Using his blade, Jack lunged at the Hydroxii, who held its arms across itself and defiantly took each hit. Charging forward, the alien forced Jack back towards the outer wall. Jack swung low and caught the alien's leg causing it to stumble. Leaning forward, he grabbed its plasma pistol from its belt and fired again and again until it was empty. Throwing it aside, Jack brought the blade upwards and into the Hydroxii's open helmet before stepping back.

The alien finally fell to the floor. Exhausted, Jack dropped to his knees and placed his hands on the ground allowing the blade to roll aside, sparking against the concrete.

"Jack?"

"Harley?"

"That was pretty insane," Harley laughed, "And we still have to get out of here."

"Agreed."

"Jack!" Jack shook as a shot was fired into the control panel on the wall and the plasma shield shimmered away, "Keep going, I'll be right with you!"

"Copy that Spider. I owe you."

"Damn right you do."

Jack stumbled towards the corridor and into Will, who propped him up.

"Not going to lie, you are made of something else."

"We can talk about that later, right now we have to go. Now! Viper One, what's your status?"

"Two accounted for so far, Jack. You might want to hurry up, the place is literally disintegrating around us."

"We're moving. Had a little altercation to deal with. Keep the door open."

"Will do!"

Jack and Will continued to stumble through the base before reaching the exit. Raising the door, Will pushed Jack on as plasma fire rattled around them.

"Jack, go! I've got you, go, go!"

Jack nodded and moved himself toward the Valkyrie dropship. Met by Dragon, he fell into his teammate who manouvered him into a seat as Draco stepped out and fired at the attacking forces.

"Don't hit Will."

"Are you kidding me?" Dragon shouted.

"No. Just. . . trust me, get him onboard."

Dragon shook his head and pushed Draco out, the pair moving forward in unison through the firefight.

Finishing off the enemy forces, Dragon pulled Will back, "Jack wants you onboard. I suggest you move before I do something I'm going to seriously regret."

Will nodded and sprinted toward the dropship as the pair turned, waiting for their remaining teammate. Dragon and Draco both stood, rifles aimed at the door ready for another firefight.

"Coming through boys!" Spider stumbled into view and ushered his teammates on, "I have company. Guys, go, go!" Behind him Lorenzo sprinted past.

The pair exchanged a quick glance, "What the hell is going on here? Aren't they the bad guys?"

"Long story. Come on, we can talk back on the ship." Spider ushered everyone on and turned to fire short bursts at the remaining enemy forces.

As everyone climbed aboard, the tension on board was palpable, the rocking of the Valkyrie preparing for takeoff barely interrupting the staring competition that was ongoing.

"Everyone hold on!" Dragon shouted in the intercom as the Valkyrie jolted. Everybody shook as the dropship took off abruptly and began to move away from the base. A few plasma blasts clattered against the outer hull, but nothing that would faze the team as they exited the planet's atmosphere and headed towards the Chicago.

What a debrief they were about to undergo, Jack thought as he leaned back in the side seat, his battered body soothed by the gentle rocking of the dropship's movement.

Chapter 25

Dragon began to adjust dials and switches on the dropship's dashboard as he prepared for their landing aboard the Chicago, "This is Viper One, Chicago you ready for us?"

"Copy that Viper. Horatio here. The Chicago awaits you. We're picking up some additional FOF tags, please confirm?"

Dragon turned to face the crew behind him and sighed, "Short answer, yes. Jack made friends with some of our alter egos. Over."

"Copy that, you're free to return home, Vipers."

Horatio pushed the button off. He stepped back and placed his hand on the communication officer's shoulder. The officer stiffened up and slowly turned to the Captain, "Sir?"

"Viper One have been compromised."

"You mean–"

"Yes. Get Viper One aboard and have them head towards the briefing room. Send a security team to meet me on route, I don't think they're going to come quietly."

The communications officer pushed a button and began to issue orders under Horatio's command. Horatio removed his Captain's hat and ruffled his hair before placing the hat back on his head and shaking himself down. His orders were to eliminate the squad as a contingency plan in order to stop the truth from coming out. If Jack and the Viper One team were to relay what he assumed they now knew, the long operation, that was going on behind the government's back, would be undone. Horatio stepped out into the corridor and began to walk down towards the meeting point. He hoped that after their last engagement the team would be an easy target and he could get his end of the job done. They were so close now to their objective. He could finally see the end after all those long, painful years.

Dragon landed the Valkyrie and sighed, flicking a switch to release the dropship's ramp and allowing the, now larger, team to slowly step out on to the hangar bay of the Chicago. Immediately, a crew of technicians swarmed the dropship and began to get to work, plugging in tablets and tutting as they admired the plasma burns scattered along the interior and exterior.

Jack spun and pulled Will towards himself, "At this point, I suggest you give me your weapon."

Will paused unsure of what was happening, "Are you sure?"

"I don't want anyone to take a shot at you before you tell your story. Once we tell everyone you won't need to be armed, for a while anyway." Jack glanced to Lorenzo who stood adjusting the rifle in her hands as a number of guards squirmed at her presence, "I chose to trust you. I need you to trust me. Please?"

Jack held out his hand and Will glanced down, placing his weapon into it. He turned to follow Spider who stood at the exit door.

Lorenzo turned to face Kayleigh, whose face gave her away

entirely as she failed to hide her emotions from the woman who she knew was the reason her partner was dead, "I can only say I'm sorry, though it won't make my actions any better. You know my story. Our story. I hope you really are the alleged good guys here."

Kayleigh took the rifle form Lorenzo as she stepped away and headed for the exit with the others. She felt confused by the whole situation. Nothing at all now made sense. In one way, she had been right the entire time, on the other, she had absolutely no idea what was actually going on out in the galaxy.

As she stood thinking, Jack stepped up to her and smiled behind his helmet, "I owe you, Crow. Really."

"Hey, we got the bad guys in the end, didn't we?"

Jack turned and looked to Lorenzo and Will, "We did, but not in the way I imagined."

Kayleigh turned to face Lorenzo, "I agree. Where do we go from here?"

"Honestly, I don't know-"

"We find out where the hell the bad guys are!" Harley butted in, loudly.

"Okay," Jack laughed, placing his hands against his chest, "But first a medic, please. I can barely move."

"I'll get one to you on route for the most tense debrief of your life, Jack. We did right, you did right. Those people, they've been lied to for so long."

"I know. Let's get their story."

Jack and Kayleigh moved back to the two teams and Jack stepped forward to take the lead, the others followed unquestioningly behind him.

Walking down the long winding corridors, the crew of the Chicago moved aside, in a mixture of fear and confusion. Every single one muttered and whispered as they stepped through the huge ship. As they teams turned a corner, Horatio and his security team met them.

"Captain Horatio, we we're just–"

"Jack Halliday, you and your team are under arrest for treason. Do not attempt to resist or we will use deadly force."

"Excuse me–" Spider stepped forward, only to be met by five security officers, who raised their assault rifles in his direction.

"I will not ask again. Now. Weapons down!"

Jack held out his arms and stepped forward, the officers changing position to aim at him, "I get it, it's a bit weird right now but. . . something is wrong. These enemy combatants are more like slave labour, they're on our side. Captain if you just–"

Horatio pulled his sidearm and fired it towards Jack's foot. Jack stopped abruptly and stared at the Captain, "I will not ask again. Weapons–"

"Captain Horatio, enemy forces just–" the radio message was cut off abruptly as the lights flickered and the ship's power waned.

Horatio stumbled back, reaching for his intercom in his ear, "Repeat–"

Harley spoke up in Jack's helmet, her voice panic-stricken, "Jack, two Hydroxii capital ships just–"

As Harley tried to warn them, an explosion rocked the ship, a second knocking everybody back. Jack groaned on the floor and turned his attention forwards; his shock turned to fear as the shape of a Hydroxii raiding ship aggressively burrowed its way ahead of him.

Horatio stumbled back and fumbled with his ear piece, "Battle stations! Return fire!"

Horatio opened fire as the raiding unit in front of him stepped out of their vessel, the ship's outer hull barging into the tight corridor, banging loudly against the interior. The boarding forces opened fire immediately and Horatio's security forces were cut down mercilessly. Horatio slid back, slamming his hand against the panel closing and locking the door ahead of him. The plasma rattled across it for a moment before attention was turned to the others.

Horatio panted loudly before pushing himself quickly off the ground, and pushing his hand against his earpiece, "Get us out of here!"

"Sir, engines are down, we're in the water."

Horatio slowly pulled his hand down his face and kicked the inner panel, screaming before pushing to a ship-wide channel, "Do not let the Vipers survive. Treat them like the Hydroxii."

Jack slid to the ground and watched as Lorenzo stepped up to Kayleigh, pulling the sidearm from her belt and returned fire. The expanded Viper team quickly drew their weapons and returned fire, quickly eliminating the boarding party.

Jack pushed himself off the floor and stepped up to the fallen Hydroxii raiders, picking a blood-covered plasma rifle from the ground. He turned and held his arms out wide, "What the hell is going on?"

"Right now, we're being torn to pieces by two Hydroxii capital ships, Jack."

"I gathered, but why did Horatio just try to have us arrested for treason?"

Spider stepped forward and picked up another plasma rifle, throwing it to Will who pushed it into his shoulder and nodded, "Whatever the hell is going on, I think we need to get off this floating coffin."

"Harley?" Jack turned as he asked the question.

"On it, Jack. Our only option is back-" As Harley explained her plan, the ship rocked violently and a siren wailed in the background.

Jack turned back to his team. The door quickly shut behind them and Kayleigh stepped up to it, slamming her fist against the metal, "Back to the hangar."

"Harley get us the fastest route there. Everyone, eyes up, the Hydroxii are the main targets."

"But what about the crew?" Spider asked, "They were two seconds from putting a shot on us?"

"Return fire only if they fire first. We assume everyone is a hostile if armed and move forward. Do. Not. Stop." Jack pushed the rifle into his shoulder, winced as the armour rubbed against a very obvious bruise beneath his suit. He wondered just how battered he really was, but he had no chance to stop, not yet.

Jack led the Viper team onwards, rocking from side to side as the ship was pummelled by the attacking forces. He had never experienced ship to ship combat, he was a ground soldier. Here, he was a few moments from being blasted into space and being left to the void. He was uncomfortable but had to press forward. As he spun round a junction in the corridor, he ducked as plasma fire splattered across his armour and the interior panelling. The team turned in response and returned fire. Jack backed up against a control panel, watching as Kayleigh loaded her sidearm and returned fire too. Her commitment was quite something, he wondered if anything was going to faze her.

Kayleigh pinned herself to the wall and took a deep breath as she dropped another empty magazine from her sidearm.

Pushing her last magazine into her weapon, she moved to return fire as the ship rocked again and the team scattered, as an explosion engulfed the corridor and another squad of Hydroxii raiders stepped onto the ship.

"Jack!" Kayleigh shouted as he twisted to face his attacker.

The raider batted the already damaged soldier aside and pulled a plasma blade from its belt.

Kayleigh fired, gaining the alien's attention. It turned to face her, raising its arm to activate a round arm plasma shield which deflected the shots. As her sidearm clicked empty, she grimaced as the alien lowered its arm and moved toward her. Kayleigh lowered herself down to the ground and curled into a ball, braced for the attack. A body stepped in front of her, and blue plasma flared all around, and the raider slumped to the ground. She pushed herself up and came face to face with Lorenzo; the pair stared at each other briefly before Lorenzo handed her a plasma rifle. Kayleigh glanced from the rifle back to the Spaniard, the person who, up till now, was her worst enemy; now she was the one saving her. Kayleigh nodded at her and Lorenzo returned the gesture and the pair turned back to the team who had finished the fight.

"Jack, we're sitting ducks here," Kayleigh shouted as she slumped against the wall.

"I know, I know. Harley, how much further?"

"Not far, if we keep following this corridor we should reach the hangar. There are only a handful of Valkyries left and then we just have to avoid the anti-air plasma batteries lining-"

"I get it, it's going to be tight. Vipers, let's move before we get left on this ship," Jack turned to his team as the rear door opened and four crew members stumbled in. Jack pushed Spider's assault rifle aside as he moved to take a shot, ushering the crew onwards.

"Thank you!" the tail crew member called out as they sprinted through.

"Why did you let them go?" Lorenzo asked standing beside him.

"They were unarmed, scared; they weren't a threat. Come on we should go," Jack stepped past Lorenzo and the Viper team followed him through the smoke and fire now filling the ship.

The team waded through the chaos and eventually reached their target. As they landed at the security chamber, linking the hangar to the hangar bay, Horatio and several security officers stepped between them.

"You can't survive this, Jack?"

"What is your problem? A decorated Captain, what is this worth to you?"

"Everything. You have no idea what is being created in the background, the lives taken, fuel to benefit humanity's next step."

"You're insane," Jack called as he aimed his rifle between the surrounding officers.

"No Jack, I'm going to be a hero."

Dragon and Draco shuffled closer together, staring at each other; they knew there was only one way Viper One was going to survive this fight.

Dragon turned to Jack and pulled him close, "Jack you need to get everyone on to that Valkyrie."

"I'm aware, Dragon."

Dragon bumped Draco who gave Jack and thumbs up, "We have a plan Jack, just move. We got you."

Jack lowered his rifle a little, understanding what they

were getting at. Nodding, he pushed Kayleigh through the security door and the others darted behind them in the chaos. Dragon slammed his hand against the control panel and Draco returned fire, knocking down several officers in quick succession. Spider spun to move back for his two teammates, pushing against Will and Lorenzo who held him back.

"No!"

Dragon and Draco stood defiantly, back-to-back as they took each hit, their bodies shaking; both committed to their final mission to kept on fighting.

"Come on, we have to go Spider!"

"I'm not-"

"Yes, you are, we are, for them, come on!"

Jack moved with the others to the final Valkyrie, watching as Lorenzo jumped into the pilot's seat and prepared the dropship for takeoff. Spider sprinted from the security door, landing on the dropship as Lorenzo raised the ramp. He stood and watched as Dragon and Draco finally succumbed and the ramp sealed the ship ready for space flight.

Lorenzo dropped the Valkyrie out of the hangar bay and spun it directly underneath the Chicago's battered hull as the Hydroxii ships continued to fire on the single human ship.

"Hold on to something!" Lorenzo sharply jolted the dropship away from the safety of the Chicago and strafed along the alien ship's hull, grazing its weaponry.

"Bit close Lorenzo!" Will called out from the co-pilot's seat.

"You try escaping two capital ships!"

As Lorenzo flew close to the enemy ship, Harley buzzed into the dropship's intercom, "Guys, there's a single ship exiting the planet's atmosphere!"

"But how? The base was destroyed." Jack pulled himself

forward and leaned against the pilots' seats, watching as a ship left the planet's atmosphere, "Who is it?"

"I can't. . . wait. It can't be!"

Jack shook as the dropship rocked from a hit from one of the enemy ship's plasma batteries, "Who is it Harley?"

"The FOF tag is Falaney's."

Jack watched as the escaping ship disappeared into hyperspace, knowing they had to follow. The endgame was coming, and they had to stop Falaney before it was too late. Whatever he had planned, they couldn't let him complete his mission, "Harley ping those coordinates, Lorenzo follow that ship!"

"Copy, hang on!" Lorenzo rocked the dropship as she aimed away from those of the Hydroxii. It shuddered as the aliens' weapons battered it, forcing her to fly in their chosen direction. Suddenly, Lorenzo flew the dropship between the two attacking ships and pushed it forwards. Jolting it away from the capital ship, Lorenzo pushed a lever on the dashboard and the space around them stretched as the ship escaped the deathly battlefield.

Horatio fell to his knees as the Hydroxii ship commander circled him, firing its plasma rifle at the struggling officer's body.

"I did everything he asked of me!"

"And he is grateful, human ship master, but this is where your value ends." The ship master turned and faced the battered human captain and handed its rifle to its ally soldier, "Besides, you allowed the humans to escape."

"Unfair, don't you think?"

"I don't care much for fair. Goodbye Horatio."

Horatio stumbled as the ship master drew its plasma blade

and cut him down, his body slumping to the ground.

"Return to your ships," the ship master turned back to his crew, "Now we wait for our victory to be assured."

Chapter 26

Everybody jolted forwards as the dropship exited hyperspace and the team were able to move around freely.

Jack stepped forward and peered out of the front window, "Harley? Where are we exactly?"

"I don't know, Jack. I don't have much data on this part of the galaxy. GMTF data suggests there is nothing of value here. No planets with viable conditions. . ."

"So, why did a mad man just fly halfway across the galaxy?"

"Wait," Harley paused for a moment, "There's something coming up. Let me magnify." The window of the ship revealed a secondary screen, on it was a magnified image of a large moon. As the team moved slowly towards it, the moon revealed a space station.

"Is that a station?"

"Looks like it but. . . it isn't human."

Kayleigh pushed her way to the front and peered at the image, "So what is it? Hydroxii?"

Mjuyr stepped behind the team as they all squeezed in to take a look, "It isn't anything I've seen before."

"I've no idea what I'm looking at here, but it feels weirdly familiar."

"Whatever it is, Falaney is there, and we need to put a stop to the lunatic. Everyone ready up, we're taking him down, today." Jack hobbled backwards and pulled a plasma rifle from the overhead locker, painfully pushing it over his back as he allowed the magnet on his armour to grip the alien weapon, "Everyone grab whatever we have left. I have a feeling we're going to need it. Lorenzo get us inside that station, I figure he knows we're coming so carefully does it, please."

Lorenzo nodded and tilted the Valkyrie toward the space station, which clung close to the orbit of the moon. She turned to Will who sat in the co-pilot seat and the pair exchanged glances, "What do you think we'll find down there?"

Will turned away, shaking his head, "Answers, I hope."

Lorenzo turned back, adjusting the controls and the ship moved steadily through space.

Jack took a seat beside Kayleigh and nudged her with his elbow, "How are you holding up?"

"Surprisingly well, despite being in a number of very close-quarters firefights." She turned to Jack, eyeing him up, "What about you?"

"I'm okay."

"Like hell you are Jack, your vital signs are all over the place," Harley shouted, "You really need to stop."

"I can't, not till we finish Falaney."

"Your stubbornness will be the death of you, you know that right?"

Jack laughed, "I know but you're here to keep me upright."

"The armour is literally acting like a crutch. If you remove it. . . I'm worried what'll happen to you."

"I didn't take you as the emotional type, Harley."

"I'm just worried, okay?" Harley sighed as Jack adjusted

himself in the seat. She wasn't wrong, Jack's body was battered and broken and even he didn't know how he was still going, "Let's finish this then."

Lorenzo adjusted the controls as the dropship entered an empty hangar bay. Everyone hovered uncomfortably inside as they waited for what would come next. As they landed, nothing happened. No attack, no defensive move. Nothing. Lorenzo knocked the panel beside her and lowered the ramp. Pulling her sidearm from her hip she held her weapon high and followed the team out.

The station became dark as the hangar door closed behind them, allowing the room to create its own atmosphere. One by one, everybody activated their flashlights and lit up the bay, the vastness engulfing the light that they shone as they slowly looked around.

Jack wandered towards a door and brushed the dust from its control panel, "Harley can you get us in?"

"One sec, reach out for me."

Jack held out his hand and watched as his hand glowed, "You still haven't explained to me what this is."

"Honestly, I don't know. Just a few things have happened, you know? I'm a really cool computer," Harley replied as the door opened to reveal a corridor. Jack held his plasma rifle high and stepped in, scanning each direction as he turned. Satisfied they were safe, Jack ushered the team to follow. As he led them inside, everyone found themselves admiring the unique architecture of the station. The build was similar to that of any species, but the markings were something nobody had encountered before.

"This is something else, is it not?" Kayleigh called out as

she brushed her hand along the panelling of the corridor, "If it isn't human or Hydroxii, then is it a species we've never met?"

"Possibly, I mean, space is pretty big by definition. Mjuyr anything here you recognise?"

Mjuyr ran his hand along a control panel and shook his head, "No. There is a story among the Hydroxii of a race who helped the first Hydroxii to fly, but it's nothing but a younglings' story."

"Maybe we are about to meet the makers, as it were."

As they wandered through the barren station, it became clear that there was to be no conflict. The station was active, but there was no living being, no signs of fighting, not even a broken panel.

"Why would a highly advanced race abandon something like this?" Kayleigh turned and watched as Jack wandered past a control panel, it's screen reacting briefly to his presence, "Hey Jack, back up a second for me."

Jack turned and lowered his weapon, "What's up?"

"Just run your hand along that panel for me."

"Why?" Jack hesitated.

"Just. . . humour me," Kayleigh insisted as she pointed to the panel. Jack stepped up to it and held out his hand. As he did so, it briefly flickered to life before activating.

"Why is it reacting to me?" Jack asked, surprised.

"I don't think it's reacting to you, Jack. Look." Kayleigh pointed back to the panel as it seemed to radiate the same gentle purple glow that Harley gave off when she was interacting with technology.

"Harley?"

"Hey, I don't know why I can do that," Harley replied sharply as the door opened to reveal another room.

Peering inside, Jack and Kayleigh walked in and discovered, what looked like, a lab. Slowly everyone joined them and began to search the newly discovered room.

Spider reached what appeared to be a water tank and brushed the thick layer of dust from its surface. Inside hovered a suit of armour, identical to the one that attacked them back at Kyreel. He moved back with his rifle raised and prepared to shoot, but nothing happened. Stepping back to the glass, he discovered it was still dormant, "Hey guys, I think I've found where our robot friend from Kyreel came from."

Everyone turned towards Spider as he wiped away the layers of dust.

"Wow, is this some kind of weapons facility?"

"No, Detective Crow, this is far more than that."

Everyone twisted round in the direction of the voice in the corner. A section of the room lowered to reveal a larger area, and there was Falaney. They all brought their weapons forward and aimed towards him. He stood alone, but with a smug defiance in his stance.

"You know what, Halliday, I'm glad you get to see the grand finale," he smiled and stepped forwards fearlessly.

"Sorry to burst your ego bubble, Falaney, but that's not going to happen," Jack also took a step but found a clear energy barrier between him and his target.

"Oh Jack, you really have no idea, do you?" Falaney held his arms wide and laughed, "You know. . . I think you should be thanking me for your job."

"Excuse me?"

"Your job, your position as team leader of the black ops squad known as Viper One. Do you want to know why?"

"Enlighten me."

"I killed their previous leader."

Spider came forward and stood beside Jack, "You bastard!" he slammed his fist against the barrier.

Falaney laughed as the shield rippled, "Yes, poor Byson stood in your position once. He thought he had me caught but you should have heard him as I watched him die. The heat from those plasma rifles. . ."

"Lower this shield, you monster, I'm going to kill you myself," Spider seethed.

Falaney stepped forward still smiling, "Though I admit, I was impressed he knew exactly who I really was. Clearly he was good at his job. You see, you all know me as the GIC operative, Falaney but. . . truth is, my name is Julian DeMarko."

Jack hesitated before replying, "You're the lunatic who gave away the position of everyone in the Foundry. You murdered them all."

"Yes Jack! Now you know who you're dealing with, a real-life monster! I'm almost disappointed how little you actually understand about the whole situation. I thought you might be the one to uncover the truth, but, in reality, your new police friend was the one who fell into that hole. Or was it. . . Greg who fell into it?"

Kayleigh stepped forward, her fist clenched as she held back from showering DeMarko with a barrage of insults, "What exactly is this grand plan DeMarko? I could never understand the need for a highly toxic drug to be on the streets? What were you doing? Kidnapping and experimenting on human beings?"

"Exactly that, Crow. I needed a steady stream of test subjects and while none were viable in Atlanta. Venom kindly struck gold in Kyreel. You see. . ." DeMarko stepped back to a workbench and pulled a cylindrical object from within it, showing it to the team, "Let me demonstrate the culmination of years of work, Vipers."

DeMarko clicked the object to reveal a large needle and injected it into himself. He let out a scream as he fell to the ground, writhing in pain. The team stood in confusion unsure what to do. DeMarko's body let out a horrific snapping sound as his body suddenly vapourised and a blue mist replaced it. The mist moved steadily below the surface of the room, and everything went silent.

Everybody turned to each other as they all considered what to do, what to say. As they stood feeling lost, the floor beneath where DeMarko fell opened up and a large suit of armour rose from it. The shield separating the two rooms shimmered and disappeared and the Viper team adjusted their aim. The suit activated as a blue glow flowed round it.

"You see Vipers, this station was once the home of a powerful race of aliens called the Lombardi. They were brilliant, but they had an enemy. Much like humans and Hydroxii, they fought against a race of god–like aliens called the Lessai. They were much like us, ignorant and claiming to be the side of good in a good versus evil war. They had discovered how to go beyond a physical form, so the Lombardi needed to devise a way to do the same, but they needed a body. They were so close to matching the Lessai until the war got the better of them. But now. . . " DeMarko's new body rose from the ground and levitated as he held out his arms, "You have provided me with the means to finish their work!" DeMarko held out his hand and pulled Jack forward.

"Jack!" Kayleigh shouted as everyone stepped into the large

room.

"Enough of this!" Spider called as he lifted his rifle, firing at DeMarko who, with his free hand, caught the bullets in midair. Releasing his grip, he dropped them to the ground and pulled the weapon from Spider's hands.

"You have no idea the power I now possess. Once I get the final piece to the puzzle, nobody will be able to stop me!"

Spider watched in disbelief as the assault rifle dismantled in the air, every part of it crashing to the ground and lying scattered in front of him.

"Now Jack, let's carry on the story, shall we?"

Jack tried to move but felt an invisible force holding him in place as he levitated off the ground, "Harley, what's happening?"

"I have no idea, I've never–" Harley stopped suddenly as Jack's armour began to glow.

"Harley!"

"You see, Jack, the Lessai sacrificed themselves to stop the Lombardi but left someone behind to ensure that their legacy was never repeated. Fast forward a millennia, and old General Kato stumbled upon an ancient artefact. Do you know what he found? Your friend Harley. What you don't know is that she isn't as simple as an artificial intelligence, no, when they discovered her, they feared her. So, they transferred her to something as primitive as a data chip and dubbed her an AI. Kato didn't understand then that she's the last of the ancient Lessai, but he knew she could not be trusted."

"So what happens now DeMarko, you're all god–like, I get it, but what's the end game here?"

"The endgame is Harley," DeMarko pulled, and everyone watched on as Jack's body began to glow purple. Jack's eyes widened as he watched Harley dragged from his body, her body appearing, manifested in her usual aura, but something was very different.

"Goodbye Jack, it was lovely to meet you," DeMarko mocked as he and Harley disappeared. Jack dropped to the ground and groaned as Kayleigh and Spider ran to his aid.

"Jack are you okay?" Kayleigh asked pulling Jack forwards.

"Been better. Where's DeMarko?"

"I don't know-"

Everyone turned as the tubes housing the alien armour popped and the armour roared to life, moving swiftly towards them. Lorenzo and Will turned, firing without hesitation as the group of combat armour moved towards them. Spider pulled his rifle from his back and rose to his feet, firing toward the approaching enemy as Mjuyr stepped into the group and joined in. Kayleigh ducked as the crossfire moved around them and the Vipers were caught in a violent firefight. Jack shuffled on to his back, moving from side to side, trying to assess the situation, watching on as everyone was becoming divided as each member of the team moved to help the other. The armour they fought against was moving in unison against them. In Jack's visor, a brief strip of purple flashed across and red indicators on his cracked HUD issued an objective for him: *Destroy.*

"Harley. . ." Jack urged himself from the floor and pulled the sidearm from Kayleigh's belt, firing the weapon and knocking one of the living armour sets to the side, "Vipers. . . new mission. Spider, take Mjuyr and Will move to this position."

Spider spun backwards briefly, "And do what?"

"You'll know when you get there. I think Harley's trying to tell us something."

Spider threw his rifle at the approaching armour, knocking it off balance, before releasing his sidearm and firing rapidly into it, knocking it down, "I hope you're right, Jack."

"As do I. Now go!"

"What are we doing Jack?" Kayleigh asked puzzled, as she hunched closer.

"Trying to stop DeMarko. I think Harley's given us a lifeline."

"But how, she's - I don't even know anymore?"

"Me neither, but she hasn't let me down yet. Come on Lorenzo, on me, let's go!"

Lorenzo nodded and the trio moved out of the room firing wildly at the remaining armour, no longer retaliating but moving with haste to their objective. Jack barely had a moment to think about what they had all just learned. Whatever was going on behind the scenes, Jack knew he had to act now.

Chapter 27

Spider led the way as the three of them finally seemed to have moved away from the attacking armour. He was thankful that it wasn't as impervious as the last lot, or they would all have been in trouble. Spider reached the objective that Jack had shared via their HUD and slammed his fist into the control panel, releasing the door lock. The three of them swept into the room and Spider stepped towards, what looked like, an energy source.

"Jack found their ping. I'm taking it this needs destroying?"

"Whatever it is, yes. There are two on my HUD, they must have something to do with shutting down the station or stopping DeMarko, I don't know but we don't have time to wonder."

"Copy that Jack!" Spider raised his weapon and fired only to find another suit of armour directly ahead of him. Stepping side, he dodged the armour's large arm and swung round it, firing at its back. The armour reacted angrily, its arm glowed blue before releasing an energy blast, knocking Spider heavily to the ground.

Mjuyr and Will both switched their aim to the armour, their bullets rattling against it. Turning to face them, the armour screamed and moved forwards with incredible speed, pinning Will to the outer wall. It fired up its cannon again and it shone brightly between itself and Will. Mjuyr sprinted for the armour, firing his plasma rifle as bullets ricocheted off it. Off guard, the armour turned, allowing Will a chance to fire his own weapon.

Spider twisted back to the energy source cycling calmly behind him and then turned to the armour as it fired another energy blast at Will, "Oi, bolts for brains!" The armour paused and faced Spider who held out his arms wide, "Think you can hit me from there, you huge, hulking bastard?"

Accepting the challenge, the armour batted Mjuyr aside and powered up its weapon, firing towards Spider. Spider dived quickly to the ground as the energy blast splintered through the air and landed a direct hit on the power source. In a mix of twisted metal and electricity crackling, the power source snapped and released a violent energy burst, piercing the armour, lighting it up as it screamed. The power source quickly dissipated, and the armour dropped to the floor.

Spider shuffled forwards and stared through the large hole in its chest. Peering inside the machine, the blue liquid had just about burnt out, but a few drops escaped the large, open wound.

"Jack. . . Job done," Spider slumped down and laid on his back, letting out a sigh, "How's it going for you?"

Jack rolled across the floor and fired his sidearm as the armour side-stepped the arena floor, firing its energy weapon repeatedly towards him, "Oh, it's going fantastic, you know?"

"Gimme a sec, we're on our way to you."

"Hurry up!" Jack jumped back as the armour slammed its

large arm down towards him, leaving an imprint in the station floor. Lifting up its arm, the armour knocked Jack flying across the room. He landed with a thud against the outer wall and sank down hard against the floor. Jack groaned as he tried to pull himself up but slumped back down again. He moved again as the armour grabbed Kayleigh, she let out a scream as the monster pushed her to the floor and began to squeeze the life from her.

"Kayleigh, no!" Jack used every ounce of his strength to push himself off the ground, picking up his sidearm and firing wildly at the armour.

Lorenzo knocked back the second enemy armour and turned to watch Jack stumbling towards Kayleigh. Firing at the armour's head, the chance to run came and Lorenzo took it. She sprinted towards them and threw down her weapon as she slid across the ground and placed her arm against Kayleigh and activated her teleporter.

Jack watched as the trio disappeared before him, "Lorenzo?"

Jack lowered his weapon and turned as they rematerialised. Lorenzo pulled Kayleigh back, away from the armour. The armour screamed and Jack sighed as he watched it burn brightly against the power source before it slumped to the ground, melted in half.

Everyone turned as Spider and the others stumbled into the room, "Damn, missed the fun."

The station shook and everyone stumbled.

"Agreed, Spider," DeMarko appeared within the room and the Viper team fired in unison. DeMarko stopped every bullet and energy blast, pushing them aside, "It's time we finish this, Vipers."

DeMarko turned as he hovered in midair and twisted his

hand. With ease, the destroyed power source twisted and pulled itself aside to reveal Harley trapped inside a beam of energy.

"Jack! Run! I can't-" Harley screamed as DeMarko twisted his hand again and the energy beam intensified.

"I'm going to strip her of her power and when I'm done I'm going to finish this! But for now. . . " DeMarko pulled his hand back and knocked the Vipers aside. As they fumbled on the ground, he continued to play god with them, throwing each of them around like ragdolls. They stretched for their weapons, but DeMarko's powers were inhuman, and they were no match for him at all.

Having had enough of toying with them, DeMarko used his power to pull Jack from the ground towards him, "I'm going to take great joy in killing you, Viper. My pleasure will be far greater than it was when I killed that fool, Byson. I hope it was all worth it." DeMarko closed his fist and Jack's body began to tighten and the armour began to whine.

The other Vipers slumped and could only watch as DeMarko slowly crushed Jack. Kayleigh pushed herself forward and sprinted for one of the weapons, but DeMarko spotted her and pinned her against the outer wall as she screamed in pain.

"Interesting Jack, we have a dilemma. You or the detective. . . who dies first?"

Harley moved forward but was kept back by the force holding her in place. She watched in dismay as Jack and Kayleigh were tortured. Jack's armour was beginning to crack, and she could sense his life was slowly diminishing, "No, no, no. . ." she whispered to herself as she struggled to get free.

Jack's voice echoed nearby as if she still had a link to the communications system built into his helmet, she listened to his dwindling breath.

"Harley. . ."

"Save your dying breath, soldier," DeMarko released Kayleigh and gave Jack his full attention, his armour finally cracking.

Jack screamed down the intercom for all to hear as Kayleigh shook desperately trying to break free. Finally the armour gave way. Harley closed her eyes, almost for the first time, and screamed, releasing a blast of energy which dissipated whatever held her in her prison. Harley hovered toward DeMarko who dropped Jack as Kayleigh stumbled over to him and began to hold him up.

"DeMarko. . . "

DeMarko turned, even in his new, more powerful body, Harley could sense the fear coursing through him, "No. . . I am the future!" DeMarko moved his arm forward, but Harley held out her own.

"Enough. . ." Harley's hand glowed in front of her, and she released a beam of energy, piercing DeMarko's once impenetrable armour. The militia General screamed as the energy beam tore through it.

Releasing his armour from her grip, Harley gently glided to the ground and leant beside Jack and Kayleigh. She placed her hand on Jack's chest, "Come on Major, one last job to do." She disappeared and her purple glow radiated softly around Jack, "Just one last job. Get off this damned station."

"I hear you, Harley, but. . . I-"

"We can talk later if we survive, you have to get up. Come on, I did the muscle work!"

The station shook and groaned as it began to break apart around them. Spider stepped up to Jack and offered his hand.

Jack took it and groaned as he was pulled to his feet, "Spider, you guys head on ahead and prepare the Valkyrie, I'll be right behind you."

"Sir?"

"Really?" Jack laughed, "It only took a near death experience to get a 'sir' from you?"

Spider laughed and shook his head, giving Jack half a salute, "Think you deserved that one. Come on, let's move out."

They headed down the corridor.

Kayleigh turned and stepped back toward Jack who was staring at DeMarko's armoured remains, "Come on, Jack, it's over. Here, give me your arm."

Kayleigh shuffled under Jack's arm and propped the battered soldier up as best she could. Jack winced as the pair carefully moved after the rest of the team. Wandering down the corridor, Kayleigh glanced at the rooms as she passed and wondered just what they were about to watch be destroyed, the history lining the station could have been quite something. What could they have learned? A falling ceiling beam gave her that answer.

As they entered the final corridor run before the hangar, Spider buzzed in through the team's intercom, "Lifeboat ready, Jack, let's go!"

"Almost there!" As Jack replied, the flooring beneath them groaned loudly and the panelling making up their floor adjusted unevenly. The pair stopped as it became unsafe, "Damn it! Spider, go, you have to go now!"

"Jack, we're not leaving you."

"That's an order!" Jack and Kayleigh separated as an explosion ripped the flooring beneath them apart and Kayleigh stumbled forward, "Kayleigh!"

Jack watched as the flooring collapsed beneath Kayleigh and

she rocked backwards. Jack moved forwards, sliding across the ground to grab Kayleigh's hand as he pulled himself closer to the edge. Beneath Kayleigh was a vast drop and without any form of protection, the drop would be fatal.

"Kayleigh, hang on!" Jack tried to move his free hand forwards, but the pain of suspending her was taking a toll on his body.

Kayleigh frantically tried to flail her body against anything to hold her up, just for a moment, but everything around her dismantled and she turned to Jack as her hand began to slip, "Jack!" Kayleigh screamed as Jack lost grip and watched as she fell.

Everything went into slow motion and Jack felt sick to his stomach as he watched her fall, the fear in her face filling his vision. He closed his eyes and turned away, unable to watch her die. Pushing himself back, he propped himself against the corridor wall. As the emotion and defeat set in, a voice interrupted.

"Someone call for a lifeboat?"

Jack rushed forwards and watched in surprise as the Valkyrie dropship hovered in between the broken station. Kayleigh closed her eyes and laughed as she rolled over and slid down the rear tail.

Lorenzo held out her hand and pulled the officer inside, "Nice theatrics."

Kayleigh laughed and collapsed into the free seat, running her hands through her hair.

Spider adjusted the dropship and twisted his aim, "Duck, Jack!"

Jack ducked as Spider fired a short burst of gunfire, shredding the broken flooring enough for him to rotate the dropship and allow Jack safe entry. Jack stepped towards the dropship with a feeling of relief.

Harley buzzed into the team's intercom with a warning, "Guys, we have a problem."

"What can be more of a problem than a space station ripping itself apart, Harley?" Spider shouted in response.

"That's just it, something is trying to stop that from happening."

Jack rocked on his feet and held his hand against the station's outer wall, "Are you telling me this isn't over?"

"Jack, there's an override in place, something in the station has triggered a program. The station is activating a failsafe."

"Elaborate faster, Harley!"

"Those suits of armour. . . they are angry Lombardi, Jack. If this failsafe re-engages-"

Jack turned and watched as two suits of armour screamed into position behind him, "They will ALL be free. We have to destroy the source. Jack or DeMarko will win posthumously."

"Damn it. Spider-"

"On it, one sec," The dropship revolved, and Spider fired up the cannons, ripping apart the enemy armour pair as he rotated it back, "So what's the plan?"

Jack shook his head and laughed, "A one way trip. Throw me a rifle. . ."

"Sir?"

"A rifle. Anything. I'll go."

"Jack, you can barely walk," Harley replied with fear in her voice.

"Are you offering to go?"

"I don't. . . really understand what I am?"

"Then I'm going."

"Then I'm going too."

"Lorenzo. . ." Jack held out his arms and ushered with his hand, "That rifle."

Lorenzo leaned down and threw a plasma rifle towards Jack, who caught it and spun it in his hands, "Jack, wait."

Jack turned and caught an object in his hand. Pulling his hand down, Jack realised he had been thrown Lorenzo's personal teleportation device and he looked back to her.

"Two-way trip. Survive."

Jack nodded and pushed the object on to his utility belt, stuffing the rifle into his shoulders as he moved back inside the station.

Spider pushed the control panel and lifted the access ramp as Kayleigh watched through the gap and held on to the side of the dropship. What was he trying to prove? He had nothing to prove. Why was he being the hero here?

Jack threw the rifle up and fired repeatedly at the armour as it roared towards him. It fell with relative ease, the variations that pursued him were not as protected as the others had been. Was this a facility to create different kinds of armoured cores for the Lombardi? Jack pondered briefly to himself before turning to fire another barrage of plasma at another armoured enemy. Jack fell into the side of the wall and stumbled down the corridor.

"Jack, your vitals are-"

"Paint these targets, Harley," Jack pushed off from the wall and continued to fire sporadically.

Harley paused before she replied, she could sense his body was becoming completely fatigued. There was no way he could sustain any more fighting. Jack was thrown aside as a large, armoured enemy groaned into the battle. Jack fired at it, but it threw aside his weapon and slammed him into the wall.

Jack groaned but couldn't bring his arms higher to fight back. His body was done, he was done, "Harley. . . I'm sorry."

"Jack? Jack, no!" Harley shouted as the armour pushed Jack into the wall. Harley hesitated as she processed what she was, how she could fight back. As she thought a beam from the ceiling fell and landed firmly on the armour, crushing its head into its body.

Jack slumped down and turned his head, just a few feet away sat a terminal, "Is that it?"

"It is! Now get up!"

Jack leaned but his body weakened, and Harley shouted again, "Jack? Come on!"

"I. . ." Jack slumped to the ground and Harley paused.

"J-Jack?" Harley moved from Jack's armour and knelt beside him, "Jack, come on, we're nearly. . . done" She hovered her hand over his body, she could feel his life fading from him. She turned to the plasma rifle, picking it up. She wrapped her fingers round it and turned to her hands. She held her hand outstretched, but this time nothing happened. The station shook and she adjusted her stance, turning to Jack and smiling before turning back to the control. As she faced the panel, several enemies materialised and roared in front of her. Harley smiled, pulling the trigger of the physical weapon and allowing it to rattle in her hands.

Chapter 28

Kayleigh pushed open the door and stepped out onto the balcony, allowing the wind to cool her face as her ponytail blew gently in the breeze. She placed her arms on the guardrail and looked out across the vast space. Ahead of her, a crew of hundreds of workers toiled away on the shell of a large, spacefaring ship. Even the sound from the shipyard barely reached her at her vantage point and she smiled, remembering her first foray into space. She reached down to her pocket and pulled out a police badge. Kayleigh carefully spun it as she stared at the object.

"Well Greg, case closed. We did it, and even better we beat Falaney; that's a whole other story but. . ." Kayleigh laughed and shook her head as she turned to the facility behind her, finding a figure standing in the doorway, "We still won. Rest easy, friend." Kayleigh turned back to the edge of the guardrail and placed the ACPD badge against the column and lowered her head. After a moment, the sound of footsteps slowly made their way towards her.

"So, what do you think of her?"

The man placed his hand on the guardrail and stood beside her.

"She's alright. What's she called?"

"Atlanta."

"Fitting," Kayleigh faced the man and stood back from the guardrail.

"It is. I think Greg would have agreed." The man's arm was slung in a cast, his body wraps hidden only partially by the military fatigues he was dressed in.

"I think so too. So tell me, did you take up Kato's invitation?"

"I did, Jack. Under someone's kind recommendation, I am officially a woman of the intelligence division."

"And well-deserved, Flight Officer Crow!"

Kayleigh watched as Harley materialised in a physical form, "Still can't get used to you. . . being a physical presence."

Harley held out her arms and laughed, "Me neither. Haven't quite got that feeling of being yet."

"Well, you have Jack for help I'm sure, he'll need it too!"

Jack smiled and turned to the shipyard, "And then you'll be out in the galaxy, leading your own team too, I hear."

"I will. But that's above your pay grade, Viper," Kayleigh laughed as she watched the Atlanta being built, "Can I call on you for a lift sometime?"

"Ring me," Jack held his hand to his ear like a phone.

"Yeah, we have a lot to do!"

Kayleigh nodded and Jack saluted her. As she watched Jack and Harley wander away, she shouted, "Jack!"

Jack turned and smiled, "Yeah?"

"Thank you for everything."

Jack smiled and turned, giving Kayleigh a wave. The pair stepped off the roof, leaving her all on her own again. Kayleigh smiled and wondered just what was going to happen next. What was there still for her to discover?

About the Author

Chris Pease is a Cumbrian born author, residing in the tail end of the Lake District. While not racing go karts or watching motorsport, Chris is a father and thoroughly enjoys helping his children write their own incredible stories.

You can connect with me on:
🌐 https://www.chrispeaseauthor.com

Also by Chris Pease

If you enjoyed Project Vanguard, then why not try one of my more modern science fiction novels. Mixing two of my favourite genres, science fiction and horror, my previous novels capture the more real horror faced in unknown situations.

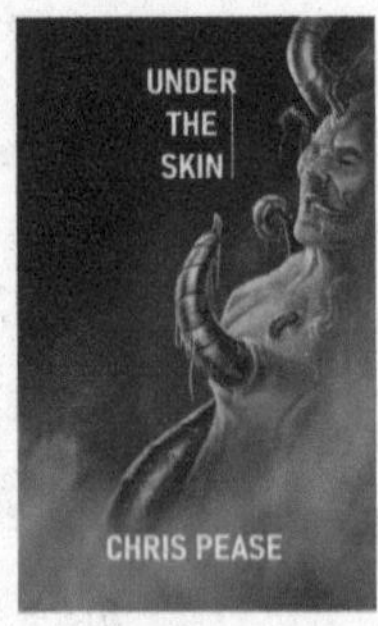

Under The Skin
Under The Skin is a Science Fiction-Horror novel set in the fictional town of Grayton. It follows the Farragher family's fight for survival, as they are thrust in to a hellish battle against dark, twisted monsters that have begun to infect the townspeople.

How far would you go to keep your family safe, in a world abandoned?

Available at Waterstones, Amazon and your local library.

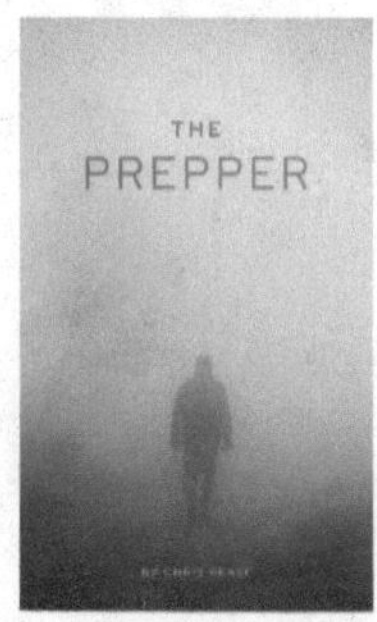

The Prepper

Lakeland Ranger, Matt Richards, lives on Lake Windermere. Struggling with his own personal circumstances, an unknown threat is lurking out in the open and threatens to change the troubled Ranger for good.

When he finds himself at a crossroad, Matt summons the courage to ask for help and finds himself thrown in to a world in disarray. Will it be too late for the troubled Ranger?

Available to read exclusively at;
www.chrispeaseauthor.com